5x 1/14 LT 9/13
7 x 5/16 LT 9/14

D0093844

Recent Titles by Peter Turnbull

* *available from Severn House*

ALL ROADS LEADETH

All Roads Leadeth

Peter Turnbull

severn House

This first world edition published in Great Britain 2003 by
SEVERN HOUSE PUBLISHERS LTD of
9–15 High Street, Sutton, Surrey SM1 1DF.
This first world edition published in the USA 2003 by
SEVERN HOUSE PUBLISHERS INC of
595 Madison Avenue, New York, N.Y. 10022.

Copyright © 2003 by Peter Turnbull.
All rights reserved.
The moral right of the author has been asserted.

British Library Cataloguing in Publication Data

Turnbull, Peter, 1950-
    All roads leadeth
    1. Hennessey, George, Chief Inspector (Fictitious character) - Fiction
    2. Yellich, Sergeant (Fictitious character) - Fiction
    3. Police - England - York - Fiction
    4. Detective and mystery stories
    I. Title
    823.9'14 [F]

    ISBN 0-7278-5970-6

Except where actual historical events and characters are being
described for the storyline of this novel, all situations in this
publication are fictitious and any resemblance to living persons
is purely coincidental.

Typeset by Palimpsest Book Production Ltd.,
Polmont, Stirlingshire, Scotland.
Printed and bound in Great Britain by
MPG Books Ltd., Bodmin, Cornwall.

One

. . . in which an exile returns from the Dominions, a skeleton is found, and an old case file is re-opened.

TUESDAY, 16 AUGUST, 10.00 A.M.

The man surveyed the house. Many people, he thought, would regard the building as unattractive, but to him it was a thing of beauty. It had been built in the mid- to late-nineteenth century in red brick, which had, over the years, become blackened with industrial pollution. It had not, could not have, blackened as rapidly as it would have had it been built in the great industrial cities of the north of England, cities like Leeds or Sheffield; but in the nineteenth century and up to the middle of the twentieth century, the United Kingdom was effectively covered in a blanket of airborne soot and grit and no building survived being blackened over time, save perhaps castles in the far north of Scotland or fishermen's cottages on the Western Peninsula. And here in the Vale of York, surrounded by lush fields under crops, or of contented cattle, and stands of woodland of thick foliage where game thrived, was a building that, despite its distance from the nearest steelworks, had been blackened. 'Cluttered', the man thought, was the only word that could describe the design of the building. For here were not the graceful lines of the great country houses of the 'Augustan' period of British history, when the magnificent house of clean, simple lines borrowed from the architecture of ancient Greece and Rome were built, here rather was Victoriana with all its elaborate fussiness.

1

A roof line that was twisted and jagged and interrupted by dormer windows; a needlessly complicated floor plan that caused the house to appear to have been bent out of shape, with rounded walls containing small ante-rooms, a small, squat entrance doorway with tiles that, when new, would have presented a 'loud', in terms of colour, very 'busy' pattern. The building was only of two floors, a ground floor and a first floor, but generous cellarage and ingenious use of the attic space nearly doubled the amount of space offered by the ground and first floor. The building, with the modest address of 2, Mill Lane, Paxton on the Forest, stood in a generous ten acres of land, most of which had been given over to woodland. The remainder of the garden had been overgrown and, as always happens in such cases, grasses had dominated. The grass now stood in excess of five feet high in places and was thickly populated with field mice, which darted hither and thither whenever the man, or his dogs, penetrated the grass. The building had been put up for sale by its previous owner having been unoccupied for the last fifteen years. The windows, of course, had been the first casualties, courtesy of village children and stones, then entry had been forced and valuable lead had been stripped from the windows, so pliable that it could be wound off the frames like plasticine. The roof lost a tile, then two, then three and, eventually, pigeons took up residence and did so in large numbers. The man, touring Yorkshire, looking for a house to buy in which to settle and live out his life, saw the building, its neglected state, the price 'to reflect the amount of work needed to restore this unique property to its former splendour and to fulfil its potential' was well within his means and he said, 'Yes, yes . . . oh my heavens, yes.'

Then he moved in, he and his two Alsatians and for the first few weeks the man camped in a small downstairs room, sleeping on a camp bed, cooking on a camping stove, reading at night by means of an oil lamp, and feeling utterly safe because of the presence of his dogs, which prowled the rooms and staircases and landings, imposing their presence on their new territory. The man laid a layer of flagstones, which he had found near the house, on the upstairs landing, outside the attic door, on which he stood a brazier, then he placed old wood and dampened vegetation and lit the contents of the brazier. He remained in constant attendance with a bucket of water to hand as the flames took hold and the smoke, as he knew it would, found its way into the loft, and the pigeons who had taken residence in large numbers left hurriedly in large numbers, flapping, it seemed to the man, their indignation at such a rude eviction.

It was then the turn of tradesmen to descend upon the house, roofers repairing the roof, electricians rewiring the property, glaziers not just glazing, but replacing the wooden window frames, all working at the same time, nodding to each other, calling each other 'mate', but generally keeping themselves to themselves and their minds on their own job, working in shirtsleeves as the sun beat down relentlessly on the Vale of York, and the man, amidst hammering and banging and the annoying presence of Radio One, insisted upon by the roofers, would ensure a constant supply of tea and would also, as agreed, pick up the 'donkey jobs', the clearing away of rubbish, for example, anything that reduced a craftsman's time and the job, and hence reduced his bill at the end of it. All of which the dogs looked upon from beneath the shade of a mulberry bush with bemused interest, having found that their barking brought a pat of approval from their master followed by a stern 'Shut up!'.

The most unpleasant task the man gave to himself: clearing the loft after years of pigeon inhabitation. It took patience, hardwearing gloves, a face mask, a hat and a strong, strong stomach. The job was eventually completed – spoil and not a few bird carcasses were removed by the bag load – and the loft was deemed by the man no longer to pose a health risk. The floor could be cleaned and sealed with a generous coat of varnish: a job to be done in the years to come. The plumbing working, the house rewired, re-windowed, the roof once again 'sound', in the words of the roofers, the central heating was installed and the man, camping in the small downstairs room, found that he was still well within budget, the relatively inexpensive purchase price saw to that. The house was then carpeted throughout at the same time that a kitchen was being installed, complete, of course, with an Aga, and all in less than one month after exchanging contracts. Furniture, if solid enough, was bought from charity shops, not out of parsimony, but the man thought old furniture, if undamaged, had a softening effect on a house, especially an older property like No. 2 Mill Lane, which was substantial enough to carry a name, but, the man thought: Number Two . . . will do. The bed, though, he bought new, and had an annoyingly long six weeks to wait before its delivery. It was mid-summer by the time the man set to, to clear the garden. Professional gardeners might, he conceded, be needed, but before then he could help his pocket by again doing the 'donkey work' in the garden, the trimming of the wildly overgrown privet, the scything of many-feet-high grass. It would also give the man something to do . . . he knew himself . . . he became fractious if he didn't have anything to do. If he had nothing to do, he would find something to do. Taking a car's gearbox apart just to put it back together again was how he had once occupied a full day, so as to feel satisfied with himself as the sun was sinking.

The woodland he was quite content to leave. Leave well alone, was, he believed, excellent advice, and he liked the idea of wild things living on his property as wild things should live. The garden proved a monstrous task and, liking fire as a good friend rather than as an agent of destruction, he burned privet and grass cuttings in fires that caused smoke to rise to great height in the still, summer air. The fires also had an additional purpose: he was letting his neighbours who lived in houses a few fields away, the closest he saw was about two hundred yards distant, that Number Two Mill Lane was now occupied, that he had now moved into the village of Paxton on the Forest.

It was in mid-August that he found the skeleton. On the fifteenth of the month, 'as near as mid as could be had' he would often say in later years, it happened, so he recalled, in this wise. The house was beginning to be 'lived in', things introduced and placed, like old newspapers on the settee, was accumulating detritus, he was settling into a routine of passing comfort . . . a relatively late rise at about nine a.m., a leisurely bath, an equally leisurely breakfast and then he would settle down to the tasks for the day. In August the tasks for the day largely meant working in the garden, clearing the last of the hay and creating a lawn, and now that the garden was once again taking on the appearance of a garden, he turned his attention to the pile of rubble. The pile of rubble was a pile of bricks, intermixed with a large number of lumps of concrete, some of which had a single smooth side. The man pondered what to do with the rubble. He did not want to throw it away because, so far as he could see, the bricks were still strong and eminently reusable and the lumps of concrete were similarly strong and healthy and free of so called 'concrete cancer'. The bricks could be used to build a non-load-bearing structure, a low wall, he thought, in the front garden, to separate the lawn from the narrow pavement that threaded down one side of Mill Lane, and the lumps of concrete could be used as an infill for some other project . . . the floor of a garage, for example. The house did not have a garage and the building of a garage was on the list he had drawn up in his mind of 'things to be done'. What was certain was that a pond had to be dug, fish and amphibia introduced – and the place where the man had decided the pond would be dug was the very place that was occupied by the pile of rubble. The task therefore on the fifteenth of August was to move the pile of rubble, one wheelbarrow full at a time, and in the process he would separate the bricks from the lumps of concrete. The bricks he would place in a neat pile in front of the house, conveniently to hand when he came to building the low wall, and the lumps of concrete could be piled close to where he planned to build the garage. A day's job he guessed, perhaps spilling over into the following morning, but a good day's job at least . . . afterwards he would shower, dress in clean clothes and walk into the village for a few pints at the Foresters Arms, where the locals had proved to be a friendly bunch, and where he was already gaining a small amount of acceptance. After a day spent under a hot sun, the beer would go down very well indeed. It was about eleven in the forenoon that he took a brick, wriggling it so as to dislodge it from a lump of concrete, eventually tugging it free, and revealed a hard, dun-coloured substance, which he at first thought was another lump of concrete, but in the next instance, he realized that it was nothing of the sort. He removed more bricks from around the object until a skull, a human skull, lay grinning, it seemed, up at him. He stared at it, then stood back feeling a hollowness inside his stomach, and noticed again how in a crisis things seem more 'real': the birdsong became louder, the green of the vegetation became greener, the sun became 'hotter'. He walked to the house and into the hallway, picked up the phone and dialled the police. He made it a three nine call but added that there was no real hurry, what he had found appeared to be human, and what he had found appeared to have been deceased for a long time. A very long time indeed. He added that the police may need directions, his house being remote in a remote village, and gave clear, explicit directions. Ten minutes later, a police vehicle turned into his driveway.

'Well, it's just as you see.' The man showed the constable the grinning skull. 'I stopped removing bricks when I found it, it's evidently a crime scene. Folk don't commit suicide by piling bricks on themselves, not that I have heard anyway.'

'Not that I have heard either.' The constable, white shirt, serge trousers, looking very young in the man's eyes, smiled at the man's joke. He took hold of his radio, mounted on the collar of his shirt, and pressed the 'send/receive' button. '241, to control.'

'Control.' The man heard the crackly reply of a female voice at the police control.

'Confirm possible Code 41 at this location. CID attendance requested.'

'Control. Understood.'

The constable released the send/receive button and asked the man if he would mind stepping away from the pile of rubble. The two men walked to the shade at the side of the house, from within which the deep-throated barking of the two Alsatians could be heard.

'Always had dogs,' the man said. 'Love the creatures. Never been without a dog . . . have two at the moment . . . both retired guide dogs . . . make a lot of noise but are not particularly aggressive.'

'I like dogs too.' The constable took out his notebook. 'Can I take a few details please, sir.'

'Of course.' The man wiped his head. 'I suppose you'd like to start with my name?'

'Yes, please, sir.'

'Francis Armstrong, aged fifty-four.'

'And this is your house, sir?'

'Yes, all mine, the monstrous rambling pile . . . all mine, bought and paid for.'

'I presume you haven't lived here long, sir?'

'Discovering the skeleton you mean . . . no, only about two months, picked up the keys in early June. Spent the last few weeks getting the house in order . . . had a little help . . . got the tradesmen in . . . started on the garden a couple of weeks ago . . . a real jungle when I came.'

'Yes . . . I know this property, sir. It's in my patch. I drove past it a few times over the years and watched its decay. I am pleased it's been rescued.'

'Thank you. I confess I like it when old buildings are rescued . . . I have no time for property developers who ruin town centres . . . but renovating old buildings, rescuing them from decay, as you say . . . well, that's in everybody's best interests.'

'Are you new to the area, sir?'

'I have returned. I grew up in York . . . left when I was sixteen . . . joined the Army, then I took a passage on a ship going to Montreal . . . took work on a building site, then got sacked for drag racing a steam roller, so set up on my own, building houses . . . "Armstrong Homes – Built to Last" – based in Toronto. Built the company up over thirty years, then sold out to a rival company earlier this year . . . returned to my roots . . . it's that tug back to your roots, it's so strong. I never left my roots in my head. If you are a builder and create housing projects . . . or estates as they are called in England . . . or schemes in Scotland, you are allowed to name the streets you create so long as the name is not already in use in that particular town or city and I always named my streets after place names in and around York . . . Minster Avenue . . . Heslington Street . . . Wetherby Way . . . not just the names of large towns but also small villages. I had an Ordnance Survey map of the York area and would select the names of obscure villages . . . Fangfoss Street, I remember . . . Towthorpe Road is another . . . planted York and its surroundings on the map of Canada.'

The constable grinned. 'Plenty of Old World names in the New World, sir, a few more won't do any harm.'

'Oh, the Canucks loved the names, especially those who had family connections in Yorkshire.' He turned as a car entered the driveway.

'This is the CID, sir,' the constable said. 'If you'll excuse me, I'll have to show them the skeleton . . . and doubtless they'll want to ask you a few more questions.'

'A bit more than my name and age.' Francis Armstrong followed the constable's gaze and watched as two men got out of the car, both tall, both comfortably dressed in light-coloured and lightweight summer jackets, but one noticeably, very noticeably, older than the other and, curiously, in Francis Armstrong's eyes, the younger of the two was the driver of the car. Nothing wrong with that, he pondered, but it did look a little unusual, a little odd.

The two plain-clothes officers approached Francis Armstrong and introduced themselves. The older of the two gave his name as Detective Chief Inspector Hennessey, the younger as Detective Sergeant Yellich.

Hennessey smiled cordially at Armstrong. He saw a muscular, well-built man, a man who had warm eyes, whose handshake was sincere, just the right amount of grip . . . not vice-like . . . not a 'wet lettuce' handshake either, but just right. 'We'll need to talk to you at some length, Mr Armstrong.'

'So the constable said.'

'Where can we find you?'

'Oh . . . just knock on the door, I'm not going anywhere . . . and don't mind the dogs, they're all bark . . . but I'll put them in the kitchen when you come to the house.'

'We'd appreciate it.' Hennessey then turned to the constable. 'All right, young man, show us what we have.'

The constable led the two CID officers down the garden to the pile of bricks and blocks of cement, to the skull revealed therein.

'The gentleman found it, sir . . . clearing the rubble away.'

'I take it he's not long in the property?'

'Just a few months, sir . . . and this he, or she, has clearly been here for years.'

'Thank you,' said dryly.

'Sorry, sir.'

'Right,' Hennessey turned to Yellich, 'if you could get Scenes of Crime here and ask the pathologist to attend. No need for a police surgeon . . . not needed in the case of skeletal or decomposed remains as you know, it doesn't need the police surgeon to pronounce "life extinct" in such cases.' Hennessey swept a fly away from his face. 'Then when they have arrived, see to the excavation of the skeleton.'

'Yes, boss.'

'Carefully, brick by brick, and take the rubble right down to the soil . . . there's room for two more skeletons in there.'

'Understood, skipper.'

'You'll need some more constables to assist you. I'll go and have a chat with Mr . . . what was his name?'

'Armstrong, sir.'

'Armstrong,' Hennessey echoed and repeated, 'Armstrong, Armstrong, Armstrong,' as he walked towards the house.

Hennessey could not drive the images from his mind, yet equally he felt enriched by them. The images of fine art at the Art Gallery . . . he had toured it the day previous, one of his days off that week, he and his lady, arm in arm, sharing the catalogue, talking in hushed tones . . . reverential tones . . . showing similar deference to other art lovers who also visited the exhibition, not crowding them, allowing them personal space. It was a collection of Victorian landscape painters. The major painters of the Victorian landscape, such as Constable and Turner, were absent. The work of painters of that ilk were clearly considered too valuable to be allowed to tour Britain as part of an exhibition. But work by lesser-known but equally impressive artists, in Hennessey's eye, was represented, works by De Wint, Géricault, Drolling and Lane, being just a few of the names that Hennessey could recall as he walked to speak to Mr Armstrong, though the images would stay in his mind. He felt given to, enriched, uplifted in a world of crime and corruption that was his daily bread. Attending the exhibition had given him something to counterbalance the cynicism present in human nature. He was pleased, very pleased, he had allowed himself to be 'dragged' there.

'About fifteen years.' Armstrong sat in a comfortable-looking armchair, a deep chair with high, wide arms and a tall back, very pre-Second World War, thought Hennessey, who sat on the matching settee. The age of the furniture seemed to contrast with the newness of the decoration and the carpet. 'It was in a bad state when I bought it, but not beyond redemption. It was better than it looked . . . no rot in the timbers, which is why I bought it . . . a small . . . I would say tolerable amount of damp in the brickwork, but that can be sorted out in time. The only occupants were pigeons in the loft . . . got rid of those, to their intense annoyance.'

'You live alone, Mr Armstrong?'

'Yes.' Armstrong looked pained. 'That is the great sadness of my life . . . never marrying . . . it isn't the absence of a partner I feel, I am a very independent man, it's the absence of issue. I worked hard to achieve all this plus money in very safe investments . . . and nobody to leave it to.' Armstrong shrugged. 'I'll have to think of something useful to leave it to, some noble cause.'

'Do you know anything of the previous owner?'

'I don't . . . believed to be a banker, or somebody who worked in the financial sector at least. I would have to refer you to the estate agents . . . Hartwells . . . they have a number of offices in York and the surrounding area. I used the office in Lower Ousegate.'

'And you discovered the skull just today?'

'Yes . . . lifted a brick, saw something that was neither brick nor cement, and lifted another and . . . stepped back . . . realizing what I had found and walked to the house and dialled three nines . . . so thirty seconds before the call was received. I understand you record the time of all such calls?'

'We do . . . and the content.'

'Really? How long for?'

Hennessey saw no harm in answering the question. 'Each 999 call is taped on to three separate recorders. One is kept for twenty-four hours, the second for a month, and the third indefinitely.'

'Never throw anything away.' Armstrong pursed his lips.

'That's a lesson I learned too late in life. When I think of the possessions I chucked away, only to regret doing so . . . sometimes immediately afterwards, sometimes only years afterwards, but I have never regretted *not* throwing any possession away. I still have a lot of stuff in storage, visit me in a week or two's time and this room will be cluttered with ornaments and bric-a-brac and paintings on the wall.'

A shaft of sunlight suddenly penetrated the room, illuminating dust particles hanging in the air.

'A few clouds today,' Armstrong said, and almost as soon as he'd said it, the shaft of sunlight vanished.

'What caused you to look inside the mound of rubble, Mr Armstrong?'

'I wasn't looking inside it, I was moving it. I want to dig a pond there . . . introduce fish . . . hope the frogs will colonize it. I like ponds and pond life.' Armstrong paused. 'I'm sorry, did that upset you?'

'No . . . it touched a personal chord . . . I'm sorry it showed. I too have a pond.'

'I see. Well, I was shifting the rubble, sorting it out, separating the bricks from the lumps of cement and . . . well, you are here.'

'You haven't noticed any other signs of suspicious goings-on?'

'I haven't . . . you are welcome to check the house over.'

'It may come to that, Mr Armstrong, perhaps not right now though. Is there a cellar?'

'Yes . . . quite extensive . . . has some junk in it. To be really truthful, I haven't fully explored it myself yet. Why, do you think? Oh . . . I should not like there to be anything in the cellar . . . I mean anything of that sort.' He nodded to his left, to the direction of the rear garden. 'That would upset me, but there is no "presence" in the house. I am sensitive to things like that.'

'Are you?'

'Yes . . . don't dismiss the supernatural too easily, Mr

Hennessey. I feel confident that if there was anything like that in this building, I would have picked it up and, moreover, the dogs are quite content in the house. Whatever happened in this property, happened in the garden. And a good few years ago as well.'

Hennessey's gaze was drawn by a movement outside. He smiled as he saw a red-and-white Riley, circa 1947, halt outside the property on Mill Lane.

'This is the pathologist.' Hennessey stood. 'I will have to show her the skeleton . . . so if you'll excuse me . . .'

'Certainly.' Armstrong also stood. 'If you have no further need of me . . . I'll have a walk in the village – too early in the day to take the dogs out, they suffer dreadfully in the heat, both long-haired Alsatians. I'll leave them in the house where it's cool.'

'There may be other questions and, as I said, we'll have to look over the house . . . especially the cellar, but as you say, whatever happened, happened a few years ago. The time pressure is off us, in a sense, but it still looks like it's going to be a murder inquiry, so we'll be asking for your co-operation in the next day or two.'

'Whatever I can do to help.'

Hennessey left the shade of the house and walked into the sunlight, shielding his eyes from the glare of the sun. He walked towards the group of officers, who stood back to allow a SOCO to take a photograph, which he did with a flash. A flash in this amount of daylight? Hennessey was surprised by that, but he was confident the man knew what he was doing and didn't allow his mind to dwell on the matter.

The skeleton had been fully exposed by the time Hennessey joined the group. It lay face up on a bed of rubble, being stared at in silence by the officers and the forensic pathologist. It seemed to Hennessey to stare back in equal and defiant silence.

'A female,' Hennessey said, noticing a gold ring on the wedding finger, 'by the ring.'

'And by the skeleton,' Dr D'Acre said. 'Wide eye orbits, flatter forehead, wide pelvis . . . that is the thing that decides sex, the ring could equally be worn by a man.' She was a woman in her mid-forties, slender, tall, close-cropped dark hair that was greying at the ends. She carried herself with poise and learned authority. When she spoke, Hennessey noted, people listened. 'And no obvious sign of trauma. No fractured skull here . . . so cause of death may never be determined . . . unless she was poisoned by means of a heavy poison such as cyanide. If that is the case, then traces will still be present in the long bones, but cyanide poisoning went out with the Victorians . . . it was the fashion when, I suppose, that house was built, but no longer the case.' She paused. 'There is little else I can do, in fact there is nothing else I can do – complete skeletalization . . . she must have been here for a considerable period of time.'

'Would you care to guess?' Hennessey turned to her, but Louise D'Acre refrained from making eye contact.

'I wouldn't guess . . . highly unprofessional. Pathologists estimating time of death is a case of life imitating art. Police series on television have pathologists pinpointing the time of death and we have allowed ourselves to be pushed into that role in real life. Strictly speaking, we determine the cause . . . the "how", not the "when". The "when" is where you and I overlap. Whilst the "why" is wholly your province. But off the record, I think she will have been here about twenty years . . . probably more. Insects would have done this. She doesn't look to me to have been deeply buried in the rubble . . . flies could easily have got to her . . . a fly can scent rotting flesh from a distance of two miles . . . that may be of interest to you, Chief Inspector?'

'The flies?'

'Well, if she was buried during the summer months, the mound of rubble would have been a buzzing hive of insect activity. It couldn't fail to arouse suspicion. Well, I would be suspicious if a mound of rubble in my garden was to become a source of attraction to large numbers of insects but if she was buried in the winter months, then decomposition would have been by primary invaders . . . bacteria in the gut and intestines, which would have eaten her from within. If that was the case, by the time the warm weather came she would have been less of interest to the secondary invaders . . . the flies . . . so perhaps she could have lain here without the occupant of the house knowing . . . it's a possibility.'

'Depending on the time of year?'

'Yes . . . also she was buried naked.'

'She was?'

'She was. Remnants of clothing would still be discernible, particularly hardwearing items . . . shoe leather for example and any metal items would remain, e.g. zips, as would plastic buttons . . . and, as you see, none are evident.'

'Murdered . . . possibly . . . no, definitely.'

'Definitely.' Louise D'Acre glanced at Hennessey, but she did so only briefly.

'Well, cause of death is still to be established, but if it is a case of accidental death being covered up, it makes no sense to remove all the clothing from the body . . . not a scientific analysis . . . but . . .'

'A reasonable deduction,' Louise D'Acre nodded. 'An eminently reasonable deduction.'

'Can you estimate her age?'

'At death, you mean?' said with a smile. 'I'll let you have her age to within twelve months. But looking at the skull, I think she will prove to be in her middle years. A fully knitted skull for one thing and what appears to be pubic scarring . . . but I will have to have a closer look at that . . . caused by multiple childbirths . . . but that is all I can do here. If you would care to have her removed to the York City, I'll do the P.M.' She glanced at her watch. 'Well, it's eleven in the forenoon, I will be able to commence at 2 p.m. Will you be representing the police, Chief Inspector?'

'Well, either myself or Sergeant Yellich . . . probably

15

myself. We'll have to excavate the rubble completely, make sure nothing else is contained within it – then check the grounds as fully as we can. Leave no stone unturned on this one, literally.'

'Not using the sniffer dogs?'

'Not if any other murder victims are also of the same vintage. Dogs cannot smell skeletons, only decomposing flesh.'

'Well that, as they say, is your department. I'll get back to the hospital now, grab some lunch and then I'll address madam here.'

George Hennessey, leaving Yellich to supervise the search of the remainder of the rubble and the grounds of the house, rode back to York in the mortuary van, sitting between the driver and his colleague with the skeleton in a black plastic bodybag in the rear compartment. He was dropped off in the centre of the city, close to Micklegate Bar Police Station. He walked into the building, pondering the fact that the age of the police station was probably the same as the house from which he had just returned, signed himself 'in' at the enquiry desk and opened the 'staff only' door by pressing the coded entry numbers. He ensured the door was firmly closed behind him and walked to the CID corridor, to his office and sat heavily in the chair behind the desk. He picked up his telephone and jabbed an internal four figure number.

'Collator.' The reply was swift and alert.

'DCI Hennessey.'

'Yes, sir.'

'Two things . . . a case number, please.'

'66/8.'

'Sixty-six crimes already this month!'

'Yes, sir,' there was humour in his voice, 'and we're only half-way through.'

'It isn't is it? All right . . . 66/8 . . .' Hennessey wrote the case number on the top left-hand side of a case record file.

'Most are petty though, sir . . .'

'Pleased to hear it or we would be overwhelmed.'

'But violence is on the increase, which is worrying . . . a spate of thefts of mobile phones . . . people just have them grabbed out of their hands, youngsters mainly . . . schoolgirls chatting to their friends . . . that's the most common victim profile.'

'I have wondered at their attraction. They can be cancelled quickly can't they?'

'Well, it might take up to an hour, sir – you can make a lot of expensive international calls in that time, none of which can be traced to you. They can be traced to a mobile, but not to the thief . . .'

'Of course.'

'And if the thief uses it for his own purpose until the phone is taken out of the system, he can still sell the redundant phone underground . . . where it can be revitalized, using legitimate numbers stolen from other phones . . . a practice known as "cloning", I believe.'

'Fascinating,' Hennessey murmured, but he also felt frightening. He was not sorry to be approaching retirement – the massive growth of new technology gave him a sense of being squeezed out of the world. Retirement had its attractions. 'The second thing . . .'

'Yes, sir?'

'Female . . . possibly middle years . . . look up the records . . . it's in connection with the case number you have just given me. Any mis per fitting that description reported about twenty years ago.'

'"About" . . . how "about" would you like me to check, sir?'

'Say twenty-five years to fifteen years . . . a ten-year span . . . from the York area in the first instance. If you don't get a result, go to the Missing Persons Helpline.'

'Yes, sir. Very good.'

Hennessey replaced the phone more gently than he had picked it up. 66/8, he thought, fortunately it wasn't June . . .

66/6 would indeed be an ominous number for a case. He stood and walked to the corner of his office and switched on the electric kettle that stood on a small table. He glanced out of the window as he waited for the kettle to boil. High summer: the season was in full swing, open-topped double-decker buses toured the streets, tourists, many, the majority foreign, walked the ancient walls, jostling each other as they travelled in opposite directions. Hennessey had often thought that a one-way system on the walls, especially at this time of year, would be no bad thing. No bad thing at all.

He left the police station and then he too joined the wall-walkers, not as a tourist but as a resident of the city, and like all residents of York, he knew that the quickest way to traverse the city was to walk the walls. To his right as he walked, was a new building, very modern yet sensitively blending with the architecture around it, but disappointingly for Hennessey it had been built on the site of the first railway station in York. Before its destruction, the first station built within the walls could still easily be discerned although it was used in its final days as a warehouse. The curved platform was visible as was the angular, glass roof. The building had, in Hennessey's eyes, been well worth preserving, but others, doubtless, he felt, who were wiser than he, decided that the building, not only the first station in York, but one of the earliest railway stations in Britain, and hence the world, should be reduced to a pile of rubble.

Rubble. The concept of rubble featured strongly in his life on that day.

He left the walls at Lendal Bridge and ate a leisurely and enjoyable lunch at the fish restaurant. From there he walked in the streets of York, bustling with people, locals and tourists, with street entertainers, musicians in the main, some very good, in his view, like the two young women in long skirts who gave an impressive rendition of a violin piece to an attentive audience and, doubtless, would earn more coinage than the young man a few hundred yards away who strummed a guitar as he shouted rather than sang a folk song. A juggler entertained children. An evangelist held a book high in the air whilst prophesying doom. A man beside him occasionally shouted 'amen'. The shops had their doors held wide open allowing in what air could be had, for the city baked under a relentless sun. An open horse-drawn carriage, yellow and black, pulled by two dapple-grey mares, clattered along the street driven by a coachman in a blue coat and a black top hat. The coach carried a family, parents and three children, the children, seemingly to Hennessey, particularly delighted by the experience of a ride in a horse-drawn coach and the parents clearly enjoying their children's enjoyment. The queue outside the Jorvik Centre was, as usual, long, and showed no discernible movement. It was Hennessey's often given advice to friends not to visit the Jorvick Centre during the summer months: the two hour wait in the queue on a hot, hot day was, in his opinion, just not worth the amount of time spent in the exhibition, interesting as the exhibition might be. The Railway Museum, he would say, was a much better bet. Yet all was not thriving enterprise and hardworking folk on holiday: a young woman sitting cross-legged with a puppy on a piece of string and a bowl in front of her containing a few coins served as a reminder that the city had an underside.

At one thirty, Hennessey ceased his wander around the streets of the ancient town, though his police officer's eye was ever vigilant, and began a purposeful walk towards York City Hospital. He walked through Bootham Bar, down Gillygate, with its string of small shops, which seemed to Hennessey to be doing steady business, though clearly not as busy as the larger stores in the city centre. From Gillygate he walked into Clarence Street and the beginnings of the city's housing, into Wiggington Road and thence across the car park of York City Hospital. As he approached the medium-rise, slab-sided, building he scanned the car park for Dr D'Acre's car and, finding it, allowed his eyes to settle on it, warmly so. Dr D'Acre had once told him of the vehicle. It had been her father's first and only car, she had inherited it and had had it lovingly serviced by a garage whose proprietor had asked her for first refusal should she ever wish to part with the car. It was a promise she had given, knowing that she was highly unlikely ever to sell. It would, in the fullness of time, be bequeathed to one of her children, probably, she said, her son, because even though he was the youngest, it was after all a 'man's car'. But the promise did have the effect of ensuring that the service provided by the garage was of the highest quality.

Hennessey entered the hospital and walked to the stairs to the basement, where was located the Department of Pathology. He went to an office, tapped on the door; a female voice said, 'Come in.' He opened the door and said, 'Good afternoon,' very formally, to Dr D'Acre.

'Ah, Chief Inspector.' She glanced at the clock on the wall. 'You are a little early but that is to the good . . . an early start . . . an early finish.' Her office was cramped but by arranging it neatly she had maximized the amount of space she had been allocated. Photographs of her children hung on the wall in expensive-looking frames, as did a photograph of her horse, the beloved 'Samson', a magnificent black stallion, which Hennessey, though he did not know horses, felt by its very image, was deserving of the name it had been given. 'Well, I'll get robed up . . . if you care to meet me in the laboratory we can begin. Though I don't think that it will be a long post-mortem – skeletal remains seldom are – and I do not promise a clear finding as to the cause of death – that is also often the case with skeletons. Even a severed skull is not necessarily the cause of death . . . it could easily have been done *post mortem*. But we shall see what we shall see.'

Ten minutes later, Hennessey, dressed in green disposable coveralls and a green paper hat, stood at the edge of the post-mortem laboratory, well distanced from the stainless-steel table, one of four in the room, all in a row, observing, as was required by law, for the police. Dr D'Acre stood beside the table and adjusted the stainless-steel anglepoise arm that was attached to the ceiling directly above the table. The ceiling itself was a battery of shimmering fluorescent bulbs, shielded by opaque Perspex sheeting. Eric Filey, the mortuary assistant, also stood in the room. Hennessey, and other police officers too, reported to each other that they liked Mr Filey – he was always found to be jovial, warm natured, cutting a short rotund figure, he was not at all sour and cynical nor was he evidently possessed of an unhealthy fascination with death as, in George Hennessey's experience, were many others of his calling.

'The remains are the skeletal remains of an adult human of the female sex.' Dr D'Acre spoke for the benefit of the microphone. 'The age at death still to be determined.' She paused and examined the skull. 'The sutures of the skull are closed, indicating a person in the thirty years plus age range at age of death, but we are reminded of observations of skulls of women of fifty years or more, which were noted to still have open sutures . . . there is evidence of pubic scarring . . . indicating that this woman gave birth more than once by breech delivery, further indicating an adult at the age of death.' Dr D'Acre stretched a tape measure along the skeleton. 'She was a small woman in life . . . only about five feet tall . . . can't be precise because the skeleton will have shrunk as the cartilage contracted and the flesh on the soles of the feet decayed . . . but not a tall woman by any means.' Dr D'Acre returned her attention to the skull and opened the jaw. It was evidently a little stiff because Hennessey observed Dr D'Acre having to prise the jaws apart; though, using only her hands, she was able to accomplish the task with ease. There was no tissue, hence no rigor. 'Always a goldmine of information, the mouth,' she said clearly for Hennessey's benefit, rather than for the benefit of the microphone, and knowing that the audio-typist would know what to omit. 'The mouth really tells us all we need to know . . . sex, age, race . . . diet even. Well . . .' Again she paused and again she spoke for the benefit of the microphone. Her voice became more formal, a little slower and admitted to no humour. 'The teeth indicate that the deceased was white European, or Caucasian . . . she had had dental work . . . including a gold-capped tooth, third molars are present. She was aged twenty-five plus . . . no wearing-down of the teeth from a poor diet, limited decay, indicating she did not eat a sugar-rich diet . . . a wealthy woman who ate sensibly. Smaller teeth than would be the case had it been male remains further indicates that the deceased was female, though the sex of the deceased is not in doubt. The skeleton shows no sign of trauma that might indicate the cause of death. There is a little erosion of the bones, which indicates that for some period of time the bones were exposed to damp, but the condition of the skeleton is near perfect, which indicates that for the greater part of the time the remains were kept in dry conditions.' She paused and spoke in a softer tone. 'Doesn't mean to say that the remains were moved, of course, Chief Inspector . . . it means that the location in which it was kept alternated from dry to damp but was mainly dry. The pile of rubble would provide that environment . . . the rubble would allow any rain water to drain from the bones . . . but a covering of snow would cause some erosion.'

'I see.'

'In terms of establishing the identity of the remains, I think you . . . we, are wholly dependent upon the dental records. That is to say, there is nothing in the skeleton that might set her apart from any other female of her race and age range . . . no healed fractures, no malformation of limbs . . . nothing missing. The teeth are loose, as is often the case in skeletons that have lain in dry conditions, but they all seem to be in place – in fact they all are in place. I can preserve the lower set, which could be matched to an odontogram . . . a dental chart . . . if her dentist has kept her records. Whoever she was, she certainly had had a dentist and knew the value of dental hygiene. I can extract one of the upper teeth, one of the incisors, which has had no work done on it at all and while its presence will be noted on any odontogram, it won't have recorded dental work. So, I'll extract one, cut it in half and that will give the age at death of the deceased plus or minus one year.'

'I would be obliged,' Hennessey said.

'And that,' Dr D'Acre said, 'is about it. Can we have a photograph of the skeleton please, Mr Filey?'

Eric Filey reached for a camera with a flash attachment and took six photographs of the skeleton from different angles.

'Do you have a case file number?'

'66/8,' Hennessey said.

'That's sixty-six stroke eight for the reference number.' Dr D'Acre addressed the pathology laboratory, but again it was clearly for the benefit of the microphone and the audio-typist who would later that day or tomorrow be typing up the commentary made by Dr D'Acre during the post-mortem. 'Quick,' she said to Hennessey, 'told you it would be a quick one. She died of causes as yet unknown but which cannot be determined by the observation of the skeletal remains alone. I will trawl for poisons, as I indicated that I would.'

'So suffocation . . . that sort of thing?' Hennessey probed.

'Yes, that sort of thing, anything which did not cause damage to the skeleton. Violence should not be ruled out . . . a bang on the head could cause unconsciousness without ‧ damaging the skull for example . . . though my report will have to be inconclusive about the cause of death, I will be able to tell you how old she was when she died.'

'That would be of considerable assistance. It would really help us determine her identity.'

'As to the age of the bones . . . that is, when she died, I won't be drawn . . . it will be more of a common-sense deduction on your part than a medical one on mine.'

Hennessey smiled and, uncharacteristically, Louise D'Acre returned the smile, and even allowed a split second of eye contact. Very, very uncharacteristic.

Hennessey walked back to Micklegate Bar Police Station. It was by then nearly three thirty, though the afternoon showed no sign of cooling. He mopped his brow and carried his jacket over his arm.

So a woman had died, most probably murdered, her body concealed in rubble in the grounds of a house that had only recently been re-occupied after being empty and unlived in for approximately fifteen years. The last occupier of the house, George, he said to himself . . . that's the next step. Upon his return to the police station, he discovered that DS Yellich had also returned.

'No other body or bodies in the rubble, boss,' he said in a spirited, sparky manner. 'Just the one. No other apparent burial in the grounds . . . any grave wouldn't be notice-able by now, the garden has been overgrown for fifteen years and any remains of the same vintage would also be skeletal.'

'And the sniffer dogs couldn't detect them, as we said earlier. Did you get back in the house?'

'No, boss. The owner . . . Mr . . .'

'Armstrong.'

'Yes, Mr Armstrong . . . he locked up and went away somewhere. I think he left us alone in the garden and went to the pub for a beer. His plans to work in the garden today were somewhat interrupted.'

Hennessey smiled. 'I'll say they were . . . you'll have to pay a return visit tomorrow.'

'Very good, sir.'

'Just to ensure there is no bad news in the bricks . . . frankly I don't think there will be, but we have to be thorough. Very thorough indeed. Strikes me one of our predecessors was not so thorough.'

'Sorry?'

'Well, if the deceased was reported as a missing person and if she was a part of the household of that house and her body was not discovered in a pile of rubble in the garden . . .

but let's not judge before we are in possession of all possible facts. Anything back from the collator?'

'Wouldn't know boss, only just got in.'

Hennessey walked to his office. He picked up the phone and dialled the collator's number.

'Collator.'

'DCI Hennessey.'

'Yes, sir.'

'Anything on those mis pers?'

'Five, sir . . . you allowed quite a time window.'

'Yes . . . any about five feet tall?'

'Let's look . . .' The collator paused. Hennessey heard the sound of files being shuffled and pages being turned. 'Yes, sir . . . one lady . . . Muriel Bradbury.'

'Have the file sent up to me, please, asap.'

Hennessey walked to the table at the corner of his office and made himself a mug of instant coffee. He glanced out of the window as the water in the kettle boiled. Tourists continued to walk the walls in droves. Hennessey returned to his desk, sat at it, and was gingerly sipping the steaming mug of coffee when a cadet tapped reverentially on his door. The cadet was tall, slim, a very good-looking boy, in Hennessey's eyes, a boy who would have little trouble attracting women, especially when in uniform.

'The collator asked me to bring this file to you, sir.' His manner was deferential, genuinely so it seemed to Hennessey.

'Thank you.' Hennessey extended his hand, the cadet handed the file to him and took a step back before turning and leaving Hennessey's office. Very deferential indeed.

Hennessey opened the file on Muriel Bradbury. He checked her height. It was given as five feet one inch tall, and a photograph showed her to be a thin-faced woman with what Hennessey believed to have been called a 'pageboy' haircut when the style was in vogue. The smile she gave to the camera seemed to be warm, her eyes though had a real look of warmth about them. Few photographs can actually

25

convey a personality, but Hennessey believed this photograph to be an exception. The woman in this photograph wearing a pink dress seemed to radiate warmth. Hennessey felt that he would have probably enjoyed meeting this woman had he been able to do so. He sipped the cooling coffee and read the file.

Muriel Bradbury, née Fallon, had been reported missing by her husband Gerald Bradbury some nineteen years earlier when she was forty-one years of age. No reason was given that might explain her disappearance. The marriage was described as 'healthy'. Mrs Bradbury was not thought or believed to be suffering from a mental illness . . . she seemed to be devoted to her children then aged sixteen, fourteen and ten. Her husband held an executive position with the York, Harrogate and Ripon Building Society. They owned the property at Number Two Mill Lane, Paxton on the Forest, in the Vale of York. Life for them was good. She and her husband had all they could hope for as a couple of their years, so it appeared. She seemed to have vanished. Her husband came home from work to find his children having returned from school unable to get into the house, no one at home. The house was thoroughly searched with the full co-operation of Mr Bradbury, as were the grounds. It was at this point that Hennessey read with interest that sniffer dogs were used to search and had cause, good cause he told himself, to reproach himself for his assumption that the investigating team had not been thorough. If the body had been concealed in the rubble, then the dogs, which were released into the grounds within twenty-four hours of Mrs Bradbury's disappearance, would have located her easily and quickly.

Hennessey sat back, causing his chair to creak. Clever, he thought, very clever . . . keep the body at a separate location, then put it in the grounds of the house once the police have searched them. Very clever. But puzzling is why they were left in the grounds until now. It was certain that they would be discovered at some point. And who owned the property prior to Mr Armstrong buying it, but was forced to abandon it, so that it lay ownerless for fifteen years?

He continued to read and saw that the file was cross-referenced to another case. He reached forward, picked up the telephone and once again spoke to the collator. He gave the collator the number of the cross-referenced file and asked that it be sent to him. Less than five minutes later, the same pleasant-of-appearance-and-of-manner cadet brought the file to him. It was with a mixture of intrigue mixed with some sadness that he read that Gerald Bradbury had been investigated for embezzlement from his employers a year before his wife's disappearance and that the embezzlement was believed to have been taking place systematically for a period of five years preceding her disappearance. The investigation had petered out because of lack of evidence but was still officially 'open'.

Two

. . . in which more is learned of the previous occu-
pant of the house and the accusing finger is pointed.

WEDNESDAY, 17 AUGUST

Yellich drove back out to Paxton on the Forest, to Number
Two Mill Lane, to the house of Armstrong. He arrived at
10 a.m., he would later recall, and parked his car on the
road and walked down the driveway. As he approached
the door at the side of the house, his eye was caught by
the flash of a camera bulb. His first thought was that the
Scenes of Crime Officers had returned to make a more
thorough documentation of the scene, but then, as his arrival
was announced by the two longhaired Alsatians, who ran
towards him, their guard-dog image being considerably damaged by wagging tails, Yellich noticed that the man with
the camera had all the artistic slovenliness of a newspaper
photographer . . . bearded, massively overweight, holding
one camera with a second wrapped around his neck. He
had clearly photographed Francis Armstrong standing in his
garden, with the house in the background. Standing next
to the photographer was a woman in her early thirties,
Yellich guessed, looking fetching in a crisp white blouse
and sand-coloured summer skirt. She had a head of tumbling
blonde hair, which seemed to explode round her face like a
sunburst and fall gently upon her shoulders. Her face was the
face of classic Nordic beauty and she served to remind Yellich
that when the Norsemen left this area of Britain, they left

28

more than their place names behind – like waterfalls called 'fosses' – they left their genes as well. Occasionally in York and its environs there is born a male or female child of classic Scandinavian appearance, even being born to parents who are both short-of-stature, dark-haired Normans . . . the Scandinavian gene had entered their bloodline, remained dormant for generations and then emerged. Sadly, suspicions about true parentage have occasionally surrounded such births and doctors have had to work hard to placate and reassure both partners.

'Mr Yellich!' Francis Armstrong beamed at Yellich as the latter bent to pat the two 'guard' dogs. 'I have all the visitors today.'

Yellich joined the group and said cheery 'good mornings' to the overweight photographer and the flaxen-haired maiden.

'This lady and gentleman are from the *Evening Post*,' Armstrong explained. 'I'm being fêted . . . they are doing a spread about me . . . local boy makes good and returns to his roots.'

'I see.' Yellich was surprised to see the woman had no ring on her finger. Not even an engagement ring. Too fussy perhaps, he thought. Surely she would not have been short of offers?

'This gentleman is from the police.' Armstrong introduced Yellich. 'DS Yellich . . . doubtless here about the alarming business I told you about.'

'Indeed.' The woman had a pleasantly soft voice, alert eyes. 'It certainly adds a spin to the story . . . bought yourself into the middle of a murder mystery. I am sorry for you, Frank, but it's a bonus for me . . . Mr Yellich, I wonder if you would care to comment on the discovery of the skeleton?'

'I wouldn't.' Yellich spoke firmly, noticing that Mr Armstrong clearly liked to be called 'Frank'. 'I believe a press release is being arranged . . . I can't pre-empt it.'

The woman smiled. 'Of course.'

'But doubtless you've got a photograph of the location . . . the pile of stones . . . now spread out . . . that's what I think is known as a "scoop", is it not?'

'It's of great use . . . we can sell it over the wire, it'll help Tom's reputation as a photographer.'

Tom, the overweight photographer, glowed with pride.

'And it'll help the paper, keep our editor and proprietors happy.'

'Could we take another of you please, Frank . . . I think I may have caught Mr Yellich in the last shot.'

'Oh, I'm sorry . . .' Yellich stepped sideways and stood behind Tom, the photographer, as he pointed his lens at Francis 'Frank' Armstrong. He noticed particularly how the eyes of the woman reported radiating warmth as she looked at Armstrong.

'Only ever happened once before,' Armstrong said as the journalists walked away, and when they were out of earshot.

'What has?' Yellich asked.

'Being interviewed for the local paper . . .' Armstrong opened the front door of the house, the dogs bounded in out of the heat. It was still not ten thirty and the day was clearly going to be hot, very hot indeed. 'Happened in Canada . . . got "profiled", as they called it, for the local newspaper when the company really established itself.'

'Sign of a successful man.' Yellich could think of little else to say.

'Frankly, I only did it for the villagers . . . the people in the village. Come in please.' Armstrong stepped across the threshold of his house, followed by Yellich. 'You see I wander up to the pub . . . but people here are cagey, keep themselves to themselves. I know they're curious about me and I can't blame them . . . not only a newcomer, but a guy living on his own . . . that's always a bit suspicious, and not only that, he's bought the rundown old house. I've had people walking down the road and just stop and stare at the house . . . then they see me and move on. There's no hostility, just curiosity. So when the *Evening Post* asked if they could do a spread about me . . . the human-interest angle . . . I agreed like a shot. They'll read about me in the village . . . then maybe all the wondering glances will stop and I'll get a game of dominos or darts in the evening.'

'It'll take a while to settle in and gain acceptance.'

'Plenty of time,' Armstrong said, 'it all goes naturally, but we never know the minute.'

'Certainly don't.' Yellich was reminded of the radio news bulletin he listened to when driving to Paxton on the Forest. The local news contained an item about a 21-year-old man who had died the previous night from injuries sustained in a pub brawl in York. A second man was assisting police with their inquiries, concluded the bulletin. It took the newscaster less than thirty seconds to read the item but a man's life had been cut off in the very bud of life, parents and family would be in a state of distress and disbelief and anger . . . You never do, he thought, you just never know the minute.

'Well, as you know, the house was pretty well derelict when I bought it. There was definitely nothing in the attic that would cause me to be suspicious. You're welcome to go up if you like, or venture in any room, but I believe it's the cellar that is of interest to you?'

'It is indeed.' Yellich thought how 'wordy' Francis Armstrong was for a self-made man and of such modest beginnings. He glanced to his left: the drawing room of the house was generously shelved, the shelves generously full of books.

'I've been down there, of course, but not searched it. There's quite a bit of junk . . . do you know what you are looking for?'

'Nope.' Yellich smiled. 'There may be nothing down there . . . of interest to us, that is, but if there is, I'll know it when I see it.'

31

'Well . . . door to your left down the hallway, opposite the kitchen door.'

Yellich went into the cellar, the steps angled sharply – a right turn into a flight of stone steps, then right again – and two steps further took him into a cool, dark cellar where daylight entering ground-level windows provided sufficient illumination.

Yellich found the cellar was of generous proportions: the floor plan of it seemed to be an exact plan of the house floor plan, forming thus a distinct 'L' shape, and was divided into 'rooms' created by the load-bearing walls of the house being extended downward to the floor of the cellar. The Victorians, he thought, certainly knew how to build.

A glance around the cellar revealed that it contained what Yellich would describe as 'junk', such as an old table of the type that was popular in the 1930s, solidly built and which folded to make a smaller dining surface and the legs of which could be unscrewed easily from a bolt by turning a wing nut. Overcome by curiosity and allowing himself to be diverted from the matter in hand, Yellich examined the table. It was dry, dusty, but was not at all rotten, nor damaged, and although dismantled into its constituent parts, all the parts were there. He thought it would clean up very nicely indeed – wipe off the dust, a coat of varnish . . . it was the perfect example of the sort of 'treasure' to be found in attics or cellars. There was an old cast-iron stove, the frame of a metal bed, neither of which intrigued him like the table, but all deeply layered in dust and clearly pre-dating Francis Armstrong's acquisition of the property. It was certain though, he felt, that Francis Armstrong had explored the cellar and anything noticeably of concern would already have been identified. If, he thought, if anything was of interest to the police in the cellar, it would be small in size and also concealed from immediate view. It was therefore a question of searching, of opening drawers of the old splintered desk, of moving the old cabin trunk to see what was behind it as well as opening it to see what it contained. It was clearly going to be a long, tiresome search.

In the event it was dusty, but not as long and as tiresome as he feared. They were found in a drawer of the desk, pushed to the back and hidden behind a hardback travel book, *A Guide to the Channel Islands*, dated 1928. What he had found were items of jewellery, a watch, a gold wedding ring, an engagement ring, a necklace. They were wrapped individually in small, clean plastic bags bearing the logo of the York, Harrogate and Ripon Building Society and were of the type used to keep small amounts of coin. On them was printed 'NO MIXED COIN' and the amount required in different denominations: ten pounds in pound coin; twenty pounds in ten pence pieces . . . but the significance for Yellich lay in the fact that those types of plastic bags were certainly not in use in 1928. So far as he was aware, such bags were introduced into British banking in the 1970s. The travel guide clearly predated the bags. The jewellery, therefore, had been placed in the drawer in the bags and the book placed after them in a wilful attempt to conceal them. Yellich put the bags in a larger 'production' bag and laid the production bag on one side. He continued to search the desk but no other drawer contained anything that seemed to be of relevance . . . old papers . . . a gas bill of many years earlier, which in the inflationary period that had elapsed since the bill was issued made the 'amount to pay' seem comically small; a few old ballpoints, but nothing of the clear significance of the jewellery. He left the cellar and in the hallway of the house called out, 'Hello.'

'Yes . . . hello . . .' Armstrong replied from the sitting room. He strode into the hall.

Yellich showed him the jewellery encased in the production bag. 'Have you seen these before?'

'I haven't. Were they in the cellar? Silly question . . . they must have been.'

'Yes . . . are any of the items in the cellar your possessions?'

'A few, easily identified . . . not much dust on them.'

'The old desk?'

'No . . . that was there when I came . . . I looked in the drawers . . . didn't find anything.'

'You found an old travel book?'

'A guide to the Channel Islands, yes . . . flicked through it, then put it back. I was moving in at the time, too much to do to be able to sit down and read old books, interesting as they may be.'

'I see . . . I actually found these in the drawer behind the book.'

'Well I never, I dare say I would have found them eventually. I intended to chop up the desk . . . can't be restored . . . mind you, there's a nice solid-looking kitchen table down there.'

'I saw it.'

'I have plans for that, but the desk is for the shredder . . . nice-looking jewellery though . . . worth a bit of money.'

'But they do not belong to you, Mr Armstrong? That is the important point.'

'They don't, regrettably . . . though legally they might, since they were in the house . . . once I signed the contract, everything belonged to me, house and contents . . . but they were not in my possession before I bought the house.'

'That's the issue. I have to remove them, they are germane to our inquiry. I can give you a receipt but I have to remove them.'

'Of course.'

Hennessey's phone rang. He let it ring twice and then casually reached forward and picked it up. 'DCI Hennessey,' he said.

'Dr D'Acre, York City.'

'Oh yes, Dr D'Acre.' Hennessey allowed an alertness to enter his voice.

'I have the results of the post-mortem.'

'Oh, excellent, excellent.'

'Well, her age at death was forty years, plus or minus one year. Now contrary to what I said yesterday, I may have come upon, chanced upon the cause of death . . .'

'Without any trauma to the skeleton?'

'Yes . . . there are indications that she drowned.'

'You can tell that from a skeleton?'

'Yes . . . I found diatoms in the long bone . . . a trace of marrow has remained in the tibia. I looked at it under the electron microscope and there they were . . . it's symptomatic of drowning, the person has to have been immersed whilst still breathing. Diatoms are microscopic creatures that live in fresh water, thrive in rivers and ponds but also occur in tap water. I have to say that diatoms are also atmosphere borne. You can breathe them in when you are walking down the road if the weather is humid, so it isn't absolute proof of drowning but it's a strong indicator . . . nine chances out of ten.'

'Strong enough,' Hennessey said. 'Certainly strong enough to set us in a promising direction . . . in fact we may have an identity.'

'Oh?'

'Yes, a lady called Muriel Bradbury . . . the height is about right . . . she had given birth . . . and now the age is right. She was forty-one when she was reported missing nineteen years ago.'

'Nineteen years,' Louise D'Acre gasped, 'that's an awful long time for a family not to know what has happened to a loved one. Her children alone will be fretting still, even if her husband bumped her off.'

'They still don't know.' Hennessey leaned back in his chair. 'We'd like a positive identification. If we can get that through her dental records it would be . . . very useful . . . in fact, if nothing else, the prosecution might hinge on the certain identity of the remains. I can see the Crown Prosecution Service refusing to prosecute unless we can establish beyond doubt the identity of the remains.'

'It's going to be a question of luck then. She definitely had had dental treatment but dentists in law are obliged to keep patient records for only eleven years. Some keep them as long as they have space to keep them; others, I understand, destroy records after eleven years and one day . . . it depends on the personality of the dentist. But that's the nuts and bolts . . . I'll fax my report to you today.'

'Thanks . . . appreciated.' Hennessey replaced the phone. As he did so his eye was caught by a movement to his right: DS Yellich stood in the doorway of his office holding a production bag. 'You look pleased with yourself, Yellich.'

'I have reason to be.'

'Come in and sit down, tell me about the contents of that production bag I see in your hand.'

Yellich sat in the chair in front of Hennessey's desk and carefully took the items of jewellery out of the plastic bag. 'Might still be prints on the bags, sir. Frankly, after nineteen years I doubt it, but I'll send them to Wetherby anyway.'

'Yes . . .' Hennessey looked at the items, turning them over with his ballpoint. 'Better chance of prints on these items if they have been kept inside plastic bags . . . no inscription that I can see. Where did you find them?'

Yellich told him.

'Well, bag them and tag them – the jewellery, the watch and the bags they were in – and send them by courier to Wetherby, then I'd like to you go to the estate agents who sold the house to Mr Armstrong, Hartwell's, Lower Ousegate . . . visit them, please . . . we have to trace the whereabouts of Mr Bradbury, they'll have an address.'

'As will the building society he worked for, boss.'

Hennessey gestured towards Yellich with an open palm. 'As you say, find his last known address . . . then you and I will pay the gentleman a call.'

'Yes, we handled that sale . . . a "snail" as we call them in the trade.'

'A snail?'

'A slow mover, but no chain . . . helps . . . going down fast though. If Mr Armstrong hadn't shown up when he did, I doubt we would have sold it.'

'Who was the previous owner?'

'I'll have to check the papers. Can I call you back? I don't wish to offend but I'd like to confirm it is the police to whom I am speaking.'

'Of course.' Yellich gave the number of Micklegate Bar Police Station and asked the representative of Hartwell's to ask for him by name: 'DS Yellich.'

His phone rang less than five minutes after had had put it down. 'Hartwell's,' said the cheery, eager to please, youthful, 'here to help you' sort of voice. The young man did indeed seem to Yellich to be excited about doing something out of the ordinary.

'Thanks for coming back so promptly.' Yellich pressed the phone to his ear with his shoulder; his left hand steadied his notepad; his right hand held the ballpoint pen.

'Well, we handled the sale for a Mr Gerald Bradbury.'

'Excellent, that's what we wanted to know. What is his present address?'

'Have to refer you to his solicitors . . . we had no direct contact with the gentleman.'

'They are?'

'Ellis, Burden, Woodland and Lake.'

'I have heard of them . . . they do a lot of criminal work . . . sort of people's lawyers, existing on Legal Aid fees . . . but still seeming to do quite well whenever I have seen them in the courthouse.'

'Well, when there are lawyers who can command one million pound fees per single brief, there are also lawyers who complain that they don't make any money and are still earning ten times the national average. Poverty is a matter of . . . something.'

'Degree,' offered Yellich.

'Is the word I was looking for.'

Yellich thanked the young man and replaced the phone. He consulted his private workplace address phonebook, much thumbed and grubby with age. Under 'E' he found the telephone number of Ellis, Burden, Woodland and Lake, solicitors. The voice on the phone when he called them was soft, gentle, feminine. Yellich identified himself and asked to speak to the partner who represented Mr Bradbury in the sale of his house a few weeks ago, and was told he was being put 'on hold'. He settled back in his chair whilst Handel's *Music for the Royal Fireworks* played soothingly in his ear. The music ended abruptly with a 'click' of the line and the soft, gentle, female voice said, 'That'll be Mr Tranter . . . only he's not a partner, though.'

Yellich smiled. 'It matters not. May I speak to him, please?' Yellich was then connected to Tranter and after the preliminaries, Yellich asked if he could be provided with Mr Bradbury's present address.

'I don't know . . .' By his voice, Tranter was young, nervous, inexperienced. 'I only recently qualified, in fact not fully qualified yet . . . I see an issue of client confidentiality here . . . this is a new one on me. I will have to take advice from one of the partners, the most senior partner I can access . . . if I can access one . . . this is a huge firm.'

'I know, I am familiar with your building . . . like an office block.'

'It is an office block,' said with humour. 'I like it . . . you can lose yourself. When I was qualifying I did part of my pupilage in a small firm which operated out of a converted house near the walls. I was in sole charge of the franking machine, amongst other duties like tea making, but there was no escape, prefer it here . . . but I'll have to take advice on this and phone you back.'

'Very good. Emphasize that it is a very serious crime we are investigating.'

'Can I say what it is?'

'Nope . . . but sufficiently serious to obtain a court order to force your firm to release the information and possibly charge your senior partners with obstructing the police in the course of their inquiries . . . but I hope it won't come to that.'

'I hope it won't either, sir. I'm sure the partners will be of the same mind. Who do I ask for?'

'Yellich, DS Yellich, at Micklegate Bar Police Station. Doubtless you'll have the number.'

'Doubtless we will. I'll come back asap.'

'Appreciate it.'

When the nervous Tranter phoned back, he gave an address in Holgate. He added that their senior partner had instructed him to contact Mr Bradbury to advise him that his address was going to be given to the police. Professional protocol dictated it.

'Rather wish you hadn't done that,' Yellich said as he wrote down the address given by Tranter.

'I was instructed to . . . sorry . . . I have to work here. I can't say too much but I doubt it will be damaging at all. He's not likely to flee the country.'

'Oh . . . ?'

'See what you think when you meet him, but the previously mentioned confidentiality issue prevents me saying anything further.'

Yellich went to see Hennessey. 'He's in Holgate, skipper.'

'Holgate . . .' Hennessey leaned back in his chair, 'well, how the mighty fall.'

'It's a solemn drop by the sounds of it . . . that house in Paxton on the Forest to YO26 . . . some descent in the social scale.'

'Some descent indeed. OK, grab your sun hat, let's pay a visit to Holgate . . . house of Bradbury . . . where exactly?'

'Retford Crescent . . . number twelve.'

The two officers decided to walk to Holgate. Turning left outside Micklegate Bar Police Station, they glanced at Micklegate Bar itself, the narrow stone-built arch that allowed only one line of traffic at a time in either direction and where once the head of Harry Hotspur was impaled and left in plain view for three years, as a warning to any who would defy the Crown, and then they turned left into Blossom Street, then right into Holgate Road and once over the railway bridge, they were in Holgate itself – its narrow streets, its rows of terraced houses, motorcycles chained to lampposts. This was a part of the city of York that the tourists do not visit. Hennessey and Yellich turned into Retford Crescent. Further along the crescent, children played soccer in the street, beyond that a woman hung washing on a line that was suspended across the width of the road. Number Twelve was close to the bottom of the street. The door was painted with green paint picked out at the edges with cream. The paint had faded in the sun over the years, and over the years had become grimy from the pollution from the railway line. The pollution was less than it would have been in the days of steam, Hennessey observed as he tapped on the door with the classic police officer's knock . . . tap, tap . . . tap . . . but diesel locomotives also leave much in their wake. The door was opened by a middle-aged man with silver hair . . . he wore a vest, a pair of baggy denims and was barefoot.

'Mr Bradbury?' Hennessey asked.

'Yes.' His voice had a certain polish about it, his bearing was of the English middle class . . . he had reserve, he had poise . . . he was defending his territory, so Hennessey read as he looked at the man.

'Police.' Hennessey flashed his ID. 'I am DCI Hennessey, my colleague here is DS Yellich.'

Yellich reached for his ID.

'It's all right, young man.' Bradbury held up his hand. 'If one of you is genuine, the other will be. How can I help you, gentlemen?'

'We'd like to ask you a few questions. May we come in?'

The interior of the house was like Bradbury himself, very un-Holgate, very neat, very clean, and while many houses in Holgate are also neat and clean, the Bradbury house had a certain learned middle-class feel to it. Solid, expensive furniture, expensive framed prints of classical paintings on the wall, but not popular classicism – here was not Constable's *The Haywain* nor a print of Van Gogh's *Sunflowers*, but two Bruegels, which Hennessey believed he recognized as *Census at Bethlehem* and *Hunters in the Snow*. His knowledge of Flemish painting did not extend to permitting him to say which of the Bruegels, the elder or the younger, had painted them. On the adjacent walls were prints of similarly impressive paintings, the sort that gave Hennessey the feeling that he should recognize them, but couldn't, though like the Bruegels, they were not likely to be chosen to be printed on the top of a box of chocolates or on the surface of tablemats. To have them appeal to you, you had to be in possession of knowledge of fine art. Hennessey thought they were those sort of paintings, just a little obscure, like the paintings he had recently seen at the Art Gallery. There were books in sight, just a few on shelves, but an indication, by their hardback nature and dull covers, that the house would contain more books, many more books. The television, too, was not the altarpiece that would be allowed to dominate the living rooms of many neighbouring houses, often too large for the room and in garish chrome and attached to a satellite dish on the outside wall. The television in the Bradbury household was, by contrast, a very simple 12″ screen that sat on a shelf in the corner of the room. Above it and below it and at either side of it were books.

'Please, gentlemen, take a seat . . . if you'll excuse me.' Bradbury left the room and returned a few minutes later wearing a clean shirt, and a pair of shoes. He sat in an armchair and said, 'How may I help you?'

'I understand you once owned the property at Number Two Mill Lane.'

'Paxton on the Forest . . .' He spoke clearly, calmly but a pained expression crossed his eyes. 'Yes, I did. In a happier time of my life.'

'You were married, I believe?'

'Twice . . .'

'Twice?'

'Twice . . . once to a lovely lady . . . once later to a less than lovely lady . . . but that is another story altogether . . . lucky to escape with my shirt though.'

'Your first wife . . .'

'Muriel'

'I understand she disappeared?'

'Yes, when two years had elapsed after her disappearance she was presumed dead, allowing her estate to be wound up . . . allowing me to remarry.'

'Your marriage to Mrs Muriel Bradbury, would you describe it as happy?'

'Very . . . we were very happy, three healthy children . . . now all adults, thirty-five years, thirty-three and the infant of the family . . . well, she's all of twenty-nine . . . and I have seven grandchildren. I keep their photographs in the back room . . . I live in the back room . . . this is the "best" room as folk say in Holgate, used for entertaining. I actually grew up in Holgate, made good, now it's come full circle.'

'Can you tell us about your wife's disappearance?'

'Again, after nearly twenty years?' Bradbury's voice trailed off, his jaw sagged. 'Oh . . . you are not going to tell me she has been found?'

'Well . . . we have some news for you, we also have some questions for you.'

'The police believed I had murdered her. I can't go through that again, I had no reason . . . no motivation.'

'People don't need reasons to kill, Mr Bradbury – premeditated murder is not a common crime. The majority of murders result from violence which gets out of hand, a row escalates to a fight which escalates to weapons being reached for. You know, the last murder I investigated was in a house which had been condemned by the Council and was going to be pulled down. The city found the two alcoholics who lived there alternative accommodation so they started to divide up the house. They could not decide on who owned the television which was inexpensive and very old . . . they argued, they fought and a knife was pulled, one was killed and the other will collect life when he appears before the Crown Court later this year. That is the usual form of murder, low-life, grubby and spontaneous . . . a motive isn't always needed, but murder is still murder.'

'Do I need a solicitor?'

'I don't know,' Hennessey replied. 'Do you?'

'I think I'd be happier with one.'

'In that case we must ask you to accompany us to the police station.'

'In that case you'll have to arrest me.' Bradbury was stone-faced. 'That means you've got twelve hours in which to charge me or release me.'

'We can always re-arrest you again.' Hennessey stood, walked over to where Gerald Bradbury sat, placed a hand on Bradbury's shoulder and said, 'Gerald Bradbury, I am arresting you in connection with the murder of Muriel Bradbury. You do not have to say anything, but it may harm your defence if you do not mention when questioned something you later rely on in court. Anything you do say may be given in evidence.'

'I like things to be done properly.' Bradbury also stood. 'I'll just get my jacket.'

Behind him he heard Yellich switch on his mobile. 'DS Yellich . . . with DCI Hennessey at 12, Retford Crescent, Holgate. We need a car. Yes . . . now . . . thanks.'

The twin cassettes of the recording machine spun slowly. The red 'recording' light glowed.

'The time is 18.30 hrs on Wednesday, the seventeenth of August. The location is Interview Room C, Micklegate Bar Police Station, York. I am Detective Chief Inspector Hennessey. I will now ask the other persons present to identify themselves.'

'Detective Sergeant Yellich.'

'Daniel Cooper, solicitor, of Ellis, Burden, Woodland and Lake and Co.'

'Gerald Bradbury. I wish it to be recorded that I was arrested at midday.'

'Gerald Bradbury, you have been arrested and cautioned in connection with the murder of Muriel Bradbury.' Hennessey spoke calmly.

'So I believe.' Bradbury remained alert.

Cooper, a slender, youthful-looking man remained silent but both officers thought he seemed utterly attentive.

'Mr Bradbury – ' Hennessey held eye contact with Bradbury – 'when you sold the house at Number Two Mill Lane, Paxton on the Forest, did you clear the house?'

'Of course.'

'Just say "yes" or "no". Completely?'

'More or less.'

'Meaning . . . ?'

'I left some few items in the cellar. Only junk . . . of no value.'

'Can you recall any items that you left in the cellar?'

'A table . . . an old cast-iron stove, a cabin trunk, a few old prints . . . nothing of value.'

'Anything else?'

'An old desk.'

'I am now going to show you some photographs.' Hennessey took a number of black-and-white photographs from a manila envelope. He laid them in front of Bradbury. 'Would you agree that these photographs show the interior of the cellar of the house at Number Two Mill Lane?'

'Paxton on the Forest. Yes, they do. When were they taken?'

'This afternoon . . . while you were eating your lunch . . . they had to be developed, which is why the interview was delayed.'

'Valuable six hours you lost there, Mr Hennessey.' Bradbury raised an eyebrow.

'Would you agree that this photograph shows the desk you recall leaving in the cellar?' Hennessey tapped one of the photographs.

'It does . . . yes.'

'Right. . . . I am now going to show you a book.' Hennessey lifted a production bag from beside his chair and placed the clear cellophane bag on the table.

Bradbury lunged for the book. 'Where did you find this?'

'You recognize it?'

'It was my father's . . . and his father's before him. The Channel Island guidebook. Of course I recognize it. My grandfather loved the Channel Islands and he infected my father with the love . . . and each year we would have a holiday in the Channel Islands. My father was a railwayman, you see . . . we enjoyed concessionary travel . . . it was only second-class but we could go anywhere free. Other kids in Holgate went to Scarborough or Blackpool for their holidays . . . we went to the Channel Islands. Cheap boarding houses when we got there but it was the Channel Islands. I took my children there too . . . we used the book a lot, though it had dated when my children were small, but we had fun using it to identify things which were contemporary with the book's publication . . . so that book links the generations of my family. I never thought I'd see it again.'

'Really?'

'Yes, really.'

'Now I want to show you some items of jewellery.' Hennessey took a second production bag and laid it on the table. 'Do you recognize these items of jewellery . . . any, or all?'

'All of them. They belonged to my wife.'

'Well, those items of jewellery were found in small change bags of the York, Harrogate and Ripon Building Society at the back of a drawer in that desk, and concealed from view by that book. Could you explain how they got there?'

'No . . .' Bradbury's voice faltered. 'I didn't put them there.'

'You didn't? Were you the sole occupant of the house at the time you sold it?'

'No, I had remarried by then.'

Cooper stirred. 'What proof do you have that the jewellery and the book were found where you say they were found? Was there an independent witness, for example?'

Hennessey shifted in his chair. He hoped his discomfort didn't show.

'No proof,' said Yellich. 'I found them, and there was no independent witness.'

'In that case, the issue of the jewellery being found where it was alleged to have been found is inadmissible in evidence. It is hearsay. You cannot continue with this line of questioning.'

Hennessey glanced at Yellich who shrugged his shoulders.

'All right,' Hennessey continued. 'Can you help us with the timescale?'

'Timescale?'

'The sequence of events . . . your wife disappeared nineteen years ago . . . in December of the year.'

'Yes . . . some Christmas that was.'

'Yes . . . you continued to live in the house for another . . . how long?'

'Five years . . . four, five . . . that sort of time. The bank repossessed it . . . it was used as collateral for a loan.'

'You had left the building society by then?'

'Yes . . .' Bradbury looked pained.

'All right, we'll return to that issue.' Hennessey paused.

'This may seem a strange question, Mr Bradbury, but tell us the story about the rubble in your garden.'

'The rubble?'

'There is a pile of bricks and lumps of concrete to the left of the garden, halfway between the house and the bottom of the garden.'

'The shelter.'

'The shelter?'

'During the Second World War, the owner of the house built an air raid shelter, four vertical lines of brick in a square and a massive concrete roof. It would have survived anything except a direct hit. There were few raids on York and none at all in the Vale, so it would have been redundant. It was poorly designed, no source of light except the door. I can only imagine that the thinking was that the design prevented light from escaping . . . but it meant the shelter was always dark. The door didn't open into the shelter, it opened into a corridor which led into the shelter. It was a dark, fearful place . . . the children were frightened of it. So I knocked it down, rather I hired a gang to do it. The concrete roof looked dangerous . . . once it started to slide off the bricks . . . anybody in the way would meet their maker. The men I employed thought the same because they demolished it from the roof down . . . used a pneumatic drill to break the roof up until there was barely room for one man to stand. Had scaffolding around it . . . no danger of it falling. Then they used the drill to demolish the bricks . . . from top to bottom, horizontal line by horizontal line. Left the bricks and concrete in a pile . . . and they stayed there despite my plans to do something with them. It was not long after that that Muriel disappeared and with her all my plans. So the pile remained until I was forced to quit the house . . . after which, everything fell into disrepair and the garden became overgrown. It's only just been sold after standing empty for fifteen years. Someone got a bargain . . . needs work but it can be restored. Had a good atmosphere . . . had an atmosphere of calm . . . of tranquillity. I sensed it as soon as I entered. I said to myself, "I want this house." Paid well over the asking price and brought up my children in it . . . until tragedy struck. The youngest was ten at the time . . . took it hard. Why do you ask about the pile of rubble?'

'Because it was where, yesterday, an adult female skeleton was found . . . within the rubble.'

Bradbury paled. 'She was there . . . all those years?'

'Apparently so.'

'But that isn't possible because the police searched the house and garden . . . they had dogs . . . the day after she went missing they searched the house and grounds. A dog would have detected her body.'

'Yes . . .' Hennessey nodded. 'So she was kept elsewhere . . . alive or dead, until the house and garden had been thoroughly searched. And then her body was placed in the one place the police wouldn't look.'

'But where it could easily be discovered . . .' Bradbury showed signs of alarm.

'Unless you had no intention of doing anything with the rubble and that points the finger of suspicion at you, Mr Bradbury.'

Bradbury glanced at Cooper who avoided eye contact.

'Did you murder your wife, Mr Bradbury?'

'No. No. No . . .'

'Which dentist did your wife use?'

'What on earth has that to do with anything?'

'Just answer the question.'

'The delightfully named, Mr Pick of York.'

'Mr Pick?'

'Appropriate name for a dentist don't you think? Like having a doctor called "O. P. N. Wide" . . . or "Sayahh". It was a family joke . . . the children thought them up . . . but Mr Pick was an excellent dentist, we were very lucky to have him. So why do you want to know who our dentist was?'

'The remains have still to be identified. We can positively identify them by matching the dental records if they are still in existence . . . but the skeleton is female, of your late wife's height and age when she was reported missing, and the remains were found in the garden of her house. It's your wife's skeleton all right, Mr Bradbury. So why don't you tell us what you know?'

A silence.

Bradbury leaned forwards. 'I have told you what I know.'

'Really?'

'Yes, really. If I didn't love my wife, I did love my children. I wouldn't deprive them of their mother.'

'Was your marriage happy?'

'Yes.'

'Will your children say the same?'

'You leave them out of this.'

'Oh, sorry . . . but they are witnesses in a murder inquiry . . . and they are adults . . . From the missing persons report you filed nineteen years ago, we have their names and dates of birth – they can easily be traced, especially if they have committed even the most minor of crimes.'

'I thought convictions were "spent" after a certain amount of time.'

'They are, but only for purposes of sentencing. The police retain all records. Why? Have any of your children come to our notice? We'll easily find out.'

'Martyn . . . our middle boy . . . he was prosecuted for disorderly behaviour when he was a teenager . . . maybe just turned twenty . . . he was fined in the magistrates' court.'

'We'll know him . . . his prints will be on file.'

'He's a university teacher – he's done the best of the three, but all have done well. His conviction didn't hold him back. He was arrested when he sat down in the middle of a road which was being built through an area of wetlands that was home to some endangered species of amphibia . . . a couple of hundred sat down, the police decimated them, prosecuted twenty and let one hundred and eighty make their own way home. Under the circumstances, the university he was at didn't expel him and because his crime was seen as not offending the moral code, it hasn't held him back . . . but he's known to the police.'

'Easy enough to trace then. So what will he tell us about your marriage? He was how old when your wife disappeared?'

'About fourteen, I think.'

'Old enough to know whether his parents had a happy marriage.'

'Yes.'

'So what will he say?'

'Why don't you ask him?'

'I think we will,' Hennessey snarled. 'I think we will.' He paused and said, 'This isn't the first time you have been in this police station, is it, Mr Bradbury?'

Bradbury sat back in his chair. 'My you have been busy, haven't you?'

'Like I said, we don't destroy records.'

'Why don't you tell us in your own words why you were previously in this police station.'

'What relevance has that to this inquiry, Chief Inspector?' Cooper glanced sideways at Hennessey.

'I believe they may be linked.'

'Why?'

'Because Mr Bradbury was investigated in connection with embezzlement at the building society in which he was employed at about the time of Mrs Bradbury's disappearance.'

'Investigated and cleared, I believe. Though I wasn't with the firm then, we represented him during the inquiry. We keep records as well, Chief Inspector.'

'Yes, investigated and cleared . . . but the embezzlement occurred and no one was prosecuted for it. It is still an open case and Mr Bradbury did leave the society after that.'

'Meaning?'

'Meaning nothing.'

'Exactly.'

'But it was an act which invites suspicion.'

'There was nothing suspicious about it.' Bradbury looked keenly at Hennessey, glanced briefly at Yellich, and then returned his keen gaze to Hennessey. 'I will take my solicitor's advice and refuse to answer questions about the embezzlement which took place, on the grounds that I was cleared and that I answered all questions put to me about the issue . . . and because it didn't take place about the time of my wife's disappearance, it took place about eighteen months before Muriel disappeared.'

'Twenty years on now . . . they occurred about the same time.'

'If you like, but the reason I left the building society was because although I was cleared, my job was safe, the nature of the thing is that I wasn't going anywhere after that, promotion-wise. Mud sticks, you know . . . so I talked about it with the board . . . and we agreed that it would be best for me and for the building society if I left. I was given a generous settlement, very generous . . . but that's why I left. No other reason.'

'I see. But things didn't work out for you quite as you had hoped?'

'That's an understatement, but I fail to see the relevance of the question.'

'As I do, Chief Inspector. Really, I must ask you to focus your questions.' Cooper spoke without looking at Hennessey. 'Frankly, I think you have taken this interview as far as it can profitably be taken. I have to ask you to charge my client or release him from custody.'

'Oh, we'll release Mr Bradbury,' Hennessey said in a calm and relaxed manner. 'We would have been happy to have had this chat in the comfort of his living room . . . it was he that insisted on being arrested. I would remind you of that.'

'So I am not under suspicion?'

'Yes, Mr Bradbury, you are under suspicion. But the net of suspicion is cast wide, other people may be caught in it. You are free to go. For now.'

Three

. . . in which a scam is described, a smallholder gives information and the gentle reader is privy to George Hennessey's home life, and personal tragedy.

THURSDAY, 18 AUGUST

'I knew it would be her. It had to be.' Martyn Bradbury sat at his desk in his study at the university. The view from his window showed the low-rise modern building, the generous green spaces on the campus . . . the small lakes with placid-looking ducks . . . the tall, angular clock tower . . . a few young people comfortably dressed in summer clothes. 'When I saw the news bulletin on the regional news . . . the house we lived in . . . the body of a woman . . . it was mother all right. I phoned my brother and sister . . . he's in London, she's in Liverpool . . . they wouldn't have seen the report. So at last we'll be able to bury her, have a place to visit. You see it's the not knowing that's the worst . . . now we know. But to think she was there all this time, in the garden.' Martyn Bradbury was lean, slender, bearded, bespectacled. To Yellich he did indeed look like a younger version of his father. 'In the rubble, it said on the news?'

'Yes,' Yellich said.

'I was fourteen when she disappeared. We were in that house for a few years after that . . . we used to play football and cricket on the lawn beside the pile of rubble . . . but don't bodies attract flies as they decay? Never saw flies buzzing round the rubble in noticeable quantities.'

53

'The pathologist, Dr D'Acre, said that if the body was placed in the rubble in the winter months it would have decayed by the spring – not fully skeletonized, but sufficient to be of little interest to flies.'

'Would it decay in the winter?'

'If the winter was mild enough, apparently so. If the mean temperature was above freezing then I believe it would, but it would be cold enough to keep the flies down. I'm sorry, I know that this is your mother we are talking about.'

'That's all right . . . it's her remains we are talking about, she was elsewhere by then. So I choose to believe. Father was going to do something with the rubble but there was no time pressure . . . the garden was vast . . . ten acres all told, not all landscaped, a lot left to waste, even a small wood. A brilliant house to grow up in but with all that room, the rubble wasn't taking up any space, any space at all, so it could be left where it was until father got around to doing something with it, which he never did. Well . . . you know that's more of a shock . . .'

'What is?' Yellich's gaze was momentarily drawn to a huge poster that was hung on the wall next to Bradbury. It was a poster of a wide square: solid, proud-looking buildings under a clear blue sky. Blue lettering at the bottom of the poster said 'Vienna'.

'The knowledge that it was where her body lay all the time. We sat around talking in anguish about where she could be, and all the time . . . she . . . her body, was under the rubble. But the police searched the ground with dogs . . .'

'Yes,' Yellich nodded. 'We know . . . the inference has occurred to us that she was placed in the rubble after the grounds had been searched and no body found. No further search would have been done . . . she was a missing person then . . . not a murder victim. We don't have the resources to search for missing people unless they are aged sixteen or less . . .'

'I can understand that. So you suspect father?'

54

'Yes, I am afraid we have to. I presume he contacted you?'

'Yes, when he got home, about 8 p.m. He said you had arrested him.'

'We did, but he's misleading you slightly . . . he refused to accompany us, even to talk to us unless we arrested him.'

'He didn't tell me that, but that's father.'

'Yes?'

'Yes. He can be very misleading if it suits him. Very economical with the truth. An awkward personality. He was a good provider but he created a stressed household. It was like walking on glass at times. No wonder we spent so much time in the garden when we were younger . . . the rows they had.'

'This is what I wanted to ask you, Mr Bradbury.'

'The nature of my parents' marriage?'

'Yes.'

'Well, I can't stand in judgement because my own marriage has had its volatile moments . . . but yes, they argued . . . fought a lot . . . never came to blows, not that I was ever aware of.'

'Can you remember what the relationship was like at the time your mother disappeared?'

'Stormy. They had one hell of a fight the night before . . . a set-to . . . shouting . . . we all sat upstairs listening to it. That was the last time I heard my mother's voice, the next morning father got us up and off to school, telling us that mother was "unwell" and sleeping in the spare room. They always slept separately after a row and "unwell" often meant mother was in a bad mood after a row, so there was nothing at all unusual in that, it was when we got back from school that we realized something was wrong. She just wasn't there . . . but her car was. You've been to the house?'

'Yes.'

'You've seen how remote it is. There are neighbouring houses but a walk into the village could take twenty minutes . . . forty minutes return . . . and carrying shopping. If mother left the home, she left in her car. So her car in the drive . . . but an empty, locked house. My sister arrived first. She was ten at the time at primary school, my brother and I arrived home later. We had much further to travel from our secondary school . . . and the three of us were waiting when father came home. He had a key of course . . . let us in . . . we searched the house . . . nothing. I remember it like yesterday, there was nothing out of place . . . nothing missing but a strong sense of "something has happened". Have you experienced that sensation?'

Yellich confessed that he had, on quite a few occasions. Adding that he had always been proved right: on each occasion he had felt the sensation, it transpired that something, usually an accident or an act of violence, had in fact taken place.

'It's almost tangible, isn't it? I have felt it again once or twice, but that was the first time, and like the first time in many things, it's the one that stays with you.' Martyn Bradbury paused. 'Well, it's the one I remember most clearly, but then I had a certain interest in it. That might be the reason why I remember it. This is difficult . . .'

'What is?'

'The absorbing of it, the implication of mother being in the rubble all the while . . . thank heavens it's not term time, I couldn't deliver a lecture . . .'

'This is the long vacation?'

'For the undergraduates . . . they're supposed to use it to study but most of them take jobs and then hitch-hike to Greece. For everybody else it's work as usual. For us teachers, it's publish or perish . . . I'm working on a paper . . . teaching doesn't start until October. But the break from teaching gives me space . . . I mean space in my head to deal with this.'

'So . . . I understand your father remarried?'

'Sandra . . . things went apart from then on. Sandra was the opposite of mother in every sense. Mother was a small, finely built lady; Sandra was big, tall, statuesque . . . towered over father. Mother was big minded, generous minded, towards her children anyway; Sandra was petty minded. Mother was a mature, strong personality; Sandra was spiteful. Even given to throwing our possessions away and letting us search the house looking for them. She was reasonable towards me and Julian but to Alyson she was the archetypal wicked stepmother. Alyson was only ten when mother disappeared and Sandra showed her no sympathy . . . had a tongue like a stingray's tail . . . used to cut her dead as well, just ignored her when she came in – glanced at her once then turned her back on her. Alyson just didn't know where to put herself.'

'How long did that marriage last?'

'As long as father's business, which is the other thing about dear stepmama Sandra . . . she was a gold-digger. Her and her mate Monica . . . What was that woman's name? Monica Wickersley . . . yes, that was it – Monica Wickersley. Always went everywhere together . . . a constant visitor to the house was Monica. Father gave up his job at the building society for some reason, which I can only describe as stupid. Heavens, he was in his mid-forties, he was the manager of the biggest branch of the York, Harrogate and Ripon Building Society, with the possibility of promotion even beyond that . . . maybe to the board, and a very nice pension at the end of it all and what does he do but give it up to start a business venture. Mid-forties is no time of life to start up a business. I was fourteen then but I thought it was an act of certifiable insanity even then and mother seemed to feel the same but accepted it for some reason. When he was employed he was relaxed, he came home each evening and had time for his family, and each weekend too. When he was self-employed he was keyed up all the time and worked at home until midnight. But the rows stopped . . . at least all the rows stopped for a while. Father had no time to row and mother's disapproval of his action took the form of icy detachment, then the old pattern set in and the rows started up again.'

'What was your father's business?'

'He set himself up as a wine importer. He had no knowledge of the wine trade . . . put up some money, but actually remortgaged the house . . . our lovely home . . . to a bank, not the building society, which in later years I saw as curious. I have often wondered whether his departure from Y. H. & R. was less than amicable but I wasn't privy to it. Sandra came into his life with indecent haste after mother disappeared . . . a matter of months . . . stayed for two years which was the length of time it took for father's business to collapse. The bank seized the house and we went to live in a little terraced house in York 26, Holgate, all except Sandra, who deserted father and went rich-man hunting. I confess it was with some joy that I watched the house fall into disrepair because the bank couldn't sell it, but father was shrewd, he kept a nest egg that the bank didn't know about . . . a nice sum with a separate bank . . . enough to keep him comfortable by Holgate standards and he'll qualify for his state pension soon. He'll survive . . . his house is dry, he has a good roof and there's a corner shop for all his wants and needs. But it's hardly the lifestyle he could have had if he had stayed with the Y. H. & R.'

'Hardly,' Yellich nodded. 'I have visited your father's house . . . cosy, I thought.'

'Oh, cosy is a perfect word to describe it, but you've also seen our old house at Paxton on the Forest, that could still have been his and my children could have visited him there and played in the ten acres . . . and our own private little wood and watched the badgers at night from the bedroom window.'

'You seem to resent your father's decision.'

'I do . . . but it was his to make . . . and he made it. We fell from grace, in a big way.' Bradbury paused. 'I have a student . . . a weird girl, she has so much potential but her head has been through the shredder and I worry about her state of mind. She once said in a tutorial group that her favourite pastime was pulling wings off angels and watching them plummet to their death.'

'Blimey!'

'She is a very strange girl and I will say no more than that. I don't think she'll graduate, in fact I don't think she'll return in October for her final year . . . but when she said that, I thought of my father . . . he was a good man . . . still is essentially . . . there is good in him. If he misleads, it's because it amuses him; if he had endless rows with his wife, it was because that was their relationship. He was an excellent provider and never displayed the slightest hint of violence to any member of his family, but somebody pulled his wings off and he plummeted to his death, financially speaking.'

'He was believed to have his hand in the till.' Mr Seymour, Sebastian Seymour by his nameplate on his desk, had received George Hennessey in his office. Hennessey had sat as invited in the leather Chesterfield armchair in front of the desk. He sat still, very still, discovering rapidly that any slight change in his posture caused the leather to squeak. He'd asked Seymour if he recalled the circumstances surrounding Gerald Bradbury's departure from the building society.

'But nothing was proved?'

'Nothing. It was essentially a very simple scam as scams go and it happens not infrequently in banking and building societies. An employee finds a dormant account, an account that has just been left to accumulate . . . often elderly people . . . or someone who has just put an inheritance on one side without wanting it to be part of their day-to-day budget, and the corrupt employee milks it.'

'Is that quite easy?'

'Too easy.' Seymour was a thick-set man. He wore a dark suit, white shirt and a black tie. His office was of dark, panelled wood, deep, dark-red carpet; portraits of men hung on the wall. Hennessey presumed they had also been senior managers in the York, Harrogate and Ripon Building Society.

'If you know what you are doing, like many things. We often only catch the felon if they are stupid enough to transfer the money in noticeable quantities to their own accounts . . . accounts in their name. But if they skim a little here, a little there and ensure the balance looks as it should look and if they open accounts in a false name, then it's difficult to trace. Now this was over twenty years ago . . . then, all you had to do to open a building society account was provide something with your name and address on and one other form of identity . . . a library card and an envelope which had been delivered to your house. Now, we want real proof of identity plus references from banks or solicitors. So then, at that time, it was very easy to open a building society account with a false name and, at the time, CCTV was virtually unknown, so we had no photographic evidence about who was paying money in or taking money out.' Seymour paused. 'So what happened was that a very large amount of money was removed from a dozen or so dormant accounts and transferred into an account, with this society, at a small branch. The money was then withdrawn in the form of hard cash.'

'Couldn't be traced.'

'Exactly . . . took place over an eight-month period . . . it was eventually discovered in the annual audit. The name and the address were traced to a lodging house . . . a huge Victorian home, broken up into bedsitters. The person had taken a room there long enough to have some mail delivered with his or her name on it and joined the library.

'His or her . . . no prefix?'

'No, just an initial, then a surname. Again, today we would insist on full first names and a prefix but twenty years ago passbooks were issued to L. Smith or D. Brown, that was just the way it was. When we saw what had happened, we froze the suspect account, but by then it was all but empty. None of the employees at the bank could identify the owner of the account because even though it was a small branch, it was in the city centre and people stream in and out. He or she just didn't "register" with any of the clerks, or tellers as they are known today, and doubtless he or she would have been heavily disguised.'

'Disguised?'

'Well, yes . . . the crime was an "inside job", as I believe the expression has it . . . and we move staff around . . . any member of staff from the small branch could have been posted to Bradbury's branch. Wouldn't have done for the thief to be recognized as a customer in a small branch. I mean, if I was doing it, I would disguise myself, if only to dress in casual clothing rather than my usual suit and tie.'

'Point.' Hennessey then asked what drew attention to Gerald Bradbury.

'No one thing as I recall. He was understood to have money problems, his house was still heavily mortgaged at the time . . . people who work in building societies are offered an interest-free mortgage as a perk.'

'Interest-free mortgage . . . well, I never knew that.'

'It's worth an awful lot of money. You pay back what you borrow and nothing more. Unlike our customers who pay back three times the amount they borrow over twenty-five years. But Bradbury had some difficulty with making his repayments and at his age he should have been further into his mortgage repayments than he was. He asked to borrow on the equity he had . . . was told "no", told he had to manage . . . he had outgoings he wasn't telling us about. The annual audit picked up the fact that the dormant accounts had been milked and it turned out the milking began shortly after Bradbury was told he couldn't remortgage.'

'The inference being that he was told he couldn't borrow from the society so he took money anyway?'

'Yes. In a nutshell.' Seymour paused. 'He was also . . . and this is strictly confidential.'

'Of course.'

'He was also believed to be carrying on a liaison with an undermanager. York is a small city, as you know, it is a city which has city status because of a charter, not because of its size . . . but by its nature it's a small town. I don't like living in York, I live out and drive in.'

'So do I,' Hennessey smiled. 'I live in Easingwold.'

'A pleasant little town. I live in Leeds. I am a city person and if I live in a city, I like it to be a proper city. Leeds suits me admirably. You can hide in a city . . . it has anonymity, it's that that I like. I like going into Leeds on a Saturday knowing that I am highly unlikely to meet someone I know. You can't do that in York and Bradbury was seen wining and dining Miss Sandra Picardie, who was . . . probably still is . . . a lady who liked the finer things in life. Was good enough at her job but she didn't earn the sort of money that could pay for those designer clothes or enable her to run her BMW.'

'Rich older men?'

'That was what was believed to be the case. Paying for a house, a family with a non-working wife and keeping the likes of Ms Picardie in the manner to which she would become rapidly accustomed would be quite a drain on anybody's income. The other thing which pointed the finger at Bradbury was that Ms Picardie didn't have a mortgage with us . . . but she had a nice address within the walls . . . a new-build flat on Cromwell Road. You may know them. They are not local authority nor housing association. If you live there, you are an owner, at least a mortgagee, or you rent it from the owner. Ms Picardie's father was a bus driver . . . she was not married . . . so again the inference was that she was being kept in a little love nest for her older lover's delectation.'

'The older lover being Gerald Bradbury?'

'Was what we believed. We notified the police of course, handed the investigation over to them. They interviewed Bradbury but he wouldn't confess to anything and nothing could be traced to him. The trail of the money went to the one account in the false name and from there it was withdrawn as hard cash. Never a money order, or a cheque that could be traced.'

'Exactly how much money was stolen?'

'Exactly, I don't know, but the value of property twenty years ago being what it was . . . enough to buy a love nest and pay the running costs of a BMW.'

'And buy more designer clothes?' Hennessey prompted.

'And buy more designer clothes.' Seymour smiled a thick-jowelled smile. Hennessey felt a warmth towards Seymour, he felt Seymour approved of him. A mutual liking, or equally, a mutual disliking, they happen. In this case, Hennessey was pleased that it seemed to be a mutual liking. 'But that was the end of Bradbury, he couldn't be dismissed but he wasn't going anywhere further in the Society. He was likely to be shunted into a siding where he could rubber stamp all day long until he collected his pension, would live under a cloud of suspicion and be constantly watched, or he could tender his resignation in return for generous severance pay. He chose the latter. He made a very clear statement that he did it under protest and made it plain that by accepting the severance pay he was not signalling his guilt. He accepted the hard fact that his career with the Society couldn't continue and the severance payment was the logical way out of the mess and best for all concerned.'

'He walked out of the tent?'

'Yes,' Seymour smiled. 'I like the reference, but whether it was the noble act of a gentleman or whether he was sneaking away into the night with his pockets full of other people's money still remains to be seen. By now we'll probably never know. After that he just disappeared. Lost all contact with him.'

'Well that has been very helpful, Mr Seymour.' Hennessey stood. 'I think we'll go and have another chat with Mr Bradbury . . . sounds like he was a little economical with the truth.'

'You've spoken to him?'

'All too briefly and in the presence of his solicitor. Tell

me, do you know what happened to the younger woman . . . Miss Picardie?'

'Oh, she left us . . . don't know what happened to her . . . I rather think the Building Society wasn't glamorous enough for her.'

'No luck with the dentist, skipper.' Yellich patted his phone when Hennessey stood in his doorway. 'Mr Pick retired some years ago and a new broom sweeping clean cleared out all of Mr Pick's files that were over eleven years old . . . but I think we can safely assume it is the remains of Mrs Bradbury that were uncovered.'

'I think we can too. If push comes to shove, we can determine the ID by DNA sampling . . . if the children give their DNA we can check it with hers. How did you find Bradbury junior?'

Hennessey walked into Yellich's office and sat down in the chair in front of Yellich's desk.

'Very co-operative . . . painted a picture of a volatile household; well, a volatile marriage – Mrs Bradbury was a devoted parent by all accounts. The picture painted was of a woman holding her family together, valiantly, so it would seem, with a difficult husband to deal with. Gerald Bradbury was one for game-playing, it would further seem . . . he enjoys misleading people.'

'A dangerous game to play.'

'But so much for his happy marriage to the first Mrs Bradbury. That myth was blown out of the water . . . the second Mrs Bradbury, Sandra by name—'

'Sandra!'

'Yes. Why, is that significant, skipper?'

'Could well be, Yellich. Could very well be . . . but carry on.'

'Well, she was a cold fish to the children . . . and stayed married until the wine-importing business collapsed.'

'Wine importing? Is that where the money went?'

'To his son's dismay. The issue of the embezzlement is not known to his family, clearly so. The son was puzzled by his father's decision to leave the building society . . . angry, really.'

'OK, we have to respect that until we can prove Bradbury's complicity with the embezzlement.'

'You think he was involved?'

'Well, I have just come from the York, Harrogate and Ripon Building Society, the head office no less. Pleasant chat with a senior director called Seymour, interesting tale he had to tell. My ears pricked up when you said that Bradbury's second wife was called Sandra.'

'Apparently she was so called.'

'Did you get the maiden name?'

'I didn't, boss.' Yellich patted the phone a second time. 'Simple call to the university, Dr Bradbury in the department of something . . . I have his extension.'

'Do that, will you? But do not be surprised if her maiden name was Picardie.'

'Picardie? Why?'

So Hennessey told him.

'Two women in his life . . . things getting expensive . . . scraps the older model and replaces her with a younger model. It's not an unknown motive.'

'It isn't, is it? In fact it's one of the best known and the oldest. Ye olde love triangle.' Hennessey looked at his watch.

'Clever of him as well . . . keep the body somewhere until the police had searched the garden, knowing they wouldn't come back.'

'Risky though . . . very risky . . . but he's a man who enjoys risks, it would seem, enjoys misleading, enjoys playing games.'

'Yes . . . yes.' Yellich spoke slowly. 'It would seem to be in keeping with what we are beginning to learn about Bradley senior but the risk becomes an act of stupidity when he left the bones in place when he had to quit the house.'

'That had occurred to me,' Hennessey said. 'He could easily have stolen back one dark night, removed the bones . . . the skull at least, though with DNA they could still have been identified.'

'If you are going back at all, you'd go back to remove all the bones. Something might have prevented him . . . something must have prevented him, and as the years went in . . . and the house began to become derelict . . . he may have allowed it to slip out of his mind.'

'I think we'll find out the reason.'

'Tell me . . . the file on the embezzlement, you've read it?'

'Yes, boss.'

'Did the recording mention anything about Gerald Bradley having an affair with Sandra Picardie?'

'I don't think it did, I think I would have picked it up if it had. It certainly mentioned that Bradbury had financial troubles, wanted to remortgage his house . . . thus he had had a motive for embezzlement, but no mention of an affair that would drain his resources. I'll go over the file and check again.'

'If you would . . . it's a puzzle why it wasn't mentioned, but twenty years on things can get confused, incidents get put out of sequence. It might have been that Bradbury was seen entertaining Ms Picardie after the police investigation, not before . . . maybe even after he had resigned from the Y. H. & R.'

'That would explain it, boss.'

'It would. And I'd still like to pick the brains of the officer in charge of the original mis per inquiry . . .'

'Bloke called Page, sir,' Yellich said. 'Retired now . . . the custody sergeant remembers him . . . he was saying this morning . . . sat with him in the canteen. Mentioned his name to the custody sergeant, telling the sergeant about the old file . . . Jim Page is only recently retired, alive and well and enjoying his retirement in Thirsk where he's taken a smallholding.'

'All right,' Hennessey stood, 'I have to go and see the Commander, got a note in my pigeonhole this morning. I think I know what it's going to be about and I will have to appraise him of this case, now it's become a murder investigation. It's eleven thirty . . . what are you doing for lunch?'

'Canteen, boss.'

'That stodge . . . don't know how you can stomach it.'

'It's cheap . . . that helps it go down very well. I've got a mortgage and two mouths to feed beside my own.'

Hennessey felt stung. 'Well, could you do those three things before lunch? Ascertain Mrs Sandra Bradley's maiden name, check the recording in Bradley's file . . . see if she is mentioned as Ms Picardie, and find out what Jim Page's address is . . . give him a courtesy call, ask if it's all right for us to visit him this afternoon.'

'This afternoon?'

'Yes . . . I fancy a drive out to Thirsk . . . lovely day like today. And you know how I detest driving.'

'OK, boss. Consider them done.'

Hennessey left Yellich's office and walked to the office of Commander Sharkey. He tapped on the door. After an imperious pause of approximately one minute, during which Hennessey knew he must not knock again, Sharkey said 'come'.

'Ah, George,' Sharkey looked up and smiled as Hennessey entered his office, 'take a pew.'

Hennessey sat in the chair in front of Sharkey's desk. 'You wanted to see me, sir?'

'Yes . . . George . . . George, I want to make it plain that your performance is not being criticized, your efficiency is not in question.'

'I am not going to a police desk, sir. I know what you are going to say . . . you've said it before.'

'You are close to retirement, George . . . I want to see you reach and enjoy your retirement.'

'I do too, sir, but I am quite content to remain in the field. Already today I heard about a chap who was offered sidelining and rubber stamping or his resignation . . . he chose the latter and I fully understand why he made the choice he made.'

'I know we've been over this ground before, George . . .' Sharkey was a small man for a police officer, he had come to the Force after a period as a commissioned officer in the Army followed by a further period in the Royal Hong Kong Police Force – two framed photographs hung on his wall told the story of his life. His desk was, in Hennessey's view, unhealthily tidy . . . unlike his, which was often a shifting sand of files and papers. Hennessey always felt uncomfortable in the presence of people with tidy desktops . . . the just-so neatness . . . the oppressive personality of such folk, the needing to dominate the world around them, or so thought George Hennessey, after a career spent observing people. He didn't envy Sharkey's wife and children. That aspect of Sharkey's life was also documented, photographically, by means of a third photograph, which hung on the wall behind him. 'We had a teacher at school, "Johnny" Taighe by name. Approaching retirement, smoked like a chimney, overweight, red nose – so he tippled in the evening. He should have been allowed to soft-pedal towards retirement . . . instead they piled on the pressure . . . and when an able maths teacher left the school to better himself, "Johnny" Taighe, who could cope with lower-school stuff, was told to teach final-year maths . . . and he couldn't, George . . .'

Hennessey listened patiently – he had heard the story before – but realized that Sharkey needed to tell it . . . he thought it was as if the man needed to purge himself.

'He wasn't up to the job . . . not his fault . . . but asking "Johnny" Taighe to teach final-year maths was not dissimilar to taking the payload from the back of an articulated lorry and putting it on to a milk float . . . the excess weight, the smoking, the drinking, the false good humour of the man . . .

he was a heart attack waiting to happen and, essentially, that's what happened. He went home, complained to his wife that he felt ill and just keeled . . . but that's not going to happen to anyone of mine.'

'I feel able to cope, sir.'

'Well, your performance tells me you are coping . . . the first sign of burnout is believing you are doing your job but in fact you are falling short. So we'll leave things as they are, but if you start falling short, George, I'm taking you out of the field, and you'll shuffle papers and rubber stamp until you collect your gold watch and if you don't like it, you don't like it . . . though it hasn't come to that yet. But I am not going to my own retirement with the knowledge that I killed one of my staff by pushing him beyond his capabilities. So if I do take you out of the field, it's for my needs as much as yours.'

'Understood, Commander.'

'The other worry . . . I know I've asked you this before.'

'I am sure there is no corruption at this police station, sir . . . as sure as I can be. Of course, we'll never know there's a bad apple until it emerges . . . but I am as confident as I can be.'

'I am relieved to hear that, George . . . I had enough of that there.' He nodded towards the photograph of a younger Sharkey in the uniform of an officer of the RHKP. 'I am proud and pleased with that but – ' Sharkey tapped the photograph of himself when in the Army – 'but that . . .' again he nodded to the photograph of himself in the Royal Hong Kong Police, 'that I keep there to remind me of a part of my life that I am not proud of. I took bribes there.'

'You should be careful, sir . . . that admission could be very costly.'

'It's an open secret. Anybody who served with the RHKP took bribes . . . it was the way of it . . . and by "it" I mean the whole Chinese mentality. They don't see it as corruption . . . it's a different thinking . . . but it wasn't corruption as we would see it in the West. Bribing officers to destroy evidence . . . or buying information about underworld opponents . . . it was a more passive sort of corruption. A sergeant would suggest I do not patrol a specific part of the Colony for the next two nights . . . so I don't, I go elsewhere . . . and a brown paper envelope full of hard cash is in my desk drawer. That's how it was . . . and that money is still in my finances, my finances are tainted.'

'It was the way of it, sir.'

'I have little choice. If I had refused to go along with the system, I would have been killed . . . I would have disappeared . . . and I wasn't there very long . . . a few months only, but I was there. I would find it difficult to deal with if it should happen here.'

'Well I have my finger on the pulse of this nick as much as anybody, sir. If I hear even a whisper, I'll let you know.'

'I appreciate it, George, I appreciate it. Now . . . the Muriel Bradbury case, where are you with that?'

'Finger of suspicion points to her husband, sir. He's shrewd, clever, sly . . . a game player . . . he seems to like toying with us. Believed to have embezzled huge amounts of money from his employers.'

'Believed?'

'Nothing could be proved, sir. Sergeant Yellich's looking at the recording as we speak but it may be that they were unaware of his motive . . . he apparently had a young lady friend who had expensive tastes and who may, or may not have become the second Mrs Bradley. This afternoon, I'm going to visit the officer on the original mis per inquiry.'

'Who is he?'

'Jim Page . . .'

'Before my time . . . but please keep me informed.'

'I will, sir.'

Hennessey returned to Yellich's office. Yellich was standing by his desk.

'Just about to go to lunch, skipper.'

'So I see. What did you find out?'

'That Picardie was indeed Sandra Bradbury's maiden name, that no mention of Sandra Picardie is made in the case file in respect of the embezzlement inquiry and Jim Page would be delighted to receive us anytime this afternoon. He gave me clear directions to "Rookwood".'

'Rookwood?'

'His smallholding, just outside Thirsk.'

'Right . . . meet you here at one thirty.'

'One thirty it is, boss.'

Hennessey walked the medieval streets of York and probably, he thought, motivated by his recent visit to the Art Gallery, he went into an art shop and purchased a framed print of a painting by Turner: *Fonthill*, believed to have been painted in 1799. He believed the print would look very well hanging on the wall above the fireplace in the living room of his house.

Later he lunched at the Ye Olde Starre Inn in Stonegate, which he accessed via a short snickelway. He sat snugly in a corner underneath a low beam and beneath a print of a map of 'Yorkshyrre' dated 1610, and with the 'moft famous, faire Citie Yorke, defcribed'. He savoured his meal of Cumberland sausage and then strolled back to Micklegate Bar Police Station, as usual taking the walls rather than the pavement.

Yellich smiled as Hennessey entered his office. He tossed a bunch of car keys into the air and caught them. 'Ready, boss?'

'We'll go in two cars as far as Easingwold,' Hennessey said. 'Leave my car in my driveway, drop me back home on the way back from Thirsk. No point in me coming into York just to drive out again . . . we'll be passing my house on the return journey.'

'OK, boss,' Yellich stood, 'that makes sense.'

Yellich and Hennessey convoyed out of York with Yellich, the junior officer, following Hennessey as protocol dictated. At Easingwold they stopped outside a solid-looking, detached

71

house on the Thirsk Road. Hennessey turned his car into the driveway, got out and walked at a brisk pace back to where Yellich had parked his car on the opposite side of the road. He got in the passenger seat and Yellich drove on across lush, flat landscape to Thirsk, and following directions to 'Rookwood', to the home of Jim Page.

'Found us all right, I see.' Page was a young-looking man for his early sixties. He had a long face, a sinewy body, and alertness about his eyes, plus a warmth, a friendliness, which said that a career in the police force had not imbued him with the cynicism, a certain hardness, that was occasionally the lot of other career police officers. He stood in his shirt sleeves and corduroy trousers and working boots at the front of his house, two spaniels at his feet who barked aggressively at Yellich and Hennessey until told to 'shut up!' by Page. 'So who's who? You'll be DCI Hennessey?'

'Yes.' Hennessey and Page shook hands. 'George, please call me George.'

'I left just as you were arriving. Came from London I heard.'

'Originally,' Hennessey said, 'but I've been in Yorkshire since I was in my twenties . . . I moved to Micklegate Bar when I was promoted.'

'I see. And you'll be DS Yellich?'

'Yes, sir.' Yellich and Page shook hands.

'Well, do come in . . . I'll get some tea arranged.'

Page entertained Hennessey and Yellich in his living room, having first conceded to the house's neatly kept manner by removing his working shoes in the porch of his house. Tea was served by a smiling Mrs Page, in an attractive blue dress, who had also evidently retained her slender and youthful appearance into her middle years and who then withdrew and was seen and heard no more. After the preliminaries, Page said, 'So you are investigating the disappearance of Muriel Bradbury?'

'Yes . . .' Hennessey stirred his tea, though it was not

sugared. 'In fact things have progressed . . . we are now investigating her murder.'

'You've found the body?'

'You haven't read the papers or watched the news, I take it?'

'Not for the last day or two . . . the smallholding keeps me busier than the police force ever did. I'm breeding pigs,' Page added proudly. 'I'm building up a herd of Gloucester Old Spots . . . so called "orchard pigs". Have you heard of them?'

'Confess I haven't.'

'Lovely beasts. Keep 'em in orchards if you can, they gobble up the windfalls . . . and their pork is of passing succulence . . . even for pork it's particularly sweet. I have an arrangement with a local butcher: I breed them and fatten them, the slaughterhouse slaughters them, and the butcher butchers. He buys from me and sells on to customers, and I get a few complimentary chops . . . a ham to hang . . . a few links of real sausages. It works quite well. I couldn't make it pay as a farming concern . . . we are pension dependent but the smallholding pays for itself without actually generating a profit . . . farming is in a bad way at the moment.'

'So I hear.' Hennessey put his cup of tea down and reached forward to take a ginger biscuit from the plate of assorted biscuits left by Mrs Page. He glanced out of the window. The Pages' house looked out across a lush landscape to a low rise of hills beyond. They gave the impression of having, still, a very successful marriage. Only a successful marriage, Hennessey thought, could cope with this relative isolation.

'So where did he put her?'

'Bradbury?'

'Who else? Always thought he had bumped her off . . . slippery customer . . . trying to get hold of him was like trying to nail jelly to the wall. He would seem to give you something then take it away . . . invite suspicion but never concede guilt. He seemed to have a sense of feeling

he was invulnerable . . . it was like a bullfight . . . he was
the matador, one hand on his hip, the other holding a red
piece of cloth . . . and I was the bull, charging and missing
him each time.'

'You remember him well, clearly so.'

'Like yesterday, George, like yesterday. You don't look
like you have long to go before you'll be collecting your own
pension . . . and it'll be the same for you . . . you'll remember
some cases, some you'll forget. I remember Bradbury.'

'Dare say that will be true . . .' Hennessey picked up his
cup of tea. 'We have of course read the recording you made
of the case.'

'Yes?'

'So this visit we are making has two purposes . . . it's a
courtesy call to let you know we have re-opened one of your
old cases.'

'I am obliged to you, George.'

'And it's also to pick your brains . . . to help the recording
come alive . . . to see if any detail which didn't seem relevant
then seems relevant now in hindsight.'

'OK, I'll be what help I can. I'll be pleased to.'

'Thank you. The house and grounds were searched?'

'Yes, thoroughly, Bradbury was very co-operative.'

'I see . . . using dogs?'

'Yes . . . in the garden; in the house we just used the
mark-one eyeball. You can't bury a body in a house. The
house had a cellar, with a concrete floor, as I recall. You
could tell at a glance if the concrete had been dug up
and resurfaced, after something had been buried in it. It
hadn't. There was a lot of furniture in the cellar, junk
mostly. We shifted it but it didn't conceal a body. We
were satisfied the body of Mrs Muriel Bradbury was not
in the house or grounds, extensive as they were.' Page
held eye contact with Hennessey. 'Go on . . . tell me what
you found.'

'Well, Sergeant Yellich here found Mrs Bradbury's

jewellery in the cellar, pushed to the back of a drawer in an old desk . . . part of the junk you mentioned.'

'Oh . . .' Page looked uncomfortable, 'but we were looking for a body, it was still a mis per inquiry. You have to accept that . . . we could only give what resources we could to a mis per inquiry. Had it been a murder inquiry . . . well, I am sure we would have fine-tooth combed the building as well.'

'I'm sure you would, Jim . . . and in fairness to you, they may not even have been there because we found the body or the skeleton of Muriel Bradbury in a pile of rubble in the grounds. Or rather the new owner of the property did.'

'You know, I think I remember that pile of rubble – Bradbury had an air raid shelter knocked down . . . . . . was that it?'

'That's it.'

'Heavens, we didn't sift through the bricks, but the dogs were directed to them. They would have detected a fresh corpse under the stones, they showed no interest in them. We presumed she wasn't there . . . oh . . .'

'She probably wasn't.'

Page looked questioningly at Hennessey.

'If you searched the grounds with dogs when she was reported missing, you would have found her body if it had been there. We presume it wasn't there.'

'Oh . . . very clever.' Page relaxed back into the sofa. 'Very clever indeed. He keeps her body elsewhere, waits until we have searched the grounds and are not likely to return to look again because without a body it's still only a missing persons case, and then places her in the one place she won't be found . . . in his garden . . . and the case file gathers dust. Still, a bit of a risk.'

'A very big risk . . . but she was deeply buried in the rubble. It would take a determined attempt to shift the rubble before the body was found, not just removing the top few bricks . . . but you'd have to really dig down to it . . . and she was reported missing in the early winter . . . in the December. She would have been well on the way to full decomposition by the spring if it was a mild winter; and your average fly is a lazy beast. It may well be able to smell decaying flesh from a distance of two miles but apparently it liked to come straight into land as it were . . . a pile of rubble may allow air to circulate round the corpse, but it will keep the flies off. Much easier pickings, especially out in Paxton on the Forest.'

'Yes, I tread in a lot of it during the day. So he sold the house?'

'It was repossessed.'

'I see . . . but he left it . . . he quit it?'

'Yes. He had to.'

'And he left the remains of his wife in a pile of rubble that would inevitably be removed, at some point in the future. That doesn't make sense. Heavens, all he had to do . . . getting rid of a skeleton is easy . . . a few bones at a time each night into the Ouse. Bones don't float . . . they would never have been found.'

'I know,' Hennessey nodded. 'And I know it doesn't make sense. He may have thought the house was turning into a ruin, so bones in the rubble in an overgrown garden would remain hidden long enough to see him out . . . maybe . . . maybe, maybe. We just don't know. We arrested him, quizzed him, released him without charge, but he's not going anywhere.'

'Did you uncover any motivation for him wanting to murder his wife?' Hennessey's eye was caught by the graceful flight of a heron as it flew from left to right in the near distance across the vista that was the view out of Jim Page's living-room window. It was losing height. Hennessey reasoned that there must be a small body of water hidden in the folds of the landscape.

'We know he had money problems, he was quite candid about that . . . and his marriage was stressed. His wife had a sister . . . it's mentioned in the file . . . she was convinced he had done her in. They had dreadful rows.'

'Yes, we read that. Did you ever hear about a love interest?'

'A love interest?' Page smiled. 'Calling a spade a spade as we Yorkshiremen are wont to do, do you mean a mistress?'

'Yes.' Hennessey returned the smile. 'To call a spade a spade, yes, I mean a mistress.'

'No. Putting it bluntly. That is news to me. That would be motivation plus, wouldn't it? Confess I briefly thought money might be a motive but insurance companies don't pay out life insurance in the absence of a death certificate and working in finance, especially in a building society, he would know that. So that really left us looking at a murder of passion . . . negative passion maybe . . . but one too many rows. Hits her over the head . . . hides the body.'

'He couldn't provide an alibi . . . that was the case, wasn't it?'

'Yes. He was on sick leave at the time, recovering from a bad cold or a bout of influenza . . . some such . . . all but over it, taking a few days extra to build up his strength, so he said. Just a bit reluctant to return to work, if you ask me. I think his working relationships were just as strained as his domestic ones. He was not a popular bunny.'

'So it seems.'

'All he would say was that he was out all day, wouldn't say where. We pressed him and he then claimed to have driven out to Marston Moor to walk the battlefield.'

'That doesn't take a day from Paxton on the Forest.'

'Doesn't, does it? An afternoon perhaps . . . but not a day . . . but he stuck to his story and wouldn't be moved from it. Saying he had lived all his life close to the location of one of the most significant battles in British history and had never walked the site. So he took the opportunity to do so while he was convalescing from his illness. And no, he didn't talk to anybody, nobody saw him. It being a week day, there were few visitors . . . in fact no other visitors at all that afternoon. Just he upon the gentle hillside on a cold December afternoon.'

'Which could be true, but not providing an alibi was clever.'

'Oh to be sure . . . give me an alibi cowboy anytime, break the alibi and you've nailed 'em. But that was Bradbury all over, like trying to fasten jelly to a wall, as I said . . . and he knew what it meant. He was all but smirking and I confess the relief that his wife had disappeared was palpable. But could we prove anything? And time went on . . . and like I have said . . . . it was still only a missing person file. Other more pressing cases came, actual murders with real corpses, and the case file of Muriel Bradbury began to gather dust. So he had a mistress after all? Well, well, well.'

'Yes . . . a young lady with expensive tastes, by all accounts, penchants for BMWs, designer clothes, and whom he kept in a costly love nest within the walls.'

'Within the walls? That *would* be costly. Renting or buying, it wouldn't be cheap.'

'And she became the second Mrs Bradbury.'

'I heard he had remarried after the two years was up . . . but that was proof of nothing. Couldn't reopen the case on the strength of that.'

'Of course not. We only found out about it this forenoon. The informant, Bradbury's employer, was convinced he had told the police, or that we knew about it. Bradbury was seen with her in a restaurant before his wife's disappearance.'

'Not passed on to me.'

'That's what we thought. Twenty years is a long time in matters like this. I thought the chap had his memory out of sequence about Miss Picardie being seen with Bradbury before his wife's disappearance. Perhaps, but after, not before the police investigation . . .' Hennessey's voice tailed off as he noticed Jim Page sink back – shrink back it seemed – as the colour drained from his face.

'Jim ...' Hennessey leant forward. 'Is something wrong ...?'

Yellich and Hennessey drove away from Jim Page's home in silence. They retained the silence until Yellich halted outside Hennessey's home in Easingwold. They spoke briefly only to say 'goodbye' to each other and that they'd pick 'this' up tomorrow.

Hennessey unlocked the front door of his house, was greeted by an excited, turning in circles, tail-wagging, barking Oscar. He stooped to pick up the post that had been delivered that day. His house being towards the end of the postman's route, any deliveries reached his house long after Hennessey had left for work. He walked down the hallway into the kitchen, by which time Oscar had run through the dog flap and was sitting on the back lawn looking at the house with his tail slowly wagging. Hennessey made himself a pot of tea and, pouring a generous mug, went out of the house and stood on the patio looking at the rear garden.

It was the garden that Jennifer had designed when he and she were newly married. They had bought the house by mortgaging themselves to the limit and Jennifer had set about redesigning the back garden, which, when they bought the house, was a flat, unimaginative expanse of lawn. She'd sat one evening while heavily pregnant with pencil and paper in hand and had drawn up her plans. The lawn, she decided, would be divided in two, widthways, by a privet hedge with a gate set in the middle. Beyond the hedge, there should be planted apple trees and an orchard was thusly created. Garden sheds should also be situated beyond the hedge, tucked away neatly in a corner. The first ten feet of the garden should be left waste to be termed 'the going forth' the term taken from Francis Bacon's essay 'Of Gardens', except that a pond be dug and amphibia introduced. George Hennessey, then still a Detective Constable, liked and approved of the design and had promised to set to and realize it. Then Jennifer had died. Suddenly. Three months after their son was born she was walking in Easingwold one hot summer's afternoon, and she was reported to have appeared to collapse. People rushed to her aid but no sign of life could be found. An ambulance was called but she was found to be 'Condition Purple' in ambulance speak, or dead on arrival. At her inquest the cause of death was found to be 'Sudden Death Syndrome'. Hennessey had always felt it to be an admission by the medical profession that they are in ignorance of the reason why perfectly healthy people, often in their twenties, should just in an instant become 'life extinct', dead before they hit the ground. Over the years he had read of similar findings in inquests, often just a filler in the side column of a newspaper, but knew only too well the anguish of the bereaved, the unfairness of it, that someone so young, so full of life, with everything to live for, should suddenly fall down dead. Jennifer had been cremated and her ashes spread in the garden, her garden. Each evening, Hennessey would stand in the garden and would talk to Jennifer, telling her of his day, telling her of their son's progress and achievements, of developments in his life – as recently, when he told her that he had 'found someone' and hoped that she would approve, assuring her that his passion for her had not diminished and when he had told her that he felt a glow, a warmth that could not be explained by the heat from the late afternoon sun. On this day, the eighteenth of August, he stood overlooking the garden and told her of that day's events . . . 'just a courtesy call to a retired officer, didn't expect to obtain any new information, clarify a question about chronological sequence but I mentioned a name, Sandra Picardie, quite an unusual name, not one that would be forgotten, but as soon as I said that, Jim Page . . . that was the retired officer . . . he looked like he'd seen a ghost. He told us to cross-check the name. He was sure he had come across it before in another very similar case. She was hovering in the background in a mis per case . . . another woman . . . wife of a wealthy man . . . also disappeared, and she took her place with what Jim Page described as "distasteful speed". If Jim Page is right . . . and the similarities are too strong to be coincidence . . . then we got more from the visit than we could have hoped for.'

Hennessey returned to the house and cooked himself a simple but wholesome casserole. Whilst the meal was infusing, he settled into an armchair and relished an account of the Welsh Regiment during the First World War. The scale and the detail were breathtaking, and he, as a well-read enthusiast of military history, regarded the book as one of the gems of his collection. Later, having eaten and Oscar having been fed, man and dog took their customary walk in the coolness of the late evening, which was comfortable for Oscar. Being a brown mongrel, he suffered in the heat, and after this, Hennessey took his own stroll into Easingwold for a pint of stout at the Dove Inn. Just one, before 'last orders' were called.

Four

. . . in which a snug is visited, an architect is visited and an old murder inquiry receives renewed attention.

FRIDAY, 19 AUGUST

'If you'd give me the nuts and bolts, please, Yellich.' Hennessey sat still in his chair. He glanced once out of his office window at the walls, already at 10 a.m. well occupied by sun-hatted, camera-wielding tourists of many and diverse nations, and then gave Yellich his undivided attention.

'Well, boss – ' Yellich nursed a case file on his lap – 'the link provided by Sandra Picardie is with this case.' He tapped the file. 'One of the last cases handled by Jim Page before he retired . . . it is also a mis per, the person concerned is, or was, Katherine (Katie) Ilford . . . spelled just as in the place name, Ilford in Essex . . .'

'Yes, yes . . .'

'She disappeared five years ago aged fifty years of age. She was the wife of one Tommy Ilford . . . a car dealer whom we know well.'

'Thought the name rang bells.'

'A few petty crimes in respect of the car trade . . . Trading Standards Office stuff, overcharging . . . charged for a new clutch when the problem was solved by a new clutch spring . . . charged the punter five hundred quid when the actual repair cost twenty . . . a few items like that. But he smells. Like you, I have heard the name before . . . he

82

smells like three-day-old fish, but have we been able to pin anything on him for the likes we suspect him of? Have we ever . . .'

'And what do we suspect him of?'

'Fencing, in the main . . . stolen cars are thought to find their way like homing pigeons to his garage, where they are quickly reduced to their constituent parts. Anything with a serial number like a chassis or an engine seems to move on to another place or places unknown, or maybe just gets chopped up and scrapped . . . too incriminating possibly, we don't know for sure. He's also believed to have financed a lot of crimes . . . provided cars . . . put up money to buy weapons from gunsmiths . . . what is known in the criminal brotherhood as an "Angel".'

'And avoided prosecution?'

'Yes . . . apart from a few Trading Standards offences, as I said, and those were a few years ago now. Spent in respect of any sentence he might receive. He learned how to keep his hands clean and did so quickly.' Yellich reached down and picked up a thin file that lay on the floor beside his chair. 'In fact this is the file on Tommy Ilford. As you see, it's . . . thin.'

'Very thin for such the felon as he seems to be.'

'Well, his wife disappeared . . . vanished into thin air . . . many people do, the vast majority turn up safe and sound . . . but a few don't.'

'A few like Muriel Bradbury.'

'Indeed, boss . . . and I fear a few like Katie Ilford. She didn't turn up again . . . no corpse has been found . . . but at the time of her disappearance Tommy Ilford's finances were being handled by one Sandra Picardie.'

'The same woman?'

'Well, the age would be right, skipper. Nineteen years ago when Muriel Bradbury vanished, the Sandra Picardie who came into the lives of the bereft household was a sprightly twenty-eight summers.'

'Years, Yellich,' Hennessey sighed. 'I don't like flowery language . . . keep it simple. And keep it serious. We could be talking double murder here.'

'Sorry, boss. She was twenty-eight years of age. Five years ago, the Sandra Picardie who was described as the financial adviser to Ilford Motors was forty-two years of age . . . right age . . . same name . . . Picardie isn't a common name. First time I have heard it in fact.'

'Me too . . . and I have significantly more summers than you.' Both held eye contact with each other and laughed softly.

'So,' Hennessey said quickly and noticeably seriously, 'Miss Picardie rapidly becomes Mrs Bradbury shortly after the first Mrs Bradbury disappears, then leaves Mr Bradbury when his business fails . . . she later turns up once again as Miss Picardie in a situation involving another disappeared lady.'

'Yes, boss.'

'And both men she associated with are believed to be involved in criminality. Bradbury embezzled money from the building society he worked for and Ilford is very bent in a trade where gentlemen are few and far between. Noticeably so.'

'But they exist . . . I have a good garage, good job for a reasonable price and not just because I'm a copper. A friend put me on to them, being going there for years now.'

'Lucky you . . . I can't wait to hang my car keys up for good. I loathe and detest motor vehicles . . . but that's for a deeply personal reason.'

'Yes, boss.'

'So where now?'

'Boss?'

'Where do we go from here?'

'Interview Sandra Picardie.'

'Not such a good idea . . . not yet . . . Heard the story of the two leopards?'

'The two *lions*, yes, boss. But leopards?'

'Two leopards, one younger, one older, lying in the grass, looking down into a valley. In the valley a herd of gazelle are grazing . . . the young leopard says, "Let's dash down there and between the two of us we could grab one," and the older leopard says, "no . . . no . . . let's creep down there and grab the lot."'

Yellich smiled. 'You are frightened of putting them on their guard.'

'Exactly . . . softly, softly catchee monkey. That's the trick. We as lions upholding the law, have a possible prey in our sights now, we don't want to startle them . . . let's get to know more about Tommy Ilford . . . and I particularly want to know about Ms Picardie . . . she pops up in all the wrong places.'

'Very well, boss.'

'What were the circumstances of Mrs Ilford's disappearance?'

'Not dissimilar to Mrs Bradbury's disappearance by all accounts . . . a marriage reported to be "happy" by the husband but neighbours reported constant rows and the lady in question, well . . . just vanished . . . no goodbye note . . . no sign of violence . . . nothing missing of hers . . . . . . she just wasn't at home when Tommy Ilford returned from his day at the garage. M.P. procedure followed . . . property was searched . . . the garden as well as the house . . . no trace.'

'Well, if there's a pile of rubble in Mr Ilford's garden, you know what we are likely to find within, don't you?'

'I think I do, boss . . . but somehow I don't think there will be.'

'Neither do I. Tell me . . . any insights in the recording?'

'About the disappearance of Katie Ilford?'

'Yes.'

'Only that Mr Ilford didn't seem too upset . . . very cagey when questioned, the inference being that he was, still is, implicated in her disappearance. Could just be a hard-nosed businessman-cum-crook who wasn't given to displaying emotion, but Jim Page didn't think so. He records his suspicions clearly . . . being that Tommy Ilford is fully implicated in his wife's disappearance . . . but without a body it's only a mis per . . . same as Muriel Bradbury was for the last nineteen years.'

'Any children of the union?'

'Yes, skipper . . . two . . . both now adults of course.'

'OK, what about relatives on Mrs Ilford's side?'

Yellich consulted the file. 'A sister . . . lives in Wetherby.'

'OK, let's pay a call on her. I am going to look some-one up.'

'Someone, boss?' Yellich raised an eyebrow and smiled.

'Someone. Someone who has been very useful in the past and I have a notion that he is going to be very use-ful again.'

Hennessey strolled around the streets of central York. As earlier in the week, he found it to be a scene of vibrancy, of colour, of activity. From Ousegate he turned into Nessgate into snaking Coppergate, right into Piccadilly, where already it was quieter, more subdued, where any shops tended to be of a specialist nature and not dependent upon passing trade. He crossed the narrow bridge over the equally narrow cana-lized and, at that moment, stagnant litter-strewn River Foss, turned left into Merchant Gate and right on to business-like Walmgate. Here was commerce, small-business premises, covered car parks. He turned right, and followed Walmgate towards Walmgate Bar, which stood halfway along the third and shortest and least-known section of the ancient walls, but stopped just before he reached the wall at Ye Olde Speculation Inn. It was inside the 'Old Speculation' that George Hennessey knew he was most likely to find the man he sought. He walked through the narrow entrance, past the nicotine-stained wallpaper, the Victorian fittings, the solid doors with their handles at waist height. He walked into the snug, with its hard upholstered bench seating round the wall, upright chairs and round circular wrought-iron tables, with framed collections of cigarette cards from pre-Second World War Britain hanging on the wall. There was a sense of time having stood still in the Old Speculation, which is how the patrons wanted it. Any and every attempt by the management to modernize the pub by introducing jukeboxes, gambling machines etc. had been met with the machines being sabotaged, but discreetly so – coins layered with superglue and pushed into the coin slot had proved particularly effective. The bar in the snug of the Old Speculation occupied just one half of one wall. On the other side of the snug bar, beyond the spirit rack, could be seen the softer, more brightly coloured lounge bar, where both a jukebox and a gaming machine clung to a precarious existence. When Hennessey entered the snug of the Old Speculation, the clock had just chimed eleven and the pub had opened for the day's business, and the man whom George Hennessey sought was sitting in the corner in front of a glass of whisky.

'Ah . . . the good Mr Hennessey,' said the man. He raised his trilby. Hennessey nodded and asked for a glass of tonic water with lime. 'No ice, thank you.' It was too early in the day to take alcohol, and besides, he knew from experience that the beer in the pipes would be tastelessly flat, having stood there all night. The landlord of the Old Speculation was a sourpuss called Nelson, known behind his back as 'Horatio' and whose parsimony was legendary in the city of York. While there were punters prepared to buy flat beer, Horatio just would not 'pull through' before the start of the day's business. So for that good reason alone, Hennessey bought a glass of tonic water with lime. 'No ice . . . but heavy on the lime, please.' He crossed the cream-and-red chequered linoleum and sat opposite the man who had greeted him warmly. The man was short, moderately finely built. He appeared to be very smartly and expensively dressed, but a closer inspection revealed a certain age about his clothing, a certain ill-fittingness, a certain ill-matchingness and thusly explained why a man who dressed like that should drink in the snug of the Old Speculation. The impression given by inexpensive purchases from charity shops could, Hennessey thought, be quite pleasing. From a distance.

'You are looking well, Shored-up.' Hennessey raised his glass.

'I do not abuse my constitution, sir.' The man smiled and raised his own glass. 'I drink to your health. It has not been my pleasure for some time, sir.'

'Nor mine, Shored-up. Where have you been?'

'Ah, a short furlough in rural east Yorkshire, Mr Hennessey.'

'Three months in Full Sutton?'

'Two in fact, following upon the perfect behaviour I can muster when placed in such circumstances. I am, Mr Hennessey, one of Her Majesty's most loyal subjects, though being her guest does not necessarily agree with me. I'm sure you understand.'

'Oh, very well, Shored-up. Was two months fair and reasonable do you think? I mean, given your lifelong experience in these matters.'

'Oh, Mr Hennessey . . . that bench . . . they were three hanging judges. They clearly had no notion of the need to temper authority with leniency. Now in the old days, magistrates knew how to be magistrates, they understood the pressure on the small man, the ordinary Joe in the street . . . the humble citizen trying to scratch a living in a world which is essentially bereft of fairness.'

'I see you made good use of the prison library, Shored-up.'

'One tries to better oneself, Mr Hennessey, at every turn, at every opportunity.' The man drained his glass, placed it on the table and then very pointedly pushed it towards George Hennessey. 'It has long been my philosophy to turn every disadvantage to my good advantage if possible and two months' absence of liberty was compensated for with a balanced diet, nourishing and alcohol-free, sleep and an immersion in the library at the institution, though the majority of books catered for tastes other than mine. *Shoot Out at Deadman's Gulch* is not my idea of satisfying reading . . . "he was deader than any cowpoke could be with six slugs in his skull". Really . . . I ask you.'

'You know, you've got more than steam between your ears, Shored-up. Your great sin in life is that you didn't use it.'

'That's what one of my teachers used to say . . . but using "it" would involve working . . . actual effort, Mr Hennessey. Could you honestly see me applying myself to anything?'

'Honestly, no. So what did they fondle your collar for this time?'

'A matter of finances, really.'

'Tell me.'

'I booked in for a three-week holiday at a hotel on the coast.'

'You've done that before. Left after two . . . without paying your bill.'

'Left after two and a half this time . . . the weather was glorious . . . and I met a popsie in the bar. Well, I didn't clean up behind me, left my fingerprints in the room. Promises to pay the money fell on deaf ears. When the true nature of my finances was displayed for the magistrates and the world to examine . . . "Never had any intention of paying, had you?" sayeth ye chief beak . . . to which I could only smile apologetically and collected three months as another sort of guest. Mind you, in terms of the quality of the food and the standard of accommodation, there was little to chose between either institution. Mine's a whisky. Double.'

'Tell me about the popsie first.'

'Widowed lady.'

'Tell me about your intentions . . .'

'Ah . . . not able to exploit that, came the time I had to depart.'

'Lucky escape for her, I say.'

'Oh, Mr Hennessey, my intentions were honourable.'

'To her body maybe . . . to her bank balance, less so. A few thousand pounds to rescue your ailing business in return for romance . . . and, being once commissioned in the Green Howards, you, of course, a gentleman, a man of honour whose word is his bond.'

'Actually, it's the Devon and Dorsets now, but that's between you and me, Mr Hennessey. I decided that if I was living in Yorkshire there was a risk of me bumping into the real thing . . . that would be embarrassing, so I settled on another county regiment. Not many old "D & Ds" in Yorkshire, I thought, so the Devon and Dorsets it is.'

Hennessey picked up the empty glass and took it to the bar and returned with it replenished, as requested, by a double whisky.

'Not blended, I hope?' The man looked disappointed. 'I should be able to expect a good malt from you, Mr Hennessey.'

'Don't push it, Shored-up.'

Shored-up shrugged.

'Ilford.'

'Small town in Essex.' Shored-up poured water into his glass from the white jug on the table, with the Bell's Whisky logo.

'And a car trader in this fair town.'

'And a man not to be messed with.' Shored-up sipped his drink. 'Probably more than you know. They don't call him the "Black Hole" for nothing.'

'I haven't heard that about him.'

'Well, that's what you get for educating the masses, and having libraries in prisons, teach them a little bit about astronomy . . . anyway, street talk has it that if you get too close to Ilford's gravitational pull you tend to disappear. And I mean disappear . . . not found floating in the Ouse.'

'But disappear?'

'Yes . . . vanish without trace or V.W.T. as the expression has it.' Shored-up sipped his whisky. 'Ah . . . the nectar of the gods . . . you came at a divine time today, Mr Hennessey. I am a little short in the old folding green department. It happens from time to time.'

'I can imagine . . . money comes in for you in fits and starts.'

'Oh it does, most assuredly.' The man took another delicate sip of the whisky. 'I do envy you salaried chaps . . . a regular income . . . we self-employed persons must take the rough with the smooth. I confess the rough tends to be more long-lasting than the smooth these days.'

'Well, there may be a drink in this for you, Shored-up.' Hennessey sipped his own drink. 'Ilford's wife disappeared about five years ago.'

'So I heard.'

'Anything else you heard?'

Shored-up pursed his lips. 'For information about "Black Hole" Ilford you pay, Mr Hennessey. The man of whom you speak is not to be trifled with.'

'So I believe . . . we have little on him but our suspicions are great.'

'Justifiably so. Believe me, justifiably so. If there's a scam in the fair and famous, he'll be involved at some point. His garage business is just a front . . . even that's dodgy . . . he tends not to keep his customers but he doesn't care, the big pennies are all bent anyway and the wheels and deals go on behind the scenes. So you're looking at him?'

'He's wandered into the frame . . . a disappearance of about twenty years ago has been partially solved.'

'Partially?'

'The body has turned up.'

'The skeleton in the pile of rubble? I saw the news report.'

'That's the one . . . well, it has been linked to the disappearance of Ilford's wife . . . a lady by the name of

Picardie is known to have had links with the husbands of both women.'

'Picardie . . .' Shored-up inclined his head to one side. 'That name rings bells.'

'Really?'

'Distantly so . . . but clearly.'

'She's believed to be Tommy Ilford's partner.'

'Ah . . . that's where I have heard the name. A woman who likes to cut a dash . . . a silver Mercedes Benz.'

'Is that what she drives?'

'At the moment . . . pops over to Leeds to buy a handbag from Harvey Nichols . . . couldn't go in anything less than a Merc. She is believed to have a taste for German tin . . . if it's not a Mercedes, it's a BMW . . . if not a Beamer, it's a top of the range Audi . . . but I think she'd turn up her nose at a VW.'

'Sounds like she would.'

'So specifically, specifically what do you want to know about Tommy Black Hole Ilford?'

'Anything and everything, Shored-up.' Hennessey reached for his wallet. He opened it and laid ten tens on the table. 'Anything and everything.'

Shored-up scooped up the notes in a swift, deft gesture. 'Couldn't do that as openly later in the day,' he said. 'Most of the boys sleep until after 1 p.m. But now it's OK.'

'I know.'

'Getting near the witching hour as it is, Mr Hennessey. Have to ask you to leave now. If I'm seen talking to you . . . well, I may live but you won't get any information. I hear what I hear and I observe what I observe because I have done time . . . I am allowed within a certain distance but not any closer. I can see who is talking to whom . . . which minion is doing what little errand for whom. I can add up . . . I can report my observations . . . my suspicions.'

'I accept that.' Hennessey stood. 'You have been useful in the past.'

'I would like to think so, Mr Hennessey. I do so loathe violence but a little venture capitalism is harmless.'

'Fleecing widows who fall for your charms is not venture capitalism, Shored-up, and you know it.'

'Ah, Mr Hennessey, you do me a disservice. But if you want to know about Tommy Black Hole Ilford, you'll have to pay . . . I mean really pay . . . in this case, you pay not for the quality of information, you are paying danger money.'

'We'll see what you come up with before we negotiate closing prices on your stock market. You know where to contact me when you have something to sell.'

'I knew my sister was dead.' The woman sat in the armchair of her modest home, arms hung limply by her side. It was a gesture of resignation, thought Yellich, of no energy left. She was in her middle years, her living conditions said 'head above the water – just'. Old furnishings, faded curtains, inexpensive clock on the wall, a small television set in the corner, which Yellich guessed was a black-and-white set. 'The moment she was missing, I knew she was dead. Even my mother . . . she's dead now, even she, who would cling to any glimmer of hope said, "Oh, she'll be at the bottom of the Ouse."'

'What do you believe happened to your sister, Mrs Hartwell? I am sorry if this is difficult for you.'

Yellich had driven out to Wetherby, shades against the sun's glare, window down. He had found Mrs Hartwell's address quite easily. He had knocked gently on her door and introduced himself. His initial impression was of a tired woman . . . a woman who had had enough of life . . . but she welcomed him into her house as if gratified for someone to talk to.

'It's not difficult.' She stared into space, not focussing on anything, it seemed to Yellich. Photographs in inexpensive frames on the mantelpiece told of children, but not a husband.

'You see, we knew it was going to be bad when Katie took up with Tommy Ilford.'

'You knew him?'

'Oh, yes . . . all Wetherby knew Tommy Ilford . . . a bad lot from a bad family . . . up to no good from the day he could walk, if you ask me. All sorts of damage was down to him in this town but he was as fly as a barrel load of monkeys . . . he could wriggle out of any tight spot. And that was when he was about ten. If that. Windows would be turned . . . locks would be forced in outbuildings . . . it would be down to him. There was one incident, a fairly posh family had a garden party . . . stalls of cakes, strawberries and cream . . . folk were mingling . . . not particularly crowded, one or two children . . . but when they were tidying up at the end of the day they found someone had been in the house, helped themselves to a few easy-to-carry-away articles, like jewellery . . . one or two people reported a "shifty-looking" boy hanging around the edge of the party, showing more interest in the house than the strawberries and cream.'

'Tommy Ilford?'

'In one . . . the police went to his house, met a tirade of abuse, couldn't find anything . . . I don't think they really expected to. Tommy would have sold them to an adult contact for a tiny fraction of their value . . . and that person would have sold them on to a jeweller or a pawnbroker for nearer their true value. That family never had a garden party again. He was just a law unto himself . . . no sense of right or wrong.'

'How did your sister meet him?'

'They grew up together . . . we lived close to each other . . . our houses I mean. Same local school . . . Katie was a pretty girl, I was the plain one . . . and I remember my mum coming home and saying she'd seen "that Tommy Ilford" looking at our Katie . . . and we knew what it meant . . . if Tommy Ilford took a shine to something or somebody, it was as good as his. We tried to talk her out of it, but he had her under his spell, he had that knack as well, probably still has . . . he can charm the birds from the trees . . . but only to put them in a cage. Anyway, she wouldn't listen . . . she was going to change him . . . when have you heard that before?'

'Often.'

'Ever heard it being done?'

'Never.'

'Me neither. But Katie was determined. Tommy was twenty-two by then, quite a good-looking boy. In fact they made a pretty pair . . . they photographed well together, but it went pear-shaped almost from the start.'

Yellich remained silent.

'You see, Tommy . . . it's hard for me to call him by his first name, I don't like doing it, it seems to imply that I approve of him. Thomas would be better, I suppose. Thomas has two levels . . . two sides . . . there is what you see and there is what there is. That phrase "the devil can assume a pleasing form", that could have been written with Thomas Ilford in mind. He was a good-looking charmer who wanted a pretty wife to complete the image of a businessman. That garage . . . a foreman and a few mechanics who may know what they are doing, but Thomas has never got his fingers dirty in his life . . . his knowledge of cars is limited to his ability to drive one. Some garage proprietor. But it was only after she had been married for a year or so did Katie realize the sort of man she had taken for better or worse and by then she was expecting her first child. He didn't waste time. It would have been possible for Katie to walk out of her marriage . . . hard, but possible . . . but being pregnant to him and subsequently the mother of his child . . . that made her captive. Number two followed within a year . . . by then she was well and truly shackled. Leonard and Norman . . . they are young men now and part of their father's business, whatever that is, and after the compulsory rite of passage in a young offenders institution. That tore Katie apart, seeing her two boys sent down . . . but what was worse for her, was the way they smiled as they were taken down to the cells.'

'I know what you mean.' Yellich spoke softly. 'I have seen that smile many times . . . you just can't be a career criminal unless you have some time under your belt. It's a different mindset.'

'Well, if I tell you that our father was a churchwarden, that may let you know how we felt about Katie marrying Tommy Ilford and how devastating it was for our parents to see two of their grandchildren become criminals.'

'I can imagine.'

'Can you?'

'I think so.'

'Well . . . and then Katie disappeared. It was not just the suddenness of it, it was the timing. She had been married for nearly thirty years . . . her children were grown up and she vanished. There was a sense that she had outlived her useful-ness and was jettisoned. Thomas Ilford is capable of doing that. He's got a glamour piece now . . . not a "sugar baby", she's in her forties . . . but has kept herself in shape and has been helped there by not having had children, so I believe.'

'You are still in contact with him?'

'Not him . . . but Leonard and Norman are still my neph-ews. We exchange cards at Christmas and birthdays. Leonard told me about her . . . Sandra somebody . . . mentioned she had been married twice before but had never had children.'

Yellich's heart thumped. 'Sorry . . . did you say "twice"? She had been married *twice* before?'

'Yes . . . well that's what Leonard said in his card. It was a year or so now . . . but yes . . . twice divorced. But Tommy wouldn't marry her, he's too wily for that, so they are a partnership, a marriage in everything but name. So I believe. That at least was the state of play a few years ago. If he has made an honest woman of her in the interim, I would be the last to know.'

'What . . .' Yellich paused, he felt his question had been

largely answered, but he asked it anyway. 'What, if anything, can you tell me about your sister's disappearance? Can you say anything other than she just vanished?'

'Such as?' The woman, clearly troubled by painful memories, opened her palms in the universal gesture of helplessness.

'Well . . . did your sister give any indication that things between her and her husband had become worse . . . or even that her life was in danger?'

'Not that I can recall. She did mention that "the new woman in the office" couldn't take her eyes off her husband. By the "new woman" I think she meant that Sandra woman who has now taken her place. My sister's husband liked her to pop into the garage from time to time . . . all part of the image, you see.'

'I see. What about her sons . . . your nephews? Did they have a close relationship with your sister . . . their mother?'

'No . . . not as they grew into late teenagers, by that time they were on their way to criminality, encouraged by their father. I wasn't welcome in the house, wasn't witness to anything but the impression I had was that Katie was trying her best to steer them away from crime. She was undermined by her husband, who drove a wedge between Katie and her two boys, and the boys saw their father as "exciting" and Katie as "dull". They had no qualifications, left school as early as they could. There's no employment to be had for young people without qualifications, not in the Vale, so they were already on their way to a life of crime as soon as they left school. Katie was in a state of despair . . . she loved her boys . . . but could offer them nothing they wanted. She could offer them everything they needed.'

'But nothing they wanted.'

'Yes . . . everything they wanted was provided by their thief, rogue and liar of a father, but nothing needed was provided by him. Then she disappeared. It was me who reported her missing. Not him. Not her husband. He didn't care, he just did not care. She hadn't phoned me for a week, so I phoned her. He answered and said he didn't know where she was, he hadn't seen her for a few days and he didn't care where she was.'

'Did he seem surprised that she had vanished?'

'Hard to tell. But I knew him by then . . . he was only interested in what or whom he could use for his own ends and by then Katie was of no further use to him. His lack of concern didn't suggest he had anything to do with his wife's disappearance, although if you didn't know him you might think that . . . but his indifference was . . . well, it was him. He's a man of little feeling . . . no conscience that I have ever been able to detect.'

'I have met the like.'

'I imagine you have, Mr . . . ?'

'Yellich. Detective Sergeant Yellich.' He paused. 'I am interested to know about Tommy Ilford's lady . . . Sandra.'

'The glamorous, youthful, Sandra . . .'

'Yes, that lady . . . I confess for reasons I would rather not tell you, I confess that when you mentioned she had been twice married my ears pricked up . . . do you happen to know what her previous married name was?'

'Mm . . .' The woman thought. 'I did know her name, and I knew her maiden name . . . my memory . . . a French connection . . .'

'Can I suggest Picardie?'

'That was it . . . it's a part of France, is it not?'

'I believe so . . . I believe the Somme river is there and much of the trench warfare in the First World War was fought in the Picardie region.'

'That was it . . . her name so reminded me of France . . . cycling holidays in younger, happier times. So she was Mrs Picardie . . . still is . . . she'll never become Mrs Ilford. Thomas is too clever for that . . . no flies on him.'

'So you said. In fact I can tell you that Picardie we believe to be her maiden name.'

'Oh, really . . . well . . . in that case her previous married name was . . . what did Leonard say? I can phone him, he'll be at the garage.'

'Rather you didn't.' Yellich held up a cautionary hand. 'We are trying to keep this discreet. We would rather they didn't know we are renewing our interest in your sister's disappearance.'

'Renewing it!' The woman stiffened in her chair. 'I never thought you had a great deal of interest in it in the first place. You just took details, asked for a photograph . . .'

'There is little else we can do. I am so sorry. I would feel the same if my wife disappeared . . . but frankly there is little else we can do . . . if it was a young child then we would search the surrounding area . . . ask for volunteers as you will have seen on such sad occasions.'

'Yes.'

'But even then, if a body is not found, we have to call off the search and wait for the body to be discovered. If it ever is. Most often it is . . . but not always . . . you can imagine the parents' anguish.'

'I am sorry I snapped. It is annoying for me. She was my sister.'

'Please, it doesn't matter . . . think nothing of it.'

A pause. Mrs Hartwell seemed to Yellich to be collecting herself . . . calming herself. During the calm Yellich heard the clock on the mantelpiece ticking. He had not previously noticed it had a tick.

'So,' she said at length. 'If Picardie is the woman's maiden name, what was her married name? Leonard did mention it. Of the two boys, Leonard always seemed to have more time for me. After Katie disappeared, it was most often Leonard who would contact me, never Norman. Norman is very like his father . . . Leonard's a bit soft. I can't see Leonard going as far in the world of crime as his father. Norman, yes . . . but not Leonard. So the name . . . mmm . . . it's on the tip of my tongue . . . a plain name . . . reminded me of the weather . . . like rain . . .'

'Frost?' Yellich threw out the suggestion. A fellow police cadet had been of that surname.

Mrs Hartwell smiled. 'Yes, that was it . . . Mrs Frost. I didn't ever hear her first name.'

'Frost,' Yellich repeated and as he did so, a chill went down his spine. Despite the heat of a mid-August day outside, a chill that was utterly appropriate to the surname in question.

'There's just a lot of smoke, skipper, a very solemn amount of smoke.' Yellich had driven sedately from Wetherby back to York. In other circumstances, he would have enjoyed the drive. A road with little traffic in the late morning, the lush green fields on either side of the road, the welcoming bundle of buildings that is York. But on that day he drove with a gnawing feeling that he would that afternoon retrieve information about yet one more missing woman, a missing woman with whom Sandra Picardie had some connection. And then . . . . and then, he thought . . . as he drove through Fulford on the outskirts of the city, there is the period before Mrs Bradbury's disappearance, the discovery of whose bones led to this investigation . . . by then Sandra Picardie was a woman of twenty-eight years, had developed a taste for the good things in life, in a material sense. Plenty of time to have been up to no good by then. He slowed behind a bus and made no attempt to overtake. Picardie . . . Picardie . . . Where did she come from? What is her history? He drove to Micklegate Bar Police Station and parked in the small car park at the rear of the station, walked across the concrete under the glare of the midday sun, feeling its heat on the back of his neck as he entered the building by the rear, 'staff only' entrance. He signed in, checked his pigeonhole, which he found contained nothing but circulars that had to be read, then signed as 'read' and put in the next pigeonhole. He then went to his office and picked up the phone and jabbed a four-figure internal number.

'Collator.' The reply was, as usual, brisk, efficient.

'DS Yellich.'

'Yes, sir.'

'Frost.'

'Sir?'

'Have any adult females of that name been reported as missing in this area within the last . . . well, let's cast a wide net . . . fifteen years.'

'Fifteen years? Leave it with me, sir. I'll get back to you asap.'

'Thank you.' Yellich replaced the receiver, gently so, though his inclination was to crash it down; an anger was beginning to displace the gnawing fear.

He went to the canteen for lunch. The hot day meant that the cold dishes had proved popular and by the time he joined the queue only lasagne remained. He didn't relish the thought of lasagne on such a hot day but his body, he reasoned, his body was an engine . . . engines need fuel. So beef lasagne it was. He ate sitting alone at a table. In other parts of the canteen police officers sat in pairs or in groups. Three constables were enjoying a game of darts, two female officers sat in the corner huddled in conversation, in the far corner an older, experienced officer was being given the undivided attention of four cadets, doubtless he was conveying 'canteen culture' to the cadets. Yellich didn't like the idea of what must be being said on that table, but he could do nothing about it. It was the way of it. If the enthusiastic young cadets were not infected by the experienced officer's cynicism in the canteen, then they would be infected by it in the patrol cars or on the beat. There was a chink of glass upon glass that occasionally pierced the hum of conversation as the barman prepared the bar for opening. The shutters would rattle upwards at 2 p.m. and the bar would remain open until 11 p.m., the first punters being the officers who would finish the six till two shift any time after 2 p.m., depending on what unavoidable overtime their particular shift had thrown up. The windows had been flung open – the sound of the traffic at the junction of Queen, Nunnery and Blossom beneath the windows further pervaded the room. It was hot and noisy and Yellich, trying to prevent the concept of 'serial killer' from entering his mind, just did not enjoy his meal. After lunch he returned to his office. He phoned the collator. He received the information he had expected, and had also dreaded. Half an hour later he was seated in the chair in front of DCI Hennessey's desk. He said there was a lot of smoke, a 'solemn amount of the stuff' . . .

Hennessey leaned back in his chair. He too felt the same sinking feeling of dread which Yellich had experienced during the drive from Mrs Hartwell's house in Wetherby back to York. 'So tell me about Mrs Frost?'

Yellich held the file on his lap. He leafed through it. 'I'd like to go over it with a fine-toothed comb, skipper . . . it's only just come from the void . . . but in a nutshell, Mrs Frost was murdered, like I said.'

'You asked the collator to check for mis pers by the name of Frost and he came up with a murder victim?'

'Yes, skipper. He's a good man. Thorough. Diligent. No mis pers by that name. A less conscientious person would have left it there, but not finding any mis pers he looked for murder victims and lo and behold.' He patted the file. 'Janet Frost, Mrs, was murdered ten, nearly eleven years ago now . . . when aged forty-five.'

'What do we know?'

'Embarrassingly little, sir . . . as you see it's quite a thin file for a murder. She was found battered to death in a snickelway. Believed, assumed to be the victim of a mugging . . . her handbag was missing.'

'Any witnesses? Any reference to the Picardie female?'

'No witnesses to the actual attack, boss . . . which took the form of Mrs Frost being attacked from behind as she walked down a snickelway, specifically Hornpot Lane, Nether.'

'That's quite a long one, if I remember.'

'It is, lots of blind corners. Nearest witness was the person who discovered her body and raised the alarm. He didn't see anything according to this recording but he passed a woman walking in the opposite direction . . . that is, away from the place where Mrs Frost's body lay.'

'A female?'

'Yes, boss,' Yellich nodded. 'I am thinking what you are thinking . . . there's a computer image in the file provided by the witness.'

'Sandra Picardie?'

'The possibility is large.'

'Inescapable, I'd say.' Hennessey ran a liver-spotted hand through his silver hair. 'This whole thing is . . . well, I don't want to police a desk like the Commander wants me to do and I don't want to retire until I have to . . . but it's cases like this that won't make me sorry to retire.'

'I know what you mean, sir. I had difficulty eating my lunch.'

'What do we know about Mrs Frost?'

'Very little, sir. Her husband was interviewed and cleared of suspicion. The trail went cold after that . . . no weapon . . . no witnesses . . . the handbag missing . . . a mugging that turned into a murder. The case remains open, of course, but it was shelved awaiting further developments. And no further developments being forthcoming . . .'

'It remained shelved.' Hennessey drummed his fingers on his desk. 'Smoke, as you say . . . three murders and she is on the playing field of all three. What was Mr Frost's occupation as given there? A wealthy man I'll be bound?'

'As given here, sir . . . an architect.'

'Wealthy enough . . . and with a position of high status . . . a senior professional, would suit Ms Picardie as we are beginning to know her.'

'That's what I was thinking, boss, except we don't know her. We don't even know what she looks like.' Yellich shifted in his seat. 'I think a spot of surveillance wouldn't go amiss here.'

Hennessey nodded. 'Be discreet . . . remember she's hob-nobbing with Tommy Ilford: he can tell a copper with a camera at one mile and he'll have his lookouts posted. How will you do it?'

'I'll drive by his garage, I think, sir. If there is a top-of-the-range German car outside, it is likely to be hers and so I'll wait until she appears.'

'Well, as I say, be thou ever so discreet.'

'If there is no such car there, I'll drive on to his house . . . we have the address – his last known address, in fact – on file. Same sketch: if there is a swanky German car in the drive, I'll wait for madam to make an appearance.'

'I think you are right, Yellich. We need a photograph of Sandra Picardie . . . but I want you to avoid the garage.'

'Too dangerous you think, sir?'

'Too reckless . . . I don't want us to show our hand until it's safe and/or necessary.'

'Very good, boss.'

'You see, Yellich . . . like finds like. Ilford's been up to his neck in bad news and all he's been nicked for are one or two Trading Standards offences . . . it seems Sandra Picardie may have murdered three women so as to take their place in the marital bed. Now she's involved with Ilford . . . but he's too cautious to allow her to marry him and she seems to accept that. They are both very good at covering their tracks. She didn't find a kindred spirit in Mr Bradbury, so she left him. She probably had the same experience with Mr Frost, but now she has Tommy Ilford, she's found someone who's on the same wavelength as her . . . so much so, that she's happy to be kept at arms' length . . . so long as she has her kindred spirit.'

'Is that how you read the situation, boss?' Yellich smiled.

'Well, it wouldn't surprise me if that was the case. But as ever, we will see what we see.' Hennessey leaned back. 'All right, onwards and upwards . . . you draw a camera from stores . . . powerful lens . . . don't get too close. I will call on Mr Frost, bereaved husband of the late Janet Frost, see what I can find out that the case records of his wife's murder do not tell us.'

It was Friday, 14.10 hours.

Yellich sighted up the house. It was as he expected it to be. New build . . . isolated . . . and surrounded by metal fencing, security lights and CCTV. The home of a frightened man. It was on two levels, a ground floor and an upper floor with a veranda, so that the floor area of the upper floor must have been less than that of the ground floor. Above the upper floor was a low-angled roof. The building seemed to sit, for that was the only word Yellich could think of, it seemed to sit in the centre of a field or meadow of short tufted grass, the sort of field where sheep or cattle can often be seen grazing. No attempt appeared to have been made to cultivate the field into a landscaped garden. It was as though cattle, or sheep, or goats might be allowed on the land to keep the grass down but the owner had no interest in the land that surrounded his house, other than that it served as a barrier between his house and the world outside. A brick-laid drive, wide and gently inclining, led from the house to the lane that ran at the edge of the field. The field itself was surrounded by high hawthorn with only one break in the hedge at the left-hand side where a five-barred wooden gate allowed egress and ingress to and from the neighbouring field and this reinforced Yellich's theory as to the means employed to keep the height of the grass surrounding the house at an acceptable level. But what interested Yellich most was the car on the drive. A silver Mercedes Benz sports coupé, at that moment parked on the drive, hood down, facing the house. Yellich accelerated

105

past the house, drove on for approximately three hundred yards, until he found a section of the lane where it was wide enough to park his car without causing an obstruction and, taking the camera concealed in a canvas knapsack, he got out of the car and walked back up the lane.

It was, he found, one of those respites from police work that occur from time to time. His mind was on his job, utterly focussed, but the walk up the lane on a hot August afternoon, of lush foliage, of birdsong, of trees offering shade from the sun . . . an observer would see a youthful, slender-looking man, white shirt with sleeves neatly folded up cuff over cuff, light-brown trousers, sensible shoes, and a knapsack over his shoulder: a townie enjoying an afternoon in the country. He reached the wrought-iron gates of the Ilford house and paused to look at it, making no attempt to hide. It was, after all, what a man or woman out for a stroll in the country would do. If he was being watched, he reasoned, it would seem to be more suspicious if he did not stop and gaze at the house, in a posture of envy and admiration for the man who owned such a property, which in estate agent speak would easily qualify as 'highly desirable' and 'viewing strongly recommended'. As he stood there a woman appeared at the window. She seemed from that distance to be tall. She had long, dark hair, she wore a blue blouse and the top of a cream skirt could be seen. She looked at Yellich, who held her gaze of over fifty yards distance and who then smiled and nodded as if to say, 'Sorry for staring,' and turned and walked on without a backward glance and was soon enveloped from view by the hawthorn hedge. That, he said to himself, that was Sandra Picardie. He walked on and put himself strongly at the small hill that the lane became and walked with some urgency because the movements of the woman had seemed to suggest to him that she was about to leave the house, as if looking for something, or as if ensuring that the house was properly locked up as per clear instructions from Thomas Ilford. Yellich reached the top of the lane and turned and saw that he had a clear view of the front and right-hand side of the property, of the driveway almost to the gate and importantly, the Mercedes Benz was in full view. He nestled beside a small tree at the side of the road and with camera – a 300 mm telephoto lens affixed – he waited for the woman he believed to be Sandra Picardie to emerge.

His wait was both short and well rewarded. Better rewarded, it would transpire, than even he could have hoped for.

He had waited for perhaps ten minutes, nestling into the shade and the branches of the tree, passing the time by counting the number of different birdsongs, only one of which, the musical blackbird's, could he identify, but never once relaxing his vigil upon the Ilford house. Then he saw the front door open. He lifted the camera and directed it at the house. A man exited first, which caused Yellich no small surprise, a stocky, bald-headed individual, dressed in a lightweight summer suit. Yellich pressed the shutter and captured the man full face, so full faced that Yellich was astounded that the man did not appear to notice that he was being photographed even allowing for the distance involved. Then the woman appeared, the same woman whom Yellich had seen at the window of the house, slender, dark haired, blue blouse, cream skirt, cream shoes. She too was captured on film by Yellich's deft pressing of the shutter button. Yellich continued to shoot frame after frame as the couple walked to the Mercedes and got into the car, she behind the wheel. Yellich put the camera into the knapsack, hurriedly so and began to retrace his steps. He heard the Mercedes approaching, dangerously fast, before he saw it, stepped nimbly on to the grass verge as the car came into view. The occupants of the vehicle, the man and the woman, glanced at him as they swept by, then dismissed him. Yellich walked on past the house, not on that occasion paying any attention, and continued until he reached his car, more humble than the Mercedes, much more humble, got into it and drove away.

He drove back into York, and in the city drove past Ilford's garage. The Mercedes was parked on the forecourt.

'They design things that reach into the sky, make people live up with the birds but they all live in renovated manor houses in Suffolk,' was as Hennessey recalled a much voiced complaint about architects. Here was the embodiment of that complaint. For Archibald Frost's house, whilst not in Constable country, of the gentle Stour and Willy Lott's cottage, was nonetheless a renovated manor house that nestled in the Yorkshire Wolds. It seemed to be tucked neatly between two small stands of woodland and at the end of a long drive, which itself was accessible only after a long drive on a B road, which required much faith, for it seemed to Hennessey to go on endlessly, though in that summer weather, not by any means unpleasantly so. After driving slowly for fear of meeting another vehicle coming in the opposite direction, he at last came across two large stone gateposts with a sign of faded paint that read 'Derrydown Manor'. There was no gate between the gateposts and so Hennessey turned between them and put his car at the winding drive between mature elms, to eventually reach the substantial, yet also squat-looking building that was Derrydown Manor House. A stone lintel over the door was carved with the date, 1615AD. Dogs barked at the sound of his arrival. The door of the house opened and four Alsatians spilled out and surrounded Hennessey's car, barking, aggressively so. Moments later, a man appeared at the door and snapped, 'All right!' and the instant he did so, the dogs quietened and returned to the house. Hennessey stepped out of the car, aware, very aware that four pairs of eyes belonging to large, hungry-looking Alsatians were staring at him.

'Mr Hennessey?' The man was short, slightly built, a straggly beard, bald head, mid-fifties, Hennessey guessed. He was dressed casually in a T-shirt, which had 'Barbados' emblazoned in red against the white background, white slacks, sandals, and expensive-looking watch on his left wrist.

'Yes.' Hennessey strode slowly but confidently towards the house. 'Mr Frost?'

'Yes. You know dogs?' Frost held out his hand.

'I have one of my own. I have always kept a dog.'

'Confident movement puts them at ease . . . they're on edge . . . thank you for that. They would be difficult to calm if they become agitated.' Hennessey took Frost's hand.

'Yes . . . had a case once . . . had to enforce a dangerous dog order, when I was still in uniform. A spaniel turned on a toddler and savaged him. The dog had to be put down but I found it to be a calm and placid animal.'

'The toddler's jerky movements had frightened the animal?'

'Yes . . . or so a vet once suggested when I mentioned the incident to him years later. Dogs display aggression towards drunks for the same reason.'

'So I believe . . . please come in . . . my directions were clear enough, I take it? You have arrived when you said you would.'

'Clear as a bell. You are quite remote. You know, I have been in remote parts of the United Kingdom . . . the highlands of Scotland, the Brecon Beacons, Thetford Forest . . . but I don't think I have ever been more deeply into cultivated countryside than this.' Hennessey followed Frost into the coolness of his house. The dogs followed.

'You couldn't be much more isolated anywhere in the Vale.' Frost shut the door behind Hennessey. 'The house is about midway between two small villages. I like it like this.'

'Your old address was in the City of York?'

'Yes, I have only recently moved here. I was able to retain my telephone number . . . we are part of the York exchange here. I have only been here about three years . . . a very lovely three years it has been.'

109

'You live alone?'

'Yes, children are grown up . . . fled the nest. I have friends, they visit, I visit them. I don't fear being burgled.' He nodded towards the dogs.

'I bet you don't.'

'Shall we sit here?' Frost indicated four armchairs neatly grouped in a circle round a coffee table. 'I like to keep the rest of the house as private as possible. That's just me. I am a private person.'

'As you wish.' Hennessey sat down.

'Tea? Coffee?'

'Well . . . a cup of tea would be most welcome. Just milk, thank you.'

Frost left Hennessey alone in the foyer of the Manor House. The four dogs kept a respectful distance from him, though not one, it seemed to Hennessey, took his eyes off him for a second. The dimensions inside the house surprised Hennessey. The roof seemed low, the stairway narrow, but he then recalled the date over the front door. To all intents and purposes, this was sixteenth-, not seventeenth-century British architecture. Even though Derrydown Manor House was of the century of Augustan England, of the great houses like Chatsworth and Hardwick Hall and Blenheim Palace with their neo-Roman design, it was, to all intents and purposes, of the vintage of Ann Hathaway's cottage in Stratford-upon-Avon. A little piece of the sixteenth century that had strayed into the seventeenth. Apart from the electric lights and the chairs in which he sat, and the low table, Hennessey could see no sign of later eras about him. He felt, as on other similar occasions, that he was touching history.

Frost eventually returned to the foyer carrying a pot of tea, cups, saucers and a plate piled high with toasted teacakes. He placed the tray on the low table and invited Hennessey to 'dig in' as he stirred the tea in the pot. Hennessey willingly 'dug in' and helped himself to a toasted teacake. Frost poured the tea, handed Hennessey a cup and poured himself a cup, added a little milk and sat back in the chair and beamed at Hennessey. 'So, how can I help the police? You indicated that it was about Janet's murder.'

'Yes.'

'Reopening the case?'

'It was never closed, sir.'

'Ah . . . rekindling your interest?'

'Well, my interest in your wife's murder was never kindled in the first place, I wasn't the investigating officer. But yes, we, the police, are taking a fresh look at it. Our interest being stimulated by developments in other cases.'

'I see.' Frost spoke with a soft accent which contained just a hint of Yorkshire. 'Am I still a suspect?'

'No,' Hennessey smiled. 'Were you?'

'Not in so many words, but I think that there was that suspicion.'

'There always is . . . please don't be offended. If a married woman is murdered the statistical probability is that her husband is responsible.'

'So I believe.'

'Even if, as in your wife's case, she was murdered somewhere other than the marital home.'

'Well, the suspicion didn't last very long anyway – my wife's death could be pinpointed in time as accurately as it could be pinpointed in place and my alibi was as reinforced as concrete. I believe there did remain the suspicion that I may have had her killed by a so called "hit man" but this is the Vale of York . . . not San Francisco, and anyway, I would not have benefited from Janet's death.'

'Well, contract killings can happen anywhere, the Vale of York included . . . but the issue of you benefiting or otherwise from your wife's death, that was not the case?'

'Saved me from a tense and difficult relationship. I will not hide the fact that things between me and Janet were not happy. There was a glimmer of passion there still, at the end, but only a glimmer . . . and that was fading. I confess that I felt a sense of relief after I had overcome the shock of the news of her murder. That was quite unexpected, the sense of relief I mean, but it was there . . . and there was peace in the house, no cold, quiet tension, no blazing, crockery-smashing rows. She was quite a violent woman . . . assaulted me on occasions . . . I was a battered husband.'

'There are not a few of those, Mr Frost, too scared to go to the police for fear of ridicule.'

'I can well imagine . . . don't need to be well built and strong to do it. Janet was quite small, but capable of throwing objects at speed and with accuracy and of pouring very hot liquid over my head, as she did on one occasion. I learned that any jobs which had to be done, which involved me having to get on my hands and knees, were best done when she was out of the house, or at least otherwise engaged. Ours was not the marriage made in heaven.'

'It doesn't sound like it.'

'You married, Mr Hennessey?'

'Widower.'

'I'm sorry.'

'But like you, I have friends. Now, I understand you remarried?'

'Sandra . . . yes . . . that was also a failure. I am twice married, both disasters.'

'Tell me about Sandra.'

'Well, Sandra worked for us.'

'Us?'

'Fawthrop and Crookes, Chartered Architects.'

'You are not self-employed?'

'I am now . . . my studio is upstairs, north-facing window . . . purer light from the north . . . and no glare to dazzle your eyes when doing detailed drawing. Artists and architects have the same requirement of pure light. Sandra was a clerical worker, started to show some warmth towards me after Janet was murdered, the old sympathy number, I reckon. A drink once led to a dinner date, which led to marriage. We were not unhappy, living in a pleasant four-bedroomed townhouse.'

'Not here . . . in this house?'

'Heavens no . . . no, there was a rough ride between the townhouse and here.' Frost sipped his tea. 'We had been married for about eighteen months . . . all seemed to be well . . . Sandra clearly enjoyed living in the townhouse though I didn't . . . too exposed. The front door abutted the pavement, not even the slightest pretence of a front garden and the back garden finished up against a section of the walls, so that we had to keep net curtains up in the bedroom, because folks on the top deck of the buses were passing our window just a few feet away and the folk who were walking the walls looked into our back garden. No privacy, but Sandra didn't mind, she had come from living in the country and before that had grown up in poverty, so she loved the townhouse.'

'What happened?'

'The firm went bankrupt. I was out of work at the age of forty plus, very plus . . . no means of keeping up the mortgage payments. Had to sell the house . . . sold it to a new firm of accountants, for whom privacy is not an issue . . . all the houses in that terrace are now in commercial hands, doctors' surgeries, dentists, accountants, graphic designers . . . no families there anymore. But anyway, when I sold the house . . . it was then that Sandra discovered the extent to which it was still mortgaged . . . which was to a great extent, and the amount of equity that was mine, which was minimal. No income, no capital . . . we were destitute and homeless. I told her so and she said, 'Well, you might be destitute and homeless but I'm not,' and walked into a solicitor's office and began divorce proceedings . . . not a woman who took kindly to poverty.'

'Few would.'

'Yes . . . but a few, more than a few, would remain loyal to their husbands. I could pick myself up, I knew I would, I could fairly ask my wife to show some support and faith in me.'

'Point,' Hennessey nodded to Frost.

'But not Sandra. Her loyalty was to the lifestyle I could provide . . . she divorced . . . went back to calling herself Picardie and I dare say she went looking for Mr Moneybags. She moved back in with her friend, one Miss Wickersley . . . I met her on a few occasions . . . very like Sandra, very cold, very calculating, very mercenary.'

'It looks like she should have stayed.' Hennessey looked around him.

'Yes. I lived on bread and jam for about eighteen months, but I was always looking for work, then I registered as an independent and designed a few extensions for houses in the suburbs and then put in a low bid for the contract to design a hotel in Saudi Arabia. Massively undercut all other bids for the project but still negotiated a six-figure fee for about twelve months' work. Bought Derrydown Manor . . . and my dogs . . . better than women any day. Sandra made noises about a "reconciliation" but by then it was clear she only wanted to reconciliate with my bank balance. Then she sued me for an increase in maintenance, but lost . . . short length of marriage . . . no progeny to support . . . no fault on my part . . . the settlement was fairly based on my wealth and income at the time. All she got out of that was a huge legal bill. Haven't heard from her since but I have seen her from time to time . . . she's found her Mr Moneybags, going by her car.'

'What do you know about her background?'

'You seem to be more interested in Sandra than Janet?' Archibald Frost smiled and raised an eyebrow.

'We are interested in both, Mr Frost.'

'Really?'

'Yes, really.'

'Well . . . now my curiosity is well up . . . but to answer your question, I know what she told me . . . and I confess that that was not a great deal. She told me she came from Wales, originally from Newport, but she didn't speak with a Welsh accent . . . not even a Welsh turn of phrase. I was at university in Cardiff, you see, so I am familiar with Welsh expressions like "by here" for "just here", and "tidy" for "good quality" or "desirable", but she never would use such phrases and so I assumed that while she may have been born in Wales, she had been long in Yorkshire.'

'Assumed? You didn't ask? I mean, she was your wife.'

'Yes, I asked, she was evasive . . . she told me she had nothing to hide but that she wanted to live for today and tomorrow, "our tomorrow," she said. But "our tomorrow" lasted only until the money dried up – "our tomorrow" in her vision of the future clearly didn't include eighteen months on the dole in a damp bedsit in an overcrowded conversion where all the derelicts and mental health cases in the city also had rooms. If she had stayed with me, I would have found better accommodation for us but even so, it would have been a substantial fall from grace, up with which she would not put.'

'Any family?'

'Me, or her?'

'Her, Sandra . . .'

'Just her. Only child of elderly parents, both well in the clay by the time she came to work with us.'

'I see. What was she like as a worker?'

'Efficient, I'd say, but she could have pushed herself more. Did not seem to me to be interested in fulfilling her potential, but she was a bit of an opportunist . . . the gold-digging propensity showed itself quite early on. Harry Fawthorp, the senior partner, became widowed and Sandra began to show him more attention than was proper for an administrative worker but Harry wasn't interested . . . he and his wife were long married and utterly devoted to each other. So she got short shrift there . . . then Janet was murdered and shortly after, Sandra started to give me the same sort of attention.' Archibald Frost shrugged. 'I suppose I just wasn't as shrewd as Harry and I wasn't as lucky in my marriage. Harry and Pauline lived for each other, no one could take her place in his life. It wasn't a question of Harry having a lucky escape . . . Sandra never had a chance with him. There was also quite an age gap between them; I was, still am, older than Sandra but the gap is/was less than it would have been with Harry. Those two would just never have become an item . . . but, I . . . well, I escaped more or less unscathed. When the firm collapsed . . . well . . . in hindsight that was the best thing that happened to me.'

'Can I ask, Mr Frost . . .' Hennessey glanced towards the Alsatians and saw four pairs of eyes still staring at him. 'Can I ask if Ms Picardie knew of your standard of living . . . the townhouse you mentioned?'

'Yes. Visited it once. She accompanied me to a meeting as a note-taker . . . and to help with a presentation . . . on the way back I had to collect something. We called in . . . had coffee. Janet was out at the time but that night we had another row . . . she, Janet, had returned home and had scented Sandra's perfume . . . seen two unwashed cups in the sink, accused me of having an affair . . . a bit prescient of her, but she was quite wrong, there was never anything between Sandra and me before Janet's murder.'

Hennessey held up his hand. 'Please, Mr Frost, I wasn't implying anything of the sort. Any children of your union?'

'Janet and I, no . . . . . . Sandra and I, no. Janet and I tried but Sandra and I didn't. I'm the last of my line.'

'Did Sandra know anything of the stressed nature of your marriage?'

'I think she must have . . . in fact, yes she did, because I complained about it long and hard in the office. Oh . . .' colour drained from Archibald Frost's face. 'You are not saying . . . not suggesting . . .'

'I am not saying or suggesting anything, Mr Frost.'

'But the implication . . .' Frost stood, the Alsatians raised their heads as one, like a line of soldiers moving on command. 'No . . . no . . . the magic had gone out of the relationship between myself and Janet . . . but if I thought that female had taken her place with premeditation.' Frost sank back into the chair. 'I . . . oh . . . I feel sick.'

'There is nothing to suggest at the moment, Mr Frost, but the possibility looms. What, can I ask, do you know of Sandra Picardie's first marriage?'

'She left because of violence. So she said.'

'She told you that?'

'Yes . . . why, are you going to tell me something different?'

Hennessey paused. He pondered. Then he said, 'No . . . I am not going to tell you anything at all. Not yet.'

'Well, it's not every day you come across a dead body, so yes, of course I remember it. Remember it like yesterday.'

'If you could remind me.'

'Well . . .' Tony Rathbone folded the clothing and placed it in the laundry basket. 'I was taking a shortcut through a snickelway . . . Hornpot Lane, Nether . . . passed someone coming the other direction, which is unusual . . . I'm sure you've walked down a snickelway, I have, many times. No matter how crowded the streets are, I always seem to have the snickelway to myself.'

Hennessey thought it a fair observation. He was not fond of the snickelways of York, but it was true, whenever he had walked a snickelway, he had walked it alone and, as Tony Rathbone said, no matter how busy the streets may be, even on Saturday afternoons, the snickelways always seem to be empty.

'But on this occasion I met someone coming in the opposite direction.' Tony Rathbone turned away from the laundry basket and tapped the ironing board. 'Don't you just love domesticity? I am a computer programmer, got bits of paper, but can I get a job? My wife is the breadwinner. She's a teacher, only primary, but we pay the bills . . . just. We might even have paid off the mortgage before she retires but that's going to be touch and go.' The kitchen was light-coloured, a large window let in the sunlight, children's paintings were Blu-tacked to the walls and doors. 'She's out with the children at the moment. August . . . the long school holidays . . . me . . . housework is never done. Sorry . . . the murder. Yes, she was coming towards me, a tall woman, quite slender, she wore dark glasses and kept her head down. I think her hair was dark but it was well done up in a bun and covered by a headscarf, but a few strands were sticking out. I'm not sure it was dark hair . . . I got and I still have a clear impression that she didn't want me to be there . . . there was a jolt . . . a distinct signal in her body language that said I wasn't supposed to be there, that my presence wasn't in the script.' Tony Rathbone stroked his beard. 'She seemed to hurry past me. I think she quickened her pace, in fact I am sure she did. At the time, I thought it was because she didn't want to be in a snickelway with a guy. I could understand that. Anyway, I carried on and saw the woman lying in a crumpled heap . . . no sign of life . . . a lot of blood in her hair . . . ran back after the woman but she had disappeared by then.'

'Disappeared?'

'Well, gone round a corner. She was going towards St Sampson's Square. There was probably a ninety-second time lapse between the time she left the snickelway and turned into St Sampson's Square and the time I left the snickelway. Time enough to get round any of the corners leading off the square or down another snickelway and anyway, I wasn't looking for her, I was looking for a phone, didn't have a mobile in those days. Got to a phone, dialled three nines . . . the rest is history.'

'The rest is an incomplete, unfinished story.' Hennessey, having sat, as invited, at the small kitchen table on a chair that he doubted would take his weight, looked out of the window across the small rear garden to the rooftops of the houses in the next street. This was Hewarth. There are worse places in York, there are better, but it was definitely the land of primary school teachers and out-of-work computer programmers. 'Can you remember anything about the woman you passed in the snickelway?'

'Anything?'

'Well, her clothing for example.'

'A dress . . . she was carrying a shoulder bag, that I do remember. I remember it because I thought to myself: 'Wow, that's some handbag. Huge, black leather thing.'

'Footwear . . . you say her pace quickened. Did you hear it or see it quicken?'

'Heard it.'

'So she was wearing heels which clicked as she walked?'

'Well, yes . . . must have been.'

'All right . . . any scent . . . anything?'

'Not that I remember. I mean, this was ten years ago and if I knew the significance of the person I passed, I would have taken more notice but at the time she was just another pedestrian walking in the opposite direction . . . coming out of the snickelway I was going in.'

'Coming out?'

'Well, she had about twenty feet to go before she reached the end of the passage, we passed about twenty feet in. Hornpot Lane, Nether, is a long snickelway as snickelways go. I reckon she was just glad to get to the end, they can be quite lonely places.'

'Would you recognize her again?' Hennessey knew it was a long shot.

'I doubt it, frankly.' Tony Rathbone pursed his lips. 'What I really remember is the dead woman . . . crumpled up . . . first dead person I saw, but I imagine you know all about her?'

'Yes, we do. But back to the woman you passed . . . she was tall?'

'For a woman . . . about my height, which is five foot ten . . . and I am sure she was dark haired.'

'Age?'

'Could only give a wide range there . . . she wasn't going to see her teenage years again, but she was a long way from her pension as well . . . thirties/forties . . . probably thirties, by her dress sense.'

'Meaning?'

'Well . . . meaning that it was trendy, fashionable rather than conservative. I recall an image of bright colours as she went by.'

'I see.'

'Why? Do you have a suspect?

'Well, probably.' Hennessey stood. He thanked Tony Rathbone for his time and drove back to Micklegate Bar.

'Could be.' Yellich looked at the photographs he had taken earlier that day which had been rapidly developed and returned for his attention. He compared them with the E-fit which ten years earlier had been compiled from Tony Rathbone's description. He handed the E-fit and the photographs to Hennessey.

'And couldn't be,' Hennessey said. 'A woman in a headscarf and shades. I am surprised they thought it worth an E-fit. The scarf and dark glasses are clearly a disguise. She won't be going out dressed like that again. In fact she would probably have discarded the scarf and sunglasses as soon as she could . . . once out of the snickelway, in fact. Was she a tall woman, would you say?'

'Sandra Picardie? Yes, she was, taller than the guy she was with.'

'Don't recognize him.' Hennessey looked at the photograph. 'But he's got "felon" written all over him. And it isn't our own beloved Tommy Ilford. So who is it . . . ?'

'Hasn't he just. He has hard eyes . . . don't see them in the photograph but when they drove past me those eyes drilled me. Then he reckoned me for a harmless guy, which I am, out for a stroll in the country, which I was.'

Hennessey smiled. 'But unbeknown to him, he and Sandra

120

Picardie had been captured on film contained within the camera contained within your knapsack.'

'That's about it, boss . . . but something is happening . . . as you say that guy has "felon" written all over him . . . it isn't Tommy Ilford but they drove to Ilford's garage. She's not playing away from home, it was more like she and Ilford are accommodating him as they work together on something.'

Hennessey remained quiet for a moment and then said, 'Saturday tomorrow?'

'Yes, boss.'

'Saturday night . . .'

'Boss?'

'I am thinking . . .'

'Yes, boss?'

'Well, if Ilford and Sandra Picardie are entertaining someone, they'll probably go out over the weekend.'

'Seems likely, sir.'

'Well people like that won't be going for a stroll in the park will they? . . . or touring museums? They'll be going out on the town . . . restaurants, night clubs.'

'Yes, boss.'

'Maybe a pub first.'

'Yes . . . you're thinking we should invite ourselves along?'

'Yes,' Hennessey smiled. 'That's exactly what I am thinking, Yellich. That is exactly what I am thinking.'

Five

. . . in which the gentle reader learns more of the private lives of Hennessey and Yellich, a houseguest is identified and a body is reported.

SATURDAY, 20 AUGUST – SUNDAY A.M., 21 AUGUST

George Hennessey woke early. His bedroom looked out over the rear garden, to the fields beyond. His bedroom, clearly unlike the townhouse once owned by Archibald Frost, could not be looked into. Nothing overlooked his house. It was, in consequence, George Hennessey's practice to sleep with his bedroom curtains open and so, in further consequence, he found he awoke with the dawn. In the summer that could be very early indeed. On that morning he awoke to birdsong and sunlight shortly after 6 a.m. He lay on one side, facing away from the window, and slumbered, allowing himself to wake slowly, restfully. He did not consider himself a sybarite, but equally he felt that wakefulness was something that one shouldn't be jostled into.

Then it happened. As always it was unexpected, the same noise or vision, and the memory returned. On this occasion it was not the sight and sound of a young man on a motorcycle, but it was the sound of one – he presumed young male, but not necessarily either – the sound of a motorcycle roaring down Thirsk Road at the front of his house, shattering the peace of the early morning. Lying there, he was suddenly back in his boyhood home in Colomb Street, Greenwich, where he and his elder brother, Graham, lived with their parents. George Hennessey worshipped his elder brother and his elder brother seemed to live only for his motorbike, which he cleaned each Sunday afternoon, polishing the chrome until it shone in the sun. Graham would take young George for a ride, down Trafalgar Road, following the Thames to Tower Bridge, through London, Trafalgar Square, Hyde Park . . . the Palace . . . all the sights . . . then back over Westminster Bridge to the south of the river and back to Greenwich. Occasionally Graham would take George Hennessey for a spin around Blackheath Common, but for the future Chief Inspector the 'trip up to town' and back was by far his favourite. Then, one night, George Hennessey, when about eight years of age, had been lying in bed, listening as his brother made ready to leave the house, saying 'bye' to his parents. His mother, as always, entreating her first born to 'be careful'. The opening and the closing of the front door . . . the few unsuccessful kicks before the Triumph roared into life; then he listened as Graham drove away, straining his ears to catch the fading sound as he drove down Trafalgar Road towards the Maritime Museum and the *Cutty Sark*. The sound of the motorbike being eventually swallowed by other sounds, ships on the river, an Irishman rolling up Colomb Street drunkenly reciting his 'Hail Mary's'. Later there was the ominous, distinct tap, tap . . . tap . . . the policeman's knock, which he would come to use in later years. The hushed conversation . . . a strange voice . . . then his mother wailing . . . neighbours coming into the house, then his father coming into his room, sitting on his bed, fighting back the tears as he told him that Graham had ridden his bike to heaven 'to save a place for us'. A few days later there was the funeral with his father being courageous in his determination to contain his emotion, but his mother utterly distraught as the coffin was being lowered. And it was summer . . . that had seemed wrong to the young George Hennessey, very wrong, and it still did. The butterflies, warm weather, the chimes of a distant ice-cream van and funerals

123

just do not marry together. Winters add to the poignancy of a funeral, just as summers add to the joy of a wedding. So George Hennessey had come to believe. But from that fateful thirteenth day of June of that year there had been a gap in his life . . . a hollow . . . a space . . . an emptiness that should have been occupied by an elder brother. In George Hennessey's mind, the space occupied by Graham upon his death was much, much smaller than the space he vacated by his death.

Hennessey levered himself out of bed, washed, shaved and clambered into casual clothes, a pair of corduroy trousers, a comfortable rugby shirt. He went downstairs and was warmly greeted by a tail-wagging Oscar, whom Hennessey noticed only barked a welcome if Hennessey returned to the house. His welcome each morning was a warm look in the mongrel's eyes, a wagging tail, but no bark. Hennessey knew that dogs eat one meal a day but always allowed Oscar a 'breakfast' of a single sliver of lambs' liver. While the animal took his 'breakfast' to savour in the garden, Hennessey made himself a huge pot of tea and drank it whilst listening to the ever reassuring, calming sounds of Radio Four. Later, he ate a leisurely breakfast while reading the *Yorkshire Post*, which had been pushed through the letterbox by the paperboy. Later still, he walked the garden, mug of tea in hand, dog at his heels, across the lawn, into the orchard . . . to the pond in the 'going forth' where he stopped and stood still, looking for frogs. They kept still, very still, but he was practised at spotting them: two eyes, just above water level, superbly camouflaged. That year, all the frogs seemed to be of normal size but a few years earlier the pond had been host to a monster. Not only was the monster four times larger than any other frog, but it had a nonchalant attitude not displayed by the others. It showed no fear and was occasionally seen making stately progress across the lawn going to or from the pond. But frogs have a short life and one spring, the monster frog didn't reappear.

A short, twin blast on a car's horn made Hennessey turn,
Oscar barked in recognition, not alarm, and Hennessey smiled
as he recognized the younger man who stood at the fence
that ran between the house and the garage and that served
to keep Oscar contained in the garden and the house during
Hennessey's absence. Moments later, the two men sat on the
porch enjoying the morning sun, sipping tea from generously
proportioned mugs.

'Completed the list yet, Dad?' the younger man asked.

'Five elude me.' Hennessey sipped his tea. 'Just five . . . all
in the middle section too . . . around the Hs.' At his secondary
school the same thirty plus names, with one or two additions
and one or two losses, had been barked out each schoolday
morning for five years and recently, George Hennessey had
set himself the task of recalling all thirty plus names. He had
been able to remember twenty-seven. He also knew that the
greatest number of pupils in that form had been thirty-two,
the least number at the end of one term had been twenty-nine.
Twenty-seven names recalled – five names eluded him. 'I'm
not pushing it,' Hennessey said, watching Oscar criss-cross
the lawn following a scent he had clearly picked up. 'I'll
remember them or I won't. If I don't, it's not the end of the
world. So what's happening in the north eastern circuit?'

'Just finished a case at Bradford . . . quite an interesting
sequence of events . . .'

'Really . . .'

'Yes . . . the police were asking questions of the girls who
work Lumb Lane . . . somebody was mugging them and one
girl mentioned a "sugar daddy" who was new to the lane and
who was throwing money around like it was going out of
fashion . . . the police watched him and followed him . . .
he led them to two mates . . . all three were councillors . . .
they have been given a huge grant to investigate poverty and
to set up anti-poverty projects . . .'

'And spent it on themselves.'

'Oh, you said it, Dad – cars, girls, gambling, foreign

holidays . . . to think the police went to the Lane trying to find a youth who was knocking the girls to the ground and stealing their handbags and they uncovered that . . .'

'Like digging for tin and striking gold. It happens from time to time.'

'Now I'm at Teesside, been there all this last week and I'll be there next week.'

'Big case?'

'Attempted murder. The gun culture has arrived in our right little tight little island. I am for the Crown in the case . . . ordinarily I don't like prosecuting but in this case I have no qualms, this is one where your lot nick 'em and we do what we can to send 'em down.'

'It's nice to be on the same side for once,' Hennessey grinned.

'It is rather.' Charles Hennessey looked out over the garden of the house where he had grown up. 'But this is as unpleasant a sort of pond life as you could think of.'

'What happened?'

'Two felons blasted a couple with a sawn-off . . . the girl has over a hundred pellets permanently lodged in her flesh and her skin is turning green from the lead which is poisoning her system.'

'Heavens!'

'Enormous weight of evidence and the defence is reduced to trying to discredit the witnesses . . . how much had you had to drink when you saw the accused? That sort of ploy. But the witnesses have so far stood up well and their credibility remains intact . . . plenty of CCTV footage . . . not of the incident itself but surrounding the incident . . . the accused buying petrol at a nearby filling station when they both claim to have been at home for example, claiming not to be in possession of a coat of a certain colour when the police have colour CCTV footage of them in the police station in respect of an earlier incident wearing just that garment. They are going down for a long time.'

'Motive?'

'Ah . . . well you might ask, the police haven't offered any . . . it is believed to be part of underworld rivalry in respect of the supply of controlled substances.'

'So the victims are no saints?'

'I think the girl was, Dad. I think, and the police officers I have spoken to believe, that the intended target was the man. They think he saw the barrel pointing at him from out of the window of the passing car and the split second before the accused pulled the trigger, he jumped behind his girlfriend and she took the full force of the blast . . . he was only slightly injured.'

'Courageous of him.'

'Wasn't it?' Charles Hennessey sipped his tea. 'Wasn't it just. So what's keeping you busy this week? Anything of interest?'

'Could well be. Well, it is interesting . . . but I mean it could well develop into something even more interesting. Started on Tuesday with the discovery of a skeleton in a pile of rubble. Identified as a lady who was reported to have disappeared about twenty years ago . . . interestingly, the body must have been placed in the rubble after the police had searched the area or the dogs would have picked up the smell.'

'Weird.'

'We quizzed the husband . . . don't know what to make of him, he is a slippery customer who allegedly likes playing games. The marriage had gone pear-shaped . . . he remarried a younger model soon afterwards.'

'Oh ho . . .'

'That's what I thought . . . a case where murder is seen as a more attractive course of action than divorce.'

'Happens often . . . more often than we know of. All those women reported "missing" . . . and not a few men either.'

'You don't need to tell me . . . but in this case the woman left the man when his business failed . . . and was then heard of as marrying another man, a successful man whose wife had been murdered . . . banged over the head in a snickelway, bag snatched . . . a mugging that went over the top. This same woman, Sandra Picardie by name, then occupied her marriage bed at a pace that might in some quarters be seen as somewhat hurried . . . he then went broke and she hopped it and is now known to have taken up with a known villain.'

'A gold-digger?'

'Seems like she might be . . . a gold-digger who is not only seeking the good life, but who is prepared to kill to get where she wants to go.'

'Puts my clients in the shade . . . they only blast people from cars with sawn-off shotguns . . . there is a marginal reduction in the muzzle velocity by the way.'

'With what?'

'A sawn-off . . . last witness to give evidence was a member of the Northern Firearms Unit.'

'Based in Manchester?'

'Yes. He said that one of the effects of sawing off the barrel of a shotgun, leaving just the barrel over the forestock is to bring about a marginal reduction in the muzzle velocity.'

'Didn't know that.'

'Me neither . . . but there was still sufficient velocity to make a real mess of that young woman's body . . . you should see the photographs.'

'I can well imagine. I have seen similar . . . in the flesh too . . . not just celluloid.'

'Of course . . . I have a much sanitized experience of crime. Rarely smell the real thing.' Charles Hennessey fell silent, then said, 'So, when am I going to meet your . . . new friend?'

'Any time now, she's anxious to meet you. I have sung your praises so much that the lady's curiosity is boundless.'

'Heavens . . . I hope I don't let you down, Dad.'

'You won't. You haven't up to now. I don't think you'll start now. And the children?'

'Well, they're at the coast today with their mum.'

'You didn't go?'

'Refused . . . it will be mobbed on a day like this.'

'You should have done . . . you should grab every minute of time with your children. These days won't come again for you.'

'Yes . . . perhaps you are right. It couldn't have been easy for you, bringing me up alone.'

'I wasn't, I had help, but I wouldn't have missed the experience for anything. Anything at all.'

Somerled Yellich spent that Saturday morning with his son. They went to the local shops and he bought Jeremy a comic and a bar of chocolate because he had been a very good boy all the previous week. They then sat together on the floor of the living room of the Yellich household in Huntingdon whilst Jeremy proudly pointed to various letters of the alphabet, as requested by his father, and delighting his father by getting most correct, though the 'Y' and the 'X' still caused some confusion. Later, they told the time by means of moving the hands on an old clock and Jeremy, again proudly, showed he could tell difficult times such as twenty-two minutes past two and thirteen minutes to twelve. He was tiring, and Yellich again wondered, marvelled at how his wife could cope each day. At lunchtime she returned laden with shopping and Jeremy rushed to her and hugged her as she entered the house. She managed to retain her footing but was forced to take a step or two backwards in order to do so. Jeremy was heavier than her, though still a few inches shorter. He was by then twelve years of age and the Yellichs had been told that with stimulation, love, nurture, he might reach a mental age of twelve or thirteen by the time he was twenty, whereupon he could live a semi-independent life in a hostel with his own room, access to a kitchen to cook his own meals, but with staff on hand if things became too much for him.

After lunch, when Jeremy had gone upstairs for his afternoon nap, Somerled and Sara Yellich sat side by side, arms around each other, on the sofa. She craned her slender neck up and kissed him . . . 'To think I gave up a lucrative and a stimulating career in teaching for this. I could have been Miss Morrison, Head of English now . . . and what did I do but let you drag me off into a bunker marked "Marriage, intelligent females for the disposal of".'

'Didn't have to do too much dragging, as I recall.' Yellich squeezed her, pulling her closer to him. 'As I recall, it was more like you running away from teaching, drawing me along behind you in your wake.'

'Nonsense, you had me by the hair.'

'What hair? I remember the first time I saw you it was from behind, I thought you were a lad. Such short hair, such a thin figure, in that rugby shirt and jeans.'

'Still thin.' She patted her stomach. 'Gone from a size ten to a whopping size twelve . . . but I still please my husband.'

'You do.'

'But all that education. Did I really spend three years at one of Britain's most prestigious universities and take a 2:1 only to stand in the aisle of the supermarket wondering whether to go for the "two for the price of one" offer on a brand of coffee we don't usually drink? Has it really come to this?'

'Would you turn the clock back if you could?'

'No.' She held her husband tightly. 'No . . . promise, promise, promise.'

'Even despite Jeremy?'

'Well . . .' She rested her head on his chest. 'We've spoken about this. I have not changed my mind. We both shared the disappointment when we realized he wasn't going to be a future prime minister . . .'

'Or a rocket scientist.'

'Indeed . . . but there is that sense of privilege . . . a world unknown to us is opening up: other parents with the same sort of child, the professionals involved, the resources available to children with "learning difficulties" . . . we would never have known about it if Jeremy had been normal.'

'And he gives us so much . . . so genuine, so affectionate . . . that sense of childhood wonder will never really leave him.'

'So, no,' Sara Yellich kissed her husband again. 'No, no . . . one thousand times, no. I wouldn't turn the clock back.' She paused. 'Are you really working tonight?'

'Yes, really, don't want to but the skipper is right, we have to watch this team . . . whatever it is they are up to, they're up to no good. Up to no good at all.'

Hennessey sat in the unmarked police vehicle, which had been parked by Yellich in the same place that he had parked his car whilst observing the Ilford house. He sat slumped back in the passenger seat with his hat pulled over his eyes. The bonnet of the car was raised, the driver's door slightly ajar. It was a ploy, a desperate ploy to appear as least like a police officer as possible. It was his suggestion, but he privately thought it might fool a teenage car thief for about thirty seconds. Yellich had moved into a position where he could observe the house whilst concealing himself behind a hedgerow. He had communicated by mobile phone to Hennessey that there appeared to be people in the house and that Sandra Picardie's Mercedes Benz and a Jaguar, believed to belong to Thomas Ilford, were indeed in the driveway. Hennessey said, all right, they would give Picardie and Ilford until 8 p.m., reasoning that if they had not left the house by then, they wouldn't be leaving at all that evening. It would be a 'quiet night in' and he and Yellich would stand down. It was then that he'd felt very conspicuous as a police officer, so he'd opened the bonnet of the car, opened the passenger door slightly and pulled his hat down over his eyes as if sleeping. The impression, he hoped, might be that of a car that had broken down, the driver having gone for help whilst the elderly passenger remained with the vehicle. It proved to be a very quiet lane and for the hour that he remained there from 6.30 p.m., not one car passed him. The only sound was the birdsong of the early evening. Then his mobile rang.

'Yes?' he responded quickly.

'They're on the move, boss.' Yellich spoke in a whisper, though Hennessey doubted he was close enough to be heard with his normal voice. 'Three of them – Ilford, Picardie and the unknown . . . looks like . . . yes, they're going in Ilford's Jag. I'm coming back.'

'All right.' Hennessey snapped the mobile shut, slid it into his pocket, got out of the car and closed the bonnet quietly. He reasoned that the 'thud' of a slammed bonnet might carry sufficiently to be heard by Ilford and friends and that the sound, amid the tranquillity of a summer's evening, could only sound suspicious. He got back inside the car as Yellich reappeared in a slow run . . . a 'jog' down the lane towards him.

'We have to hope they don't come this way, boss.' Yellich turned the key in the ignition. 'Yon is the quickest way into York and that was the way she went yesterday.'

'It's one way or the other. We can but hope.'

'Well, if they haven't passed us in thirty seconds, they've gone the other way.'

The two officers waited in silence, a short, brief silence broken by Yellich as he engaged first gear. 'They've gone the other way.' He drove off, passing the entrance to Tommy Ilford's house a few moments later, allowing Hennessey to glance at it.

'Gone in the Jag all right,' Hennessey said. 'Only the Mercedes there now.'

Yellich didn't reply. He drove the car at the fastest speed he deemed safe along the narrow lane. At a long stretch of the lane he saw the rear bumper of Ilford's Jaguar, just glimpsed it before it disappeared round a bend.

'Don't want to get too close.' Yellich eased his foot off the accelerator.

Ilford drove the Jaguar towards York on the A64, turned off the bypass to join the Malton Road into the city. Yellich followed, always ensuring that at least two cars were between the police vehicle and the Jaguar. In the city, Ilford found a parking place between two other vehicles in George Hudson Street. Yellich drove past, pointedly not glancing at them, and as he did so, halted at the junction with Tanner Row, where, without speaking, Hennessey got out of the vehicle and walked back towards the place where Ilford had parked the car. He slowed his pace as he watched Ilford ensuring the Jag was locked, the anti-theft alarm set, and to his relief walking away in the direction he too was walking, so that he immediately began to follow them. The three, the two men and Sandra Picardie, strolled in the warm evening, down winding Micklegate and entered the Unicorn. Hennessey halted and took out his mobile. He keyed in Yellich's number.

'Yellich,' Yellich's reply crackled. Hennessey heard the sound of the car's engine.

'They've gone into the Unicorn on Micklegate,' Hennessey said. 'Join me in there, when you can.'

'Will do, boss. I'm parking in Leeman Road car park. I'll be with you in a minute.'

'OK. What are you drinking?' Hennessey laughed. 'You can have whatever you like, so long as it isn't alcoholic.'

'See you . . .' Yellich replied, also laughing.

Yellich parked the car and strolled back along Rougier Street, into George Hudson Street, and turned left into Micklegate. He entered the Unicorn and saw Hennessey sitting modestly, it seemed, in a corner, with two glasses of pale-looking liquid in front of him. Yellich sat opposite him.

'Tonic water with lime,' Hennessey answered the unasked question. 'Extra shot of lime . . . a perfect drink for weather like this, rehydrate you and give you a vitamin C boost.'

'Really?' Yellich drank deeply. The drink was indeed refreshing. Tonic water with lime. He committed it to memory. Refreshing and very appropriate for the weather. Hennessey the Wise was right, he thought, right yet again. 'Where are they?'

'Far corner.'

Yellich didn't turn round.

'I can see them clearly . . . huddled in a group . . . interesting . . .'

'Talking business, you mean . . . as opposed to relaxing?'

'That's the impression I have. They are going somewhere after this . . . they're dressed for a restaurant or the casino . . . but they are not relaxed, very intense conversation there, and Sandra Picardie's right in there.'

'Part of the gang?'

'Very definitely . . . she's more than just the glamour-piece to set the scene off, to be looked at while the men do the doing.'

The Unicorn was an old pub that had been modernized in the late-twentieth century to look space-age and then, as public tastes changed, had been remodernized at the turn of the century to look old. The wood had been stripped of paint or varnish, the floor had been sanded down to the bare floorboards and sawdust spread each day for 'authenticity', the tables and chairs were an ill-assorted collection, not at all uniform as in many pubs, but a desperate purchase from second-hand furniture dealers of anything solid and wooden. Music . . . very late-twentieth/early-twenty-first century, though mercifully for both Hennessey and Yellich, but most mercifully for Hennessey, who thought the music 'weird', it was played at a bearable volume. A Space Invader machine whirred and buzzed; a television screen, mounted on the wall adjacent to where Hennessey and Yellich sat, was tuned into a satellite sports channel, but equally mercifully, its volume was turned off. The bar staff were uniformed with 'here to help you' name tags. Hennessey had been served by 'Benjamin, here to help you'. The Unicorn strove to suggest antiquity but could not resist the modern. The pub, in Hennessey's view, just didn't work, unlike his beloved Dove Inn in Easingwold with its timeless charm. Now there was a pub.

'Give anything for a mike on that table, skipper.' Yellich drained his glass.

'Take it steady,' Hennessey growled.

'Why?' Yellich was puzzled. 'It's not alcoholic.'

'Because I don't want us to be noticed. If you go up to the bar you'll be noticed, if you sit too long in front of an empty glass you'll be noticed.'

Yellich winced. 'Sorry, boss, I wasn't thinking.'

'Just keep sitting there . . . they can't see your glass. But yes, a microphone on the table would pick up an interesting tale . . . an interesting job in the planning . . . an interesting job going on right now as we speak.' Hennessey turned his gaze away from the group. 'The stranger's buying a round.' He glanced at his watch. 'Eight thirty . . . if they're going on somewhere, this will be their last round. Soon we will find out if we know the stranger, by which I mean if he has any track.'

'How's that, boss?'

'By grabbing the glasses they've been using before the staff can clear them away.'

Yellich beamed at him.

'Soon as I tell you they're moving, move to their table . . . walk across the opposite side of the room, don't look at them, but get to the table before the bar staff.'

'May not come through this evening.' Hennessey glanced out of his office window. Night had fallen: he saw his reflection and beyond his reflection, he saw the ribbon of lights that was the street lighting and passing headlights of the cars. 'Even with all this modern technology at the hands of computer wizards . . . there are millions of prints to search through, as you know.'

Yellich glanced at his watch. 10.10 p.m. He had privately

hoped to have been home by then, enjoy a little more quality time with Sara when the house was peaceful. But Hennessey had insisted on remaining in case the fingerprints that had been lifted from the glasses 'got a result'. 'Aye' he said, 'Aye.' He hoped his voice didn't sound too irritated, too exasperated.

'Don't be so exasperated, Yellich,' Hennessey smiled. 'We'll give it until ten thirty and if—'

Then the phone on his desk rang. He glanced at Yellich, whose heart sank, as he thought, If you haven't got a family to go home to, boss.

'Hennessey.' He held the phone in a tight grip.

'Collator, sir.'

'Yes.'

'We have received the results from the fingerprints from the Police National Computer . . . only Thomas Ilford's were held locally, we had to send the other two down to Hendon . . .'

'Yes . . . yes . . .'

'Well the other two came back with interesting results . . . the female is known to the West Midlands police as Tracy Morrison.'

'What?'

'Yes, sir, she is a.k.a. Tracy Morrison. With convictions for theft, minor stuff . . . shoplifting in the Birmingham area, quite some time ago now although Sandra Picardie is believed to be her real name.'

'How did she manage to do that and still get a job in a building society?' Hennessey thought aloud as he looked at Yellich.

'Don't, know, sir . . .' The collator sounded nervous. 'I didn't know she did work in a building society.'

'It's all right, my fault, I was thinking aloud. How old was she when she was convicted?'

'Seventeen . . . an adult, so she could have given a false name . . . and date of birth, the police might not have checked. So when she gave her name as Sandra Picardie to her employers she would have passed the vetting procedure, and explained the absence of employment in those years by some uninvestigable excuse . . . backpacking in Australia for example . . . that could explain it, sir.'

'Could do, but that's interesting anyway, something we can chat to her about when the time comes.' He cupped his hand over the phone, and smiled at Yellich. 'And the time will come.'

'Have to see what they are up to first,' Yellich replied feebly, feeling tired, for sleep was coming upon him fast.

'OK,' Hennessey spoke into the phone. 'Who is the second guy?'

'Big-time crook from London, sir. He goes by the name of Kennedy . . . Harold Kennedy, aged forty-five . . . a.k.a. "Passover".'

'Passover?'

'Yes, sir, Harold "Passover" Kennedy . . . he has serious track for armed robbery. He's on the Met's "most wanted" list. There is an interested officer against his name, one Detective Sergeant Sherrie, Whitechapel Police Station.' The collator gave Hennessey the phone number of the police station in East London.

'All right . . . well, thank you for that information, that will give us something to work on on Monday. Thanks again.' Hennessey replaced the phone.

'Known to the police, I take it, sir?'

'Well . . . I'll say . . . if you didn't pick it up, Sandra Picardie is a.k.a. Tracy Morrison with track for petty stuff, which she clearly concealed in order to take her job at the building society . . . and the guy you suspected of being bent is as bent as you can get . . . armed robbery . . . has the handle of "Passover".'

'Passover?'

'Harold "Passover" Kennedy.' Hennessey paused. 'What is happening, Yellich? What is happening?'

'Beats me, boss . . . but something is going down.'

'It has to be. People like that don't visit each other for a holiday. They're going to pull a job.'

SUNDAY

The man and woman walked slowly along the lane, arm in arm. It was a twisting lane, a winding lane, which wound through fields of wheat, shortly to be harvested. An ancient hedgerow ran on either side of the lane. Above was an expanse of blue sky and a sun that beat down. The man was grateful for his straw hat, the woman too wore a hat, also of straw, wide brimmed and with a blue ribbon round it, but in her case the hat was for fashion and style; for the man, his headgear was functional. His hair was not only silver but it was thinning . . . exposure to the sun was a source of danger: bad headaches then heatstroke. He was also finding out that being sunburned upon one's scalp was very uncomfortable indeed. A cyclist passed them travelling in the same direction and held up a hand in greeting as he passed. A rambler, striding out forcefully and clearly with distance to go, passed in the opposite direction. The three people nodded and said their 'hello's' as they passed by each other.

'He's got a strong tooth.' The man spoke when the rambler was safely out of earshot.

'A what?' The woman turned and smiled. She squeezed his arm, pulling it closer to her.

'A strong tooth . . . it's a German expression. I was walking the walls once . . . a long time ago now, with a woman whose father was German, English mother . . . she was bilingual, utterly fluent in both languages. I went striding ahead, didn't realize I was leaving her behind, waited for her more or less opposite the railway station. When she caught up with me, she said that I had a "strong tooth" . . . it means I am a strong walker. So I gather.'

'Strong legs? I could have told her that.'

138

The man and the woman walked on for another fifteen minutes until the lane reached a road on which there was clearly a large amount of traffic.

'Sun brings 'em out,' said the woman.

'All off to the coast, I expect,' the man replied and guided the woman round. She didn't resist and they began to retrace their steps. Walking, strolling slowly, enjoying the morning air . . . the rural morning air especially, and the birdsong . . . and the hawk that hovered and then dived on to the verge at the side of the lane some hundred yards ahead of them, and then flew away along the lane, then higher, over the hedgerow, over the wheat, towards a small stand of trees with a small rodent in its talons. Both the man and the woman watched the event, of the natural world in action, of death being taken so that life may be lived, of the importance of raptors in keeping down the rodent population, but neither commented and, not commenting but knowing the other had also witnessed the event, felt a communion, a closeness. The man and the woman fully understood each other.

Half an hour later the couple reached the village where they had parked the car and did so without encountering another walker or cyclist. Village? Hardly, thought the man . . . a small collection of cottages. At the first one they passed, a woman was digging her garden and said a cheery 'good morning' as her Border collie barked ferociously at them. The man raised his hat and said, 'Good morning'; the woman merely smiled politely. Amid the collection of cottages was the pub, the Green Man, and Hennessey assumed that it must rely on passing trade, or on folk driving out to it in the evenings. It could not, he thought, it could not possibly survive on the trade generated by the few cottages which clustered around it. 'Come on,' he said, 'I'll buy you a drink.'

The inside of the pub delighted the man. Having been driven out to the hamlet by the woman, who would often stroll along the lane if she had an hour and a half to herself and when there was nothing pressing to be addressed, he was there for the first time. Initially welcoming was the cool of the interior. It was very refreshing after the growing heat outside. Then he relished the silence . . . not the silence, but the silence created, cultivated, by the absence of early-twenty-first century public house amusements, which, in his view, had wrecked the ambience intended by the designers of the Unicorn on Micklegate. For in the Green Man were no Space Invader machines, no jukebox, no television screen permanently tuned into a cable or satellite network. Here was . . . well, a pub, as a pub in the man's mind ought to be. Any noise in this pub would be later that day: a hum of soft, amiable conversation, a rattle of dominoes, the thud of darts into a cork board, perhaps a clock that chimed the hour. But there would be nothing else. The wooden benches that ran round the side of the pub seemed to the man to be original, dark-stained and polished with age . . . occasionally burnt here and there; the tables were wooden, circular and had two chairs round each. Just two. This pub would never become crowded. He turned to the woman. 'Excellent,' he said. 'Excellent.'

'I thought you'd like it – ' she smiled – 'knowing your preferences in these matters.'

He bought his lady a gin and tonic. He contented himself with a tonic water and lime, as he had done in different circumstances the day previous. He didn't drink at all during the day, under any circumstances, even when on holiday, for he found it always cost him the afternoon. He would never drink alcohol until after sundown and even then, only when all duties had been discharged. After the drink, after returning their glasses to the bar and thanking the barman, they walked out of the pub across to where the lady's distinctive red-and-white car had been parked in the shade of a tall lime tree. The woman slid gracefully into the driver's seat, bottom first, twisting, bringing both knees and ankles into the car together, then closing the door. The man sat in the front passenger seat and slung his hat on to the rear seat.

They sat in silence, a contented, pleasant silence, as the woman drove to Skelton, north of York, with its delightful eleventh-century church and its ancient yew tree.

'Thank you for the walk.' The woman turned to the man as she switched off the engine and applied the handbrake. 'I often walk on that lane but it's always better if I've got company. And now we have the house to ourselves . . . until ten o'clock, when the children will be back from their father's.'

'Lovely,' said the man, 'eight or nine hours to ourselves.'

'So what do you say? A quick snack then straight upstairs?' Louise D'Acre placed her hand on his knee. 'Sound all right?'

'Sounds . . . sounds just perfect,' said George Hennessey. 'Sounds about the most perfect thing to do on this perfect day.'

Yellich read the report on Harold 'Passover' Kennedy that had been faxed up from the Metropolitan Police for the attention of Detective Chief Inspector Hennessey, Micklegate Bar Police Station, York Division, North Yorkshire Police. He relaxed in his chair as he read the report, written by an officer with a clipped, laconic style.

Harold 'Passover' Kennedy was by all accounts an East End villain of the first order. He had accumulated track for robbery with violence from the age of fourteen, spent two years in youth custody, come out, gone back in, come back out, gone back in until he was twenty-one, when he went back in. He went into Wormwood Scrubs. He came out after his last stretch when he was twenty-five and never went back in. 'Not reformed,' read the report, 'just learned how to escape detection.' Kennedy was believed to have to date accumulated a substantial sum of money, in excess of one million pounds by orchestrating a series of armed robberies in the Greater London area. Warehouses were a particular favourite, and would be cleared out with skill and dismaying ease. Three million pounds worth of fur coats in one raid, without anyone knowing anything was amiss until the warehouse was noticed to be suddenly empty. The security guard patrolling the premises with an Alsatian and a mobile phone had to work very hard to convince the police that he wasn't part of the operation. That was Harold 'Passover' Kennedy – 'very, very good at villainy'. He continued to read the report: 'Likes to avoid violence if he can. Most villains do. But not afraid to use it. Most villains aren't.' The report went on to detail bullion robberies, complex and successful burglaries of prestigious homes, theft of prestigious cars for export to the Middle East. The latter being very lucrative: the dripping-with-wealth oil sheikh who cannot wait the years involved for a new Rolls Royce has one that is just a few months old, stolen to order, at twice the list price of a new model, placed in a container and shipped to the Gulf. 'Popular job,' read the report. 'Many, many thousands of pounds worth of money for a few hours work and nobody needs to get tapped. But the word is always that Kennedy is behind it, behind them, a good many of such jobs. No longer, at least rarely on the jobs himself . . . but orchestrating them, controlling the strings, negotiating the deals, putting the teams together. And ruling with fear. People who cross him, people who grass him up . . . disappear, and blood, rumoured to be their blood, is spilled liberally on the doorstep of their house; hence his nickname. The report concluded that the North Yorkshire Police were correct to be suspicious. The man does not take holidays and, like most Londoners, dislikes the north of England, believing that the tundra starts at Potter's Bar, and so it is safe to conclude that if Kennedy is in York, he is 'there for business'. The report also offered the services of Detective Sergeant Sherrie, the author of the report, and an officer who knows Kennedy well.

Yellich laid the report on his desk, and strolled to the window and glanced out of it. Sunday afternoon, mid-August. The ancient city basked in sunshine; the walls, clearly seen from his office window, were crowded with tourists. He rolled up his shirt sleeves, military style, cuff over cuff, and made himself a cup of tea. Sundays, he found, were often like this – a quietness descended on the police station. There was no logical reason for it – crime is an animal that never sleeps, and with stores and markets and cinemas opening on Sundays, there was really little to separate Sunday from the days preceding it and the day succeeding it, but nonetheless, Sunday still happened to be a day of calm. Relatively speaking. He settled back down behind his desk and addressed the paperwork that had accumulated in the week. It was the great benefit of drawing duty on a Sunday. If things kept quiet, it was a very useful day to do a lot of catching up. His tea was still warm, too warm to drink unless by sipping it, when his phone rang. It sounded the usual ringing tone, it was indeed the same ringing tone, but there seemed to Yellich to be an urgency about it.

The body had not been dead very long. Yellich could see that. He glanced around. The body was lying in a meadow, hidden from the road by a hedge. A path beside the field led towards a wood in the distance. He looked again at the body. The deceased looked peaceful. He had a deathly pallor but that was only to be expected – he was, after all, life extinct. The police surgeon had said so. The pleasant-mannered Sikh, Dr Mann, had confirmed life extinct at 13.32 hours. Coincidental almost with Yellich's arrival. The sergeant placed the heavy-duty plastic sheeting over the head and face of the victim. He stood and walked the road, dipping beneath the blue-and-white police tape that cordoned off the corner of the field in which the body lay. He approached the police constable.

'Member of the public found the body, sir,' the constable said. 'Out walking . . . up the path here.' The constable nodded to the path that drove beside the field towards the wood. 'It's part of Pilgrim's Way . . . an ancient right of way. The path connects York Minster to Selby Abbey . . . allegedly, and has become known as Pilgrim's Way.'

'And he was walking Pilgrim's Way?'

'So he said. He didn't want to be interviewed.'

'He didn't?'

'Gone by the time we got here, sir. He called us on his mobile, gave us precise details as to the location, said there was nothing he could do . . . said the feller was dead . . . said he didn't see anything that appeared to be connected to the body, it was just lying there like the feller had gone to sleep in the grass. When he checked, he saw the gentleman was deceased, so he phoned in and went on his way.'

'I see.' Yellich thought that mobile phones did indeed have their uses, unless one happened to be on a train journey sitting next to a teenage girl who insisted on phoning all her friends to decide such matters of monumental importance of what they were going to wear that evening. 'He did give a name and address, I trust?'

'Bruno Wedgewood, of "The Spires", Conisborough Road, Lesser Howton, Vale of York.'

'That has to be fictitious,' Yellich said. 'Bruno Wedgewood, "The Spires" . . . I ask you. Well . . . I dare say I had better ask Dr D'Acre to come out, if she's still free.' He reached for his mobile and dialled a number he called up from the phone's memory.

They, upon her insistence, did not close the bedroom curtains, believing that it would only advertise to the neighbours what was going on in the room that afternoon. They lay there, side by side, calmly, not talking, again just enjoying each other's presence and the warm glow that follows successful loving. Her phone warbled, she sighed, rolled out of bed and across the floor to the phone, whilst he marvelled at her slender body and superb muscle tone, which had been developed by her passion for horse riding. He realized that on a day like this he was indeed being paid a compliment by being put before Samson, her magnificent stallion. He watched as she listened and then sank resignedly to the bench beside the phone, reached for a pad and pen and began to take notes. She said, 'I'll be there directly,' replaced the phone and said, 'I bet you can't guess who that was and what it was about?'

'Can't guess,' said George Hennessey with unusual sarcasm, 'I have no idea . . . honestly. Where is it anyway?'

'Other side of York . . . a village called Escrick. I can drop you in York.' Louise D'Acre left the bedroom and walked to the bathroom.

Six

*. . . in which George Hennessey is rudely robbed
and Yellich learns the ways of Harry 'Passover'
Kennedy.*

SUNDAY, 21 AUGUST – MONDAY, 22 AUGUST

Louise D'Acre drew her car to a halt behind the police
vehicles and the black, windowless mortuary van. She left
the car with practised ease and, carrying her black bag, she
walked to the entrance of the field, to where Yellich and the
other officers stood.

'Afternoon, ma'am,' Yellich nodded his head deferen-
tially. 'I do apologize for asking you to come out on a
Sunday.'

'Think nothing of it,' Louise D'Acre smiled. 'I am on call
and I wasn't doing anything anyway.'

'Very good, ma'am. This way please . . .' Yellich
escorted Dr D'Acre to the police tape that was strung
from four posts surrounding the body and that hung limp
in the still, warm air. Yellich folded back the plastic sheet
revealing the head and shoulders of the deceased. As he
did so, flies appeared as if from nowhere and descended
on the pallid flesh.

'Those beasts can smell rotting flesh from a long way,'
Dr D'Acre said as she knelt by the deceased. 'Their mates
will be on their way here in droves, we'd better get this done
as soon as we can . . . hate fighting swarms of flies.'

'Don't we all?' Yellich kept a reverential distance.

'Well, male, west European – ' she removed the rest of the plastic sheet – 'appears well nourished, clothed appropriately for the weather . . . shirt . . . slacks . . . barefoot though . . . . . that's odd, didn't get out here without footwear, so he died elsewhere and was brought out here and dumped. Could you roll him on his front, please?'

'Constable!' Yellich yelled for assistance, and he and a constable, who, to Dr D'Acre's eyes, seemed young and inexperienced – it was probably his first corpse, but it would not, she pondered, be his last – rolled the deceased on to his front and then, again at Dr D'Acre's invitation, removed the deceased's lower garments, allowing Dr D'Acre to take a rectal temperature reading.

'I know that you always want to know the time of death,' she said. 'We shouldn't really give it, we have been forced into being the source of that information . . . all those television police series . . . the forensic pathologist conveniently pinpoints the time of death to within a few minutes . . . really, how fanciful! And you lot have come to expect it.'

'Seems like we have,' Yellich conceded.

'Quite honestly, a simple observation of the last authenticated sighting of the person alive and the discovery of the body is more of an accurate time window as to the time of death than any scientific deduction I can make.' She noted the reading of the rectal thermometer. 'That's interesting . . . he's cooler than I thought he would be in this heat. This is a low core temperature . . . very low . . . with corpses of this temperature I would expect to see evidence of decomposition, rigor at least . . . but – ' she flexed the left wrist of the deceased – 'no rigor . . . totally flaccid, he is at Stage One of decomposition.'

'The first stage?' Yellich asked.

'Yes . . . there are five stages . . . fresh, bloated, decayed, post-decayed and dry, and the insects will attack in five different waves corresponding with the five stages of decomposition. Here, the bluebottles are the first stage, looking for places to lay eggs which will hatch and begin to feed on the bloated corpse. By the time the corpse has reached the decayed stage, the insect activity will be within the body, not on the surface. The insect activity will move beneath the body at the post-decayed stage . . . there are different insects or invertebrates at each stage . . . the dry stage is the stage of microscopic activity, removing the last traces of tissue before the corpse becomes a total and complete skeleton.'

'I see.'

'But this corpse is as cold as I would expect a corpse to be in Stage Three, yet it's evidently very fresh . . . it could have been kept in a deep freeze – I have come across that means of confusing time of death – or left in a house wherein the central heating was turned off so it kept the temperature in the house at minus three Celsius . . . just froze the corpse at the point of death . . . but this is altogether different.' She brushed a fly from the face of the deceased. It seemed to Yellich to be a reflex action rather than to serve any pathological purpose, nor did it have any effect: the bluebottle flew a few inches away, turned and descended to the man's forehead and walked to the eye socket.

'They look for cracks and crevices.' Dr D'Acre seemed amused at the futility of her action, for she made no further attempt to brush off the insect. Further, as she predicted, more and more flies were arriving by the second. 'I think we had better put him in a body bag and get him to York District Hospital. I'll conduct the post-mortem as soon as.' She replaced the rectal thermometer in her bag and took out another thermometer with which she took the ground and air temperature, whilst two constables placed the body in a body bag. They seemed to fumble and bundle the body in the bag prompting Dr D'Acre to comment that they were having it easy with 'this one'. 'The next one,' she said, 'could be stiff with rigor, or bloated . . . or worse.' The body was lifted on to a stretcher by the driver and mate of the mortuary van, conveyed to the van and placed inside it and driven away.

'Will you be representing the police, Mr Yellich?' Louise D'Acre consulted her watch. It was by then nearly 3 p.m.

'Yes . . . there's only me on duty, the boss has his day off.'

'Really?'

'Yes . . . doesn't often get Sundays. I expect he's spent the day in his garden.'

'Well, we'll let him continue with weeding his herbaceous borders then . . . shall we say 4 p.m. at the York District Hospital, Department of Pathology?'

'Yes, ma'am, 4 p.m. it is.'

The woman was inconsolable. Distraught. Waiting with no indication of remission. The crowd gathered, the police officers, just two of them, fought desperately to keep the neighbours, more curious than concerned, at bay. Yellich turned into the road and halted his car behind the police vehicle. He pushed through the crowd and saw an open door, he saw a massive dark stain on the doorstep and on the lower part of the door.

He knew immediately what it was, he knew immediately that he was going to find the identity of the man who had been found dead in the field near Escrick. 'Passover' Kennedy was living up to his reputation.

He nodded to the constables and walked up the short pathway from the road to the house. This was Tang Hall. Violence was not unknown on this estate, but this was another league . . . another dimension. He tapped on the door and entered. It was a small council house – the door led to a narrow corridor, on the right of which was a door that opened into the living room, within which a large, middle-aged woman sat in an armchair in floods of tears. She was being comforted as best she could by a very junior female police officer who seemed to Yellich to be out of her depth. She smiled with relief at Yellich's arrival. 'Lady's beside herself, sir.'

'So I see.' Yellich sat on the settee. The woman was in no state to invite him to sit down, and he didn't want to intimidate her by standing in the room. 'Do we have a name?'

'Rosemary Petty, sir . . . by her neighbour's information. She has not been very forthcoming.'

'Not in any state to be, as you say.' Yellich read the room. It was not, he thought, untypical of many north of England, working-class homes in council land: inexpensive furniture, lightweight frames, easy to lift, covered with black PVC; inexpensive shelves containing video tapes, many pre-recorded. Yellich could not understand people's predilection for purchasing prerecorded video tapes of feature films, which can always be taped when they are screened on television, or rented for a fraction of the cost from a video library or borrowed freely from a public library. The fire grate had accumulated a large amount of combustible material, empty cigarette packets in the main, doubtless to be ignited on the first chill evening. A framed print of a painting of an idyllic nineteenth-century rural scene hung on the wall above the fireplace. The mantelpiece was cluttered with inexpensive glass ornaments and souvenirs from the south coast of England, Ramsgate being particularly prominent, but Portland Bill, Beachy Head and Herne Bay were also represented. It was unusual in Yellich's experience that the residents of Tang Hall should favour southern resorts, being more at home in Scarborough or Bridlington, or Blackpool. Then the woman spoke.

'My man . . .' she cried, burying her head in her hands. 'My man.' But pronounced man as 'mayne' and Yellich's curiosity as to the reason for the plethora of souvenirs from the south coast was answered. Mrs Rosemary Petty was a southerner. Not from this lady the short clipped vowels of the north of England, where 'man' was pronounced as it is spelled, but here were the elongated vowels of east London.

'My man,' she wailed, 'my man.'

'What can you tell us, Mrs Petty? I am Detective Sergeant Yellich by the way.'

'He said he wouldn't come . . .'

'Who?'

'My man said it.'

'But who wouldn't come?'

'Passover.'

'Kennedy?' Yellich said. 'Harold Kennedy?'

'You know him?'

'By reputation.'

'All the way up here? Passover is known up here?' The woman began to control her tears. 'My man said he wouldn't leave London.'

'Well, he's here.'

'I know . . . I know . . . that's my man's blood on the doorstep, that's Passover. Only Passover could do that, that is Passover's trademark. I had to step over it to get in . . . phone the police . . . my man is dead.'

'Are you able to come down to the station, Mrs Petty? We have to take a statement from you, then we will have to ask you to identify the body of the man we believe may have been your husband.'

'Have been . . . I am going to have to get used to that.' She took a deep breath and fought back tears. 'Thanks, thanks that Thomas didn't see this . . . this outside.'

'Thomas?'

'Our son. He's on remand right now in Brixton.' The statement was said with no small measure of pride. That her son was entering the criminal fraternity by doing his 'apprenticeship' in Brixton, getting known to the London underworld. That you are not 'in' unless you've 'done time', been 'banged up', 'done bird', was clearly a source of gratification and reassurance to Rosemary Petty. 'Yes . . . I want to . . . I want to get out of the house . . . away from that . . . I'll have to do it, won't be raining for a while.'

'Do what?'

'Scrub my husband's blood off my doorstep, all eight pints of it.' The woman struggled to her feet. 'How many women can say they've done that?' And that, again, to Yellich's astonishment, seemed to be said with a deep pride.

'Well, not until we've photographed it and taken samples for testing . . . have to make sure that it isn't sheep's blood.'

'Oh, it's my man's blood all right.' The woman looked round, she appeared to be in shock . . . . . . then said she wouldn't need a coat in this weather, would she? Yellich said he doubted that she would and that she would be driven home anyway. He asked if she had a neighbour, a friend who could sit with her?

'No. We haven't made many friends round here . . . get left alone, but we've no friends.'

'You'll need someone . . . surely?'

'My sister-in-law. She's in London but she's got a car . . . she can be up here by tonight. Could you phone her for me . . . I wouldn't know what to say. It's her brother, you see. My man, is her brother.'

'Of course.' Yellich stood aside as Mrs Petty walked to the door. He followed her and then turned to the WPC, who was smart in a crisp white blouse, blue skirt and stockings, blonde hair done up in a bun. 'Secure the house, will you, please?'

'Yes, sir.'

'Then remain here, outside the door, until S.O.C.O. have been and also the forensic chemist. Have to get the doorstep photographed, and samples of the black stuff taken for analysis.'

'Yes, sir.'

'When that has been done, you can vacate the scene and return to duties. I'll make sure your sergeant knows where you are.'

'Thank you, sir.'

It was difficult. It was sometimes just difficult and sometimes it was very difficult but it was never, ever easy.
This time it was the woman, shaking with fear and dread,
fighting back tears. There was the soft, as if accidental,
rattle of the trolley from behind the screen. Then a door
opened and a nurse with a sombre, serious expression, a
slightly built woman in her twenties, entered the room
and shut the door behind her. She looked at Yellich, who
nodded, and the nurse pulled a sash cord. Two heavy velvet
curtains slid open. Silently.

They revealed the face of the man Yellich had first seen
that afternoon lying, as if asleep, in a field. The head was
concealed in a tightly wrapped bandage, the body lay on a
trolley tightly tucked up with blankets and by some trick of
light and shade, the body, with only the face visible, appeared
through the glass screen as if it was floating peacefully in a
black infinity.

'Yes . . .' the woman sniffed as she continued to fight
back tears, 'yes, that's him . . . that's my man . . . Michael
Petty.'

Yellich nodded and the nurse pulled the cord and the
curtains silently closed.

The woman sat – sank, it seemed to Yellich, as if her legs
gave way – on to a hard, but upholstered bench that stood
against the wall opposite the curtains and the pane of glass.
'It wasn't like you see in the films.' She breathed deeply. She
seemed to Yellich to be struggling valiantly to keep a grip on
her emotions, as if refusing to be defeated. He thought her a
courageous woman. Many women, and not a few men, would
be, and have been distraught in that very room. 'I thought they
put them in a drawer, pulled them out and lifted a sheet from
their face.'

'They used to do that, Mrs Petty. It's more sensitive
this way.'

'Like he was floating . . . at peace. It's how I'll remember him. He was a warm man – a thief from his earliest days . . . but we all were. I was . . . his dad was . . . taught him the art, his dad . . . he went out with his dad when he was nine or ten. His dad would feed him through a crack in a window . . .'

'"Feed" him?'

'Just the smallest crack . . . and my man would be in there either tossing out jewellery or going downstairs to open the door and his dad would come in . . . very civilized like . . . didn't do no damage to the house . . . . very proper team of thieves, him and his dad made.'

'Very proper.' Again Yellich repeated the sentiment, having difficulty, still, grasping an utterly alien attitude.

'Did a pub once . . . stole ten thousand pounds.'

'That's a lot of money.'

'It was even more money when my man was ten years old, could buy a house outright with that money. This publican . . . not on our manor . . . wouldn't do a pub on the manor, you always go off the manor to do a pub . . . thieves' honour, see.' She sniffed. 'Anyway, this geezer was known to be hoarding money, kept it in a suitcase under his bed. Reckoned it was safe because he had a Rottweiler . . . kept the dog in his bedroom during opening hours. His bedroom window was above a sloping roof over the car park at the back of the pub. They went there early one night, my man and his dad in a pickup with a ladder in the back . . . went to get the right place in the car park . . . then went home for a few hours, went back at ten o'clock. A Saturday it was and the pub was heaving by then . . . took the ladders . . . put them up from the back of the pickup against the window. My man shins up then opens the window, feeds the dog a stick of liquorice . . . it may be a Rottweiler but it knew my man.'

'How?'

The woman tapped the side of her nose and forced a

smile. 'My man's dad watched the publican take his dog for a walk . . . same bit of woodland, by the railway line. Made sure my man was there with a stick of liquorice . . . gave the dog the liquorice . . . dog and boy got to know each other, dog got to know the boy's scent. So when he appeared at the window that night, well, it was a woof of delight, not a bark of warning. The lad hopped into the window, grabbed the suitcase, slid it down the ladder, followed it down. They folded the ladder, put it back in the pickup and drove away . . . ten thousand quid for a few minutes work and a few sticks of liquorice . . . "only fools and horses work", that's what my man said, that's what his dad told him. Didn't last long, though, that ten thousand . . . about a month.'

'A month?'

'So my man says, but he wasn't to know the exact length of time and he was always exaggerating, so it could have been six months . . . the dogs and the boozer, but mainly the dogs . . . terrible one for the dogs was my man's old man . . . terrible one.' She paused. 'And him just forty-five and cold.'

'Well,' Yellich allowed a note of solemnity to enter his voice. He thought he had allowed Mrs Petty time to gather her emotions, allowed her to reminisce, but then began to suspect something else lay behind the story of Petty the younger. 'If you would care to accompany me to the station, I'd like to ask you a few questions.'

'Yes . . .' Rosemary Petty stood. 'Sorry I went banging on, young man . . . you should have stopped me. I'll answer what I can. I don't think I'll be able to help you though . . . my man didn't tell me a lot.'

'He told you about Passover,' Yellich raised an eyebrow.

'Pass . . .' the woman stammered, 'Who mentioned Passover?'

'You did . . . a few times, at your house, just about an

hour ago. You were probably too upset to realize what you said but you mentioned Passover.'

'I did?'

'Yes . . . so listen . . . I think you'd better tell me what you know, and don't come this "I don't know anything" or entertain me with tales of what the deceased, your late husband, did when he was still in short trousers. I won't be sidetracked.'

The woman looked at him with an expression of dawning realization.

'This isn't "Twenty Questions",' Yellich emphasized the point he was making. 'There's no time limit . . . you can't play this out until it's time for the ten o'clock news. We want answers . . . and we're going to get them.'

Rosemary Petty nodded.

'I'm not under arrest then?' Rosemary Petty swilled the coffee around the white plastic beaker.

'No,' Yellich smiled, but the smile also transmitted a warning: that this was serious. 'You are here of your own volition, giving information in respect of the death of your husband. I should say, the murder of your husband.' He drained his coffee and placed the empty beaker on the black vinyl surface of the table that stood between him and Rosemary Petty. 'But I will tell you now, Rosemary, that I won't get sidetracked by tales of your man when he was a youngster in Whitechapel. Understand?'

'Yes, sir.'

'Right, so now we understand each other. So tell me, what connection your late husband had with Thomas Ilford.'

'Thomas Ilford?' Rosemary Petty's voice failed.

'Yes.' Yellich's jaw set firm. 'Look, we know this fellow "Passover" was staying with Thomas Ilford . . . we were watching Ilford's house in connection with another matter . . . a woman we are very interested in, very keen to talk to in respect of a number of serious crimes, when who should turn out to be their houseguest, but none other than Harold Kennedy a.k.a. "Passover".'

'A.k.a.?'

'Also known as . . . because of his tendency to pour the blood of his victims on the doorstep of their houses. If I remember my Sunday School lessons, that's what the Jews did to the lambs they slaughtered on the feast of the Passover. I presume that is the reference?'

'Dunno . . . just know they called him "Passover" and never asked why. Did know he did what you said with his victims' blood . . . he's had a few victims. That's how I knew it was Passover's doing.'

'So, Passover trailed your man from London to York?'

Rosemary Petty shrugged.

'Is there something we don't know? Something we should know?'

A silence. Rosemary Petty glanced round the room: the polished veneer of the ribbon of wood that ran at waist height along the wall, the matching veneer of the door, the painted plaster, a dark red beneath the ribbon of white, very businesslike, while above it, the white ceiling, the light in the ceiling, not at that time turned on because ample daylight surged through the window, which looked out on to the rear of Micklegate Bar Police Station.

'So?' Yellich prompted. 'You know, I have been doing this job long enough to know when somebody wants to tell me something, but for some reason is afraid to do so. I think that's your position. So who are you protecting? It could only be yourself now. Your husband is deceased . . . I saw no sign of children, dependent children anyway, at your house. So there's just you. Are you frightened of Passover coming after you?'

Rosemary Petty shook her head.

'What then? Who then?'

'Suppose there isn't anybody, is there?'

'So spill. I presume you want us to catch the person who

did that to your husband . . . forty-five . . . half-way through his life. You are clearly fond of him.'

'Well . . . daresay we could break the rule.'

'Yes?'

'We were under the police Witness Protection Programme.'

'I see.'

'My name isn't Petty . . . well it is, Petty is my maiden name, my married name is Oates.'

'Oates.' Yellich scribbled the name on his notepad.

'My man has track under that name.'

'I see.'

'He was one of Passover's boys . . . in the Kennedy Gang . . . a foot soldier but well in . . . trusted . . . years of service with them. He'd been on a lot of missions . . . they were known as the Cable Street Boys after one of the main drags through Whitechapel. "Passover Kennedy and the Cable Street Boys" . . . sounds like a band. Anyway, they were out on a mission . . . which went pear-shaped . . . the Old Bill had 'em cold . . . they were waiting for the boys . . . they'd been grassed up.'

'So Passover Kennedy thought your husband had grassed him up?'

'No, my man was never in any kind of bother like that. In fact, they found out who grassed them up and it wasn't my man . . . he was in the clear. The guy who grassed Kennedy up, well, he was cooled . . . his body was found in the Old Father . . . and his blood . . .'

'I can guess . . . on his doorstep.'

'In one.' Rosemary Oates née Petty . . . now Petty again, sighed, drew breath and continued. 'Anyway it was an armed robbery. They went in heavy, sawn-offs, ammonia spray . . . one guy, a security guard, was hurt bad . . . I mean really bad, they were lucky it wasn't a murder charge . . . but they were still looking at a twenty-five stretch. No one can survive that . . . no one can do more than ten. You get so you need prison to survive and even if you do come out . . . things have moved on, your contacts have gone. My man . . . he was thieving all his life . . . he never got any real dosh out of it, like his dad, it just slipped through his fingers, so he was looking at a twenty-five stretch . . . him and about four others. The Old Bill offered them all the same deal . . . . . . turn Queen's on Kennedy and no action will be taken against you and you'll get witness protection . . . new name, new ID, new address . . . clean start . . . even fix you with a job if you want one. The others were sensible, told the Old Bill where to put their offer, they knew Kennedy wouldn't let them go down . . . but my man . . . all he could see was twenty-five years of porridge and slamming metal doors and slopping out and the odd razor attack to put him in the prison hospital and he jumped at the offer. Gave the Old Bill all they wanted to know which was nothing new because they knew all about Kennedy. They'd had him under surveillance for years . . . tried to infiltrate the gang . . . but he did stand up in court, number one court at the Old Bailey when Kennedy and the boys who did the job were in the dock, sitting there, listening to my man give evidence.'

'And?'

'Well, Kennedy walked, didn't he . . . ? And so did the others that refused to take the offer the police made. My man's evidence wasn't enough to convict them, his evidence was . . . what's that word? . . . discredited . . . by the defence brief . . . and other prosecution witnesses disappeared, so it was all down to my man's word against Kennedy's and the word of the others. My man said Kennedy was behind it all . . . he said he wasn't . . . can't convict on that . . . and the witnesses that put the gang at the scene, they disappeared . . . bottom of the Thames most like.'

'You said the police were waiting? You're not telling me that the police officers disappeared too?'

'No . . . the gang knew they'd been rumbled, made a good bid for an escape . . . got arrested the next day . . . got as far as coshing the security guard, then it was all blue flashing lights . . . so nothing actually to put 'em at the scene, unless one at least turned Queen's evidence. The Old Bill played a game, told my man they had enough without his evidence to put them all away and my man believed them. Anyway, the judge threw the case out "with regret," he said. But by then, my man was marked . . . price on his head . . . so he went north. The police found us a council flat in Nottingham – it was the worst flat in the city . . . but we had to take it and we changed our name to my maiden name, so we became Mr and Mrs Petty. Living on the dole in a damp-infested house on a really bad estate in Nottingham . . . really bad . . . the Old Bill, they'd done what they said, rehoused us, but in worse conditions than we had on the manor. They got what they wanted, they weren't bothered about us. Kept to the letter of the agreement but not the spirit . . . made my man angry . . . he felt let down . . . turned to crookin' . . . thieving, was getting close to being lifted by the Nottingham Police. So we packed our bags and moved further north . . . came to York, one winter's day. I tell you, we knew what was meant by the frozen north . . . that wind.'

'Winter easterlies,' said Yellich, 'they can bite all right.'

'Anyway, that was about four years ago . . . the council gives us our flat in Tang Hall, which wasn't as good as what we had in the Smoke, but it was better than what we had been given in Nottingham . . . so we settled in, and my man did what he was best at.'

'Thieving?'

'And such like . . . anyway . . . he got into the network and found himself working for the Man again.'

'The Man?'

'The local Godfather . . . every town has one . . . more if the town is big enough . . . in Whitechapel it was Harry Passover Kennedy . . . York, it's Tommy Ilford. And my man was a foot soldier. After that I don't know what happened . . . maybe my man was clocked . . . all the crims know each other . . . the jungle telegraph, and I tell you something, it would take a lot for Harry Kennedy to come north of the Smoke. You know the way folk in the South look at the North . . . for somebody to go and live in Yorkshire, they're as good as dead . . . they're out of the game. If Kennedy came north, it was for something more than killing my man. If he's teamed up with the local man, something big is going down. Something very seriously big . . . and no . . . I wouldn't know what it is.'

'Your husband never said anything?'

'No. He wouldn't anyway. But whatever it is, it is going to be big.'

'All right . . .' Yellich drummed his fingers on the table top. 'Something big . . . and Kennedy's form is robbery,' he thought aloud. He paused. 'All right, we'll have to come back to that. When did you last see your husband?'

'Sunday today . . . day before yesterday . . . Friday . . . he went to work.'

'Work?'

'Well, he went to Ilford's garage . . . he was needed for some jobs, he was a foot soldier. Ilford wanted a job doing . . . he'd send for one of his "gofers". My man was a "gofer" for Ilford . . . go for this . . . go for that.'

'I know what a "gofer" is.'

'It was the only thing my man knew, thieving.'

'So where were you?'

'When?'

'Between the time you last saw your man and when you returned home to find black stuff all over your front step?'

'Well . . . was home alone until this morning . . . nothing unusual in that, my man could be away for a few days. I learned to expect him when I saw him. So today I went to my work . . . I have a job behind the bar at the Fort.'

'"The Fort?"' Yellich looked puzzled. He hadn't heard of that pub. 'Is it a social club?'

'No . . . It's the Heron on the Tang Hall estate . . . brick-built pub in the middle of a massive concrete car park. I mean, who on the estate has a car to drive to a pub which anybody can walk to in ten minutes? To anyone on the estate the pub is called "The Fort", all bricks and a flat roof, small windows with metal frames . . . it looks like it's built to be defended not built to attract beer drinkers . . . but anyway, I have a job there pulling pints part-time. I work Sundays, it's double time and the regular staff get the day off to be with their families. Suits everybody.'

'I see.'

'So I finished my shift at three . . . got home and there was the black stuff all over my doorstep . . . *that*, that was the last time I ever saw my man. When I came home today, his blood was on my doorstep. You'll be doing those house-to-house enquiries . . . well, you can do, but you needn't bother, nobody will have seen anything. The only thing you can tell was that my man was killed this afternoon . . . blood gets solid quickly once it's out of the body.'

'I have thought the same,' Yellich said. 'Very well, we'd better get this down in the form of a statement.'

It was Sunday, 21st August, 18.35 hours.

MONDAY

'Only too pleased to help.' DS Philip Sherrie proved to be a young-for-his-rank, very serious-minded individual, so thought both Hennessey and Yellich. 'Been after Kennedy for a long time. A very long time. Never gets his hands dirty . . . slithery customer . . . The really clever criminals never see the inside of a prison, let alone the inside of a police station.' He sipped his tea. Yellich, sitting beside him, did the same. Hennessey, sitting behind his desk, facing Yellich and Sherrie, contented himself by cradling his mug of tea in both hands. 'And now he's in York . . .

that's quite a departure for our boy, it'll take a lot to bring him to the North. He belongs to that mindset in the south that thinks that all transport north of Watford is by husky-drawn sledge, and that herds of mammoth roam the Pennines.'

'That's what Mrs Petty said.' Yellich drained his mug. 'She said that it would take more than an old score to bring Kennedy out of London. She also said that he would regard Petty as being deceased if he was living in Yorkshire.'

'So the inference is that Kennedy came north for something other than exacting revenge on Petty for turning Queen's evidence, but since he was here, he tidied up that loose end for form's sake.' Hennessey sipped his tea.

'It would seem so, boss.'

'All right. Well, can you summarize the case for us, please – more for our friend's sake than mine. Then we will see where we go from here.'

'Very good, sir.' Yellich adjusted his position in the chair, leaned forwards and consulted his notebook. 'It's really a case of all roads leadeth to Rome—'

'All roads lead?' asked Sherrie.

'Right. In this case, plural roads turn out to be lanes of a motorway, singular. It began with the discovery of a skeleton in a house, or the grounds of a house in the Vale of York . . . this was on Tuesday last . . . a week ago tomorrow. We have almost certainly identified the body as being that of the lady of the house when the house was in its previous ownership . . . we interviewed the husband.'

'Before you look at the outlaws, look at the in-laws?' Sherrie smiled.

'Indeed. He was a little suspicious but in the event, he was a game-player . . . he liked the attention he was getting. It turned that he was also suspiciously close to a case of embezzlement in the building society he worked for. Anyway, he left his employment under a cloud and started out on his own and took up with a young woman called Sandra

Picardie, who also worked for the building society. She was
quite happy to take his wife's place in the marital bed and
with some rapidity, according to his children, but when this
gentleman's business venture failed, she was equally speedy
in her departure from said bed.'

'Greedy for the good life?'

'Seems so,' Yellich continued. 'Because she next turns
up as the wife of a man whose wife was murdered in a
snickelway—'

'A what?' Sherrie glanced at Yellich.

'Snickelways are unique to York,' Yellich told him. 'In the
medieval part of the city, which is essentially the centre of the
city, there are quite a few narrow covered alleyways which
lead through the buildings from one street to the next . . .
some are quite short, some are quite long . . . few people
walk in them, though they are not considered dangerous
places. Visitors can walk past them without noticing them,
the entrances are low and narrow . . . it's like a street system
within a street system.'

'I see . . . I must take a stroll down one before I return to
the Smoke.'

'I'll be pleased to show you one or two.'

'Thanks – ' Sherrie smiled – 'I might take you up on that
if there's time.'

'Right . . . anyway this lady was murdered in a snickelway,
Hornpot Lane, Nether, to be specific . . . nearest thing we
have to a witness is the guy who found the body. He passed
a woman who was coming out of the snickelway as he was
going in.'

'Sandra Picardie?'

'Well anticipated.' Yellich was impressed.

'Been a copper too long.' Sherrie inclined his head at the
compliment.

'But you are correct. Well, we assume you are correct,'
Yellich continued, 'because Sandra Picardie became the
wife of the man whose wife was murdered in Hornpot

Lane, Nether, and enjoyed a good living until his income also dried up, whereupon she was bags packed and off. She should have stayed, because that man's fortunes soon picked up again . . . he's an architect and has a very nice house indeed. Keeps dogs, prefers them to women, he said.'

'But a pattern emerges,' Sherrie said. 'Wealthy men's wives get murdered, she takes their place . . . and when the men can't afford to keep her in the manner which she wants to be kept in, she's up and gone.'

'Yes . . . that was our thinking – ' Hennessey leaned back in his chair – 'and because of that, we want to talk to her about the embezzlement of some twenty years ago now, but it's still an outstanding crime.'

'Yes, I think I would too,' Sherrie said. 'Quite a dangerous-sounding female.'

'Well, we found out that she is presently the female in the life of one Thomas Ilford, who is too shrewd to marry her . . . like has found like, if you ask me . . . and here is where the roads converge. Thomas Ilford is York's version of Harry "Passover" Kennedy.'

'Ah . . . ha,' Sherrie smiled. 'Talk about like finding like.'

'Yes . . . we watched the Ilford house and saw that Ilford had a guest whom we didn't recognize but who looked like a villain . . . followed them into York on Saturday evening, we expected them to go out on the town if they had a guest . . . followed them to a pub, not too far from this building in fact, collected the glasses they were drinking from before the bar staff could collect them and lifted the prints.' Yellich paused and looked at Hennessey. 'The glasses have been returned with thanks, skipper.'

'All right.'

'The prints we lifted from Sandra Picardie's glass told us she was a.k.a. Tracy Morrison, with small-time track for shoplifting.'

'Cutting her teeth before the big time?' Sherrie remarked.

'Seems so . . . hid the Morrison name in order to get her job in the building society. And the prints we got from the other beer glass led us via the Police National Computer database to Harold "Passover" Kennedy . . . known to the Metropolitan Police.'

'And the courtesy call to ourselves. Thank you. My Inspector phoned me at home, told me to get the 7 a.m. from King's Cross. I left my luggage in Sergeant Yellich's office. I will need somewhere to stay . . . I have a budget which is reasonable.'

'We'll help you there,' Hennessey said. 'We use a guesthouse run by a couple, both former police officers, they keep a small boxroom permanently free for a small weekly retainer.'

'Neat.'

'Now –' Hennessey allowed a note of seriousness to enter his voice – 'I understand there was a development yesterday.'

'Yes,' Yellich replied. 'Yes, there was quite a bloody development . . . and I mean bloody.' He paused. 'I had just read the report about Harry "Passover" Kennedy faxed to us by the Met when I got a Code 41. Attended at the scene . . . one deceased male . . . pronounced life extinct by our police surgeon, called out Dr D'Acre.' Yellich turned to DS Sherrie. 'That's our forensic pathologist.'

'Thank you.' Sherrie smiled his appreciation.

'Dr D'Acre made observations at the scene, took temperature recordings and had the body conveyed back to the York City Hospital to do the post-mortem. I was on my way there to represent the police when I received another call which diverted me to an address in Tang Hall. A lady had returned home to find her doorstep awash with what appeared to be blood. You understand, sir, that just an hour earlier I had read that that was one of "Passover's" calling cards—'

'More than his calling card,' Sherrie interrupted. 'That's how he earned his name.'

'Indeed . . . so I put two and two together – fresh body, fresh pool of blood, separated by only a few miles – and so I phoned Dr D'Acre and explained the situation and asked Dr D'Acre if she could postpone the PM because we possibly had a next-of-kin who could make an identification and so the body was prepared for the ID . . . which was positive. So he is . . . was Michael Oates a.k.a. Michael Petty.'

'So the PM wasn't done at all yesterday,' Hennessey groaned. Yellich thought he looked crestfallen.

'No, sir . . . sorry.'

'What did Dr D'Acre do?'

'I believe she went home, sir . . . no other reason to remain in the hospital . . . it was her day off. She only attended because she was on call.'

'Yes . . . yes . . .' Hennessey turned his head to one side.

'I was following procedure, skipper.'

'It's all right, Yellich . . . carry on.' He collected himself and tried to dismiss the thought of the lost opportunity from his mind . . . but the idea of him alone, save for his dog, all the previous afternoon and evening, and Louise D'Acre alone until her children returned at about 10 p.m. . . . he knew he would be irritated by that for some time to come.

'Well, I interviewed Mrs Oates and she told me that her husband was once one of "Passover" Kennedy's foot soldiers or "gofers" and that he turned Queen's evidence and testified against Kennedy . . . but the case collapsed. So he came north under the witness protection scheme, changed his name to Petty, being his wife's maiden name. First to Nottingham, then fixed up better accommodation in York . . . but couldn't keep out of crime.'

'Petty by name, petty by nature,' Sherrie said, sourly – thought Hennessey, but he didn't respond.

167

'So the rest is to be explained but it is Mrs Oates' or Petty's belief that once back in among the thieves, her husband ran into Kennedy and his blood was spilled. Literally.'

'I see. Thank you for that, Yellich.'

'I think it's worth adding that Mrs Oates believes that Kennedy came north for some other reason than to murder her husband because, as has been said, Kennedy sees the North of England as a graveyard anyway . . . Not being able to live in London is to him a form of death.'

'So he's up here for some other reason?'

'Seems so, sir . . . whatever it is.'

'He's a thief,' Sherrie said. 'He's not up here to murder somebody, though he appears to have done that anyway . . . he's not up here to kidnap, that's not his field of operation, he's going to rob something. It won't be a bank . . . no, something that requires local knowledge, otherwise he wouldn't have teamed up with the local villain, Ilford.'

'So . . .' Hennessey rested his elbows on his desk top. 'We have the murder of Mrs Bradbury, whose skeleton was found in the pile of rubble, the murder of Mrs Frost . . . found in a snickelway . . . possibly the disappearance of Tommy Ilford's wife.'

'Ilford's wife disappeared?' Sherrie's ears pricked up.

'Yes . . . sorry . . .' Yellich stammered, 'we didn't tell you that. Ilford's wife disappeared shortly before Sandra Picardie became "financial adviser" to "Ilford Motors" . . . but she never made it to become Mrs Ilford.'

'So the pattern is strengthened,' Hennessey added, 'wife disappears or is found murdered and shortly afterwards Sandra Picardie takes her place . . . not once but thrice?'

'Heavens . . .' Sherrie raised his eyebrows. 'Methinks madam has some explaining to do . . . there comes a point in law where circumstantial evidence becomes so overwhelming that it is admissible.'

'Indeed,' Hennessey growled. 'And now there is the murder of Michael Oates, a.k.a. Michael Petty, whose blood, as you said, Sergeant Yellich, was quite literally spilled. So four murders, if you include Mrs Ilford's disappearance as murder . . . and she will have been murdered . . . the embezzlement of funds from a building society many years ago . . . and something in the offing . . .The case has switched from past to future . . . and I sense we're moving into the fast lane . . . all right, what's for action?'

'Still to interview the witness who reported the finding of Michael Petty's body, skipper. He might have seen something . . . maybe something he didn't see the significance of . . . if he exists . . . fanciful name and address he gave us.'

'All right.'

'And the PM has still to be done and that will need a police representative.'

'I'll represent the police at the PM.' Hennessey scribbled on his notepad.

'We'll have to interview Ilford,' Yellich said. 'He'll know we will have IDed Petty by now . . . and that Mrs Petty will have told us where he works.'

'Yes,' Hennessey nodded.

'They'll be expecting us to call . . . they'll be waiting for us and they will be suspicious if we don't call, so we'll have to call.'

'Good point.' Hennessey nodded and smiled at Yellich.

'I'd better not be seen there,' Sherrie offered. 'If Kennedy's there, if he sees me . . . he knows me, that will tip them off that you, that we, know more about them than they think. I'd like to interview the witness, the feller who found the body . . . would that be possible?'

'I should think so.'

Then Hennessey's phone rang. He said, 'Excuse me,' and picked it up. As he listened, he wrote on his pad. Then he put his phone down and said, 'That was Shored-up.'

'Shored-up?' Sherrie asked.

'An informant who has been useful in the past.'

'Ah . . .'

'Wants to meet me.' Hennessey glanced at his watch. 'I'll have to see him after the post-mortem. I want to find out how Petty was murdered before anything else.'

'He was drained of his blood,' Sherrie smiled. 'It's Passover's way.'

Hennessey's jaw sagged. 'He was what?'

'Drained of his blood.' Sherrie shrugged. 'The story is that when Kennedy was holidaying in Tunisia quite a few years ago . . . a body of a European tourist was washed ashore . . . no injuries on his body except two little nicks in his ankles . . . and no blood in his system at all . . . he'd been mugged for his blood.'

'Heavens . . . !'

'The local hospital would have bought it . . . no questions asked. Anyway, the idea appealed to Kennedy, so he employed it . . . strings his victim up, opens him up with a cut in the right place and the victim bleeds to death. Painless . . . but utterly terrifying for the victim. You can only imagine what it must be like hanging there, getting colder and colder as your blood leaves your body. That's "Passover".'

Leaving Hennessey's office, Sherrie asked Yellich about his Christian name.

'Pronounced "Sorley",' said Yellich. 'It's Gaelic apparently. At least I know that. My surname . . . well that's obscure eastern European. I know nothing about its origins and I suspected it was corrupted somewhere along the way to make it pronounceable in English. But at least I avoided being called "Ruby" or "Diamond" because that's what one of my ancestors was wearing when they arrived in the UK as refugees from some dreadful pogrom or another. That's the only possible origin for surnames like that . . . there is no alternative derivation.'

'Really?'

'So I believe. I'll take you to the guest house. Then you can interview the witness. Sounds an interesting character. An eccentric by all accounts. If he exists.'

It was Monday, 22nd August, midday.

Seven

. . . in which details of a dreadful death are uncovered, Inspector Hennessey strongly disapproves of a rendezvous, and the police must content themselves with a partial success.

MONDAY, 22 AUGUST, 14.00 – DAWN, TUESDAY, 23 AUGUST

'He has no blood.' Louise D'Acre rested her hands on the stainless-steel dissecting table. The body of the man identified as Michael Oates, a.k.a. Petty, lay face up on the table, a starched white towel draped over the coyly termed 'private parts', his right forearm having been opened at vein and artery by Dr D'Acre's scalpel. 'I have never seen anything like this.' She shook her head. 'I thought I'd seen everything . . . but this is a first for me.'

'We were advised that that might be the case.' Hennessey stood at the edge of the room, dressed, as Dr D'Acre was, in disposable green coveralls, a disposable hat and latex gloves.

'There are no other injuries on the body apart from ligature marks round the wrists.' She turned to Paul Fry, the usually jovial mortuary assistant, who, on this occasion, was ashen faced at the sight of a man who had been wilfully drained of his blood. 'Can you get photographs of the wrists, please, Mr Fry.' She stepped back as Paul Fry closed with his camera. She once again turned to Hennessey. 'He appears to have been suspended by his wrists and two small incisions cut in his ankles. The ankles themselves appear quite clean, which

172

is interesting because it suggests that a catheter was inserted and the blood drained via a tube into a vessel or two . . . they had to find storage space for eight pints or so of the stuff. I take it this gentleman is believed to be the previous owner of the blood which was poured over some poor lady's doorstep?'

'Yes,' Hennessey grimaced.

'Sergeant Yellich told me about it by means of explanation. He asked me if I minded postponing the PM.'

'Yes . . .'

'Frankly, I am pleased he did.'

Hennessey looked at her questioningly.

'Well, I would have been upset about it – no warm welcoming company for my children. At least this way I had an inkling of what I was going to find. I was able to prepare myself first.'

'I see.'

'Well . . . nothing much else that I can add. The time of death . . . again, difficult to determine but if it was his blood, it wouldn't have remained in a liquid state for very long . . . blood has a fairly rapid-acting coagulant . . . probably no more than an hour before the blood was poured over the lady's doorstep.'

'And we have no actual witness to that,' Hennessey said. 'We just believe it to be some time yesterday.'

'I'll see if I can help you there, Detective Chief Inspector.' Dr D'Acre took the scalpel and clearly for the benefit of the microphone which was attached to a stainless-steel anglepoise, she said, 'I am performing a simple mid-line incision to open the stomach cavity.' Dr D'Acre drew the scalpel down from the breast bone to the navel, then from the navel down towards each thigh, thus creating an incision which took the pattern of an inverted 'Y'. She then peeled the skin back in three sections and exposed the outer wall of the stomach. She smiled at Hennessey but it was a smile of professional seriousness. 'You might care to take a breath,' she said. 'It won't be a bad odour, the corpse isn't old enough, but there will be an odour.'

Hennessey returned the smile and drew a deep breath. He noticed Paul Fry doing the same. Dr D'Acre took the scalpel, punctured the stomach wall and the air within escaped with a distinct hiss.

'Well, smelled worse – ' she turned her head away – 'much worse in fact . . . so . . .' She opened up the stomach. 'Let's see what we have . . . well, partially digested food is noted. In fact I can identify what appears to be bread – ' she poked the contents of the stomach – 'bacon . . . and egg . . . a bacon-and-egg roll. Most possibly it's what he had for breakfast . . . his last meal. So he didn't eat lunch. Didn't or couldn't. Probably disinclined to eat if he knew what was going to happen to him. Not a death I would choose if I had any say in my end.'

'Nor I,' Hennessey said. 'How long would it have taken?'

'Could have been about half an hour. If his heart was beating strongly because of fear, then less than that . . . but it's what must have been going through his mind . . . feeling his blood being drained away like that . . . . . . it does not do to dwell on it.'

'Doesn't at all,' Hennessey replied, then asked, 'What sort of premises would be required to do that?'

'Well. Your guess is as good as mine, Detective Chief Inspector . . . but I would suspect not the living room of a family home, nor anywhere within a family home, I would have thought. The gentleman was suspended by his wrists . . . so beams would be required . . . the ligature marks on his wrists are deeply cut and seem to tug towards the hands, so that indicates that as he died he was taking his weight on his wrists. That would have been quite painful and it may even, mercifully, have caused him to lose consciousness . . . and then there would have to have been room beneath the feet for the containers into which the blood was drained. So I would say a commercial premises rather than domestic premises.'

'And some time yesterday?'

'Yes . . . after breakfast, it would seem.'

'You don't sound like a Yorkshireman.'

'That's because I am not,' Sherrie replied. 'Thank goodness.'

'Where are you from?'

'London, Putney to be precise, but I would prefer to ask the questions.'

The man shrugged. 'Orl Korrect,' he said, 'but spelled with a "K".'

'What?'

'Orl Korrect. Believed to be the origin of the expression "OK". A foreman in an American factory with limited English would write "Orl Korrect" on goods fit to be sent off . . . got shortened to "OK". So you want to ask the questions? OK, ask.'

'You found the body yesterday?'

'Yes . . . in the field . . . near the gate.' Bruno Wedgewood sat in the armchair in the front room of his cottage. Sherrie sat opposite him in another ill-matching armchair. The entire cottage seemed to Sherrie to be furnished from charity shops or junk shops and decorated with items obtained from similar sources, yet he conceded it made for a very comfortable room, a room in which he felt relaxed.

'You were walking?'

'Yes.'

'Doing the Pilgrim's Way?' Sherrie did indeed find Bruno Wedgewood an 'interesting' character – a 'dazzling' character in yellow trousers and red waistcoat with a handlebar moustache and a cloth cap, which he clearly insisted on wearing indoors, heavy boots worn even indoors, purchased clearly for durability and no thought, it seemed, to fashion, comfort or appropriateness for the weather. The man reminded Sherrie of the story of a similarly ill-dressed man who, after recounting his woes and worries to a friend, said,

'Can you now give me one good reason why I shouldn't commit suicide?' to which said friend was alleged to have retorted, 'Yes . . . because no one would want to be seen dead dressed like that.'

'I do it each year . . . no particular day of the year, but once a year I do the walk from York Minster to Selby Abbey, a distance of about ten miles, perhaps twelve. It's a pleasant walk and I take about four hours over it. A gentle pace, you see more. So I saw the body . . . thought it was a man asleep but realized it was a man dead. Nothing I could do, so I reported it with my mobile. Dislike the things really, but useful if you are isolated. Think they should be banned in public places but very useful if you are a long way from help. They've saved lives.'

'So I believe. Now, what did you see, if anything, prior to discovering the body?'

'Of relevance?'

'Well yes . . . of relevance.'

'Like a car speeding in the opposite direction containing four men, one young who looked to be very, very upset . . . very shaken?'

'Yes,' Sherrie nodded, 'yes, something like that.'

'Would you even be interested in a photograph?'

Sherrie jolted in his seat. 'You photographed it?'

'Yes – ' Wedgewood smiled – 'always carry a small pocket camera . . . never know when it might come in useful . . . so I snapped the car after it passed me . . . close enough for you to enlarge it to read the number plate. Do you know why they call such a photograph a "snapshot"?'

'No.' Sherrie shook his head but, having learnt the origin of the expression 'OK', he felt he was about to find out. Moments later, fully edified, he asked what Wedgewood had meant when he described a passenger in the car as 'upset' and 'shaken'.

'Pale . . . glancing down and out of the car window

176

as though he didn't want to be a member of the group within the car . . . as though he had seen something he had rather not have seen. Far be it for me to tell you how to proceed, but I would have thought if there is a weak link in their chain, a crack in their armour . . . that it is he.'

'You think so?'

'Well I worked for many years as a psychologist, I'm quite mad, you see . . . completely eight stops after Upminster . . . out to lunch. It's quite nice actually . . . eccentricity is a perfectly rational adjustment to an insane world . . . many mad people will tell you that it's the world, not they, who are mad . . . but in my case it's true, but anyway, I can read people . . . body language, facial expression. That boy was not a boy – late twenties, I'd say, possibly older . . . but not made of the stuff to be part of what he had witnessed . . . too sensitive . . . not a hard man.'

'Could you describe him?'

'Well . . . thin faced, short, light-coloured hair . . . wearing a green T-shirt, but he won't have that on today . . . really nothing to set him apart, I'm afraid.'

'You'd recognize him again, though?'

'Indubitably, my dear fellow, indubitably.'

'Would you be willing to attend an identification parade?'

'Love to – ' Wedgewood beamed – 'love to, dear boy, love to. Anything to help the boys in blue.'

'How much time elapsed between the car passing you with the unwell-looking passenger and you discovering the body?'

'Well . . . a few minutes only. I turned a bend in the road after the car passed me and then saw the entrance to the field, which was the next leg of Pilgrim's Way . . . two minutes . . . three?'

'So you didn't actually see the car leave the field?'

'No . . . if it was in the field at all . . . they could have parked at the verge, carried the body into the field . . . broad

Peter Turnbull

daylight but there was nobody about . . . except little I of course, but they dismissed me.'

'You saw the driver?'

'Yes . . . oh yes . . . and the front-seat passenger. Looked at me once and then forgot me . . . just a harmless old guy – ' Wedgewood smiled a smile of triumph – 'but they underestimated my powers of observation . . . it's one of the great advantages of being an eccentric, nobody competes with you, nobody sees you as a threat.'

Sherrie smiled, he was warming to Wedgewood. 'So, the driver? Can you describe him?'

'Late-middle-aged, dark hair and a dark-skinned complexion, definitely a European but with an olive skin as some Europeans are . . . hard eyes. . . . he pierced me with piercing eyes then looked away . . . looked ahead. If he had looked at me for just a second longer I wouldn't have dared take the snapshot because he would have been clocking me in his rear-view mirror but his eyes were all on the road ahead . . . so I took a risk.'

'We are grateful.'

'If it comes out . . . it's not an expensive camera. I'll get the spool for you in a minute.'

'Age?'

'The driver? Same vintage as me . . . late fifties . . . about . . . had a ring in his right ear.'

Sherrie smiled.

'Why do you smile? Does this description mean anything to you?'

'Yes – ' Sherrie nodded – 'yes, it does. I don't want to contaminate your evidence by suggesting anything . . . but yes . . . it means something.'

'He had quite a set of jewellery.'

'Jewellery?'

'Gold chain round his neck . . . ring on every finger. They were curled round the steering wheel . . . his fingers, I mean.'

178

'You took all this in in an instant?'

'Yes.' Wedgewood looked pleased with himself. 'Impressed, I hope?'

'I am. I am very impressed.'

'Comes of a working life as a person-watcher. But that's all I can tell you about the driver.'

'The passenger . . . front-seat passenger?'

'Another male of the same age. Well built. Bald-headed guy . . . he was second fiddle to the driver, they were not equal partners . . . they were boss and lieutenant. The passenger was serious-minded by his facial expression but he had a distant look about him . . . as though he too was a little out of his depth . . . not quite the sickened look of the rear-seat passenger, but not the grim, determined look of the driver either.'

'Would you recognize him again?'

'Oh yes . . . no problem at all. He wasn't wearing any decorations . . . no necklace or earring . . . didn't see his hands of course . . . nothing to set him apart in that sense, but I'd recognize him again.'

'And just in case the photograph doesn't turn out, what sort of vehicle was it?'

'A Range Rover . . . fawn coloured . . . black vinyl roof . . . burning oil, too much smoke from the exhaust. Quite an old vehicle . . . seemed to have more working life behind it than before it, but plenty of life left in it still though, oh yes, plenty of life.'

'Plenty of life,' Sherrie echoed.

'But not for the chappie in the field.' Wedgewood read Sherrie's thoughts. 'Not for him. I'll go and get the film for you. If you'll excuse me.'

The darts thudded into the cork of the dartboard. The glasses at the bar 'chinked' as they rattled together; one or two people sat alone, heads buried in newspapers, others sat in groups drinking beer, talking, playing cards or cribbage, or darts. It was the canteen above the work stations at Micklegate Bar Police Station. The bar had been opened, the 6 a.m. till 2 p.m. shift were 'coming down' before going to their homes and families. Yellich and Sherrie, still on duty, sat in a corner away from the beer drinkers and contented themselves with a mug of instant coffee each.

'Not hard and fast evidence.' Sherrie reclined in his chair. 'He did exist and was a most entertaining witness as you thought he might be . . . but wholly circumstantial evidence, even if the photograph identifies the vehicle as belonging to the prime suspect or suspects, it's still circumstantial.'

'But that's useful.' Yellich sipped his coffee contained in a white plastic beaker. 'All adds to the weight of evidence . . .'

'That's true.' Sherrie watched an attractive young female police officer throw a dart. He thought, but did not comment, that her arm and wrist action was more akin to that of men than women, who, when he had observed them in pubs, never seemed to him to know how to throw a dart, trying, it seemed, to 'put' them into the board rather than to launch them with precision. He turned to face Yellich. 'Very true. I can think of a couple of cases like that . . . no single piece of evidence offered was an unbroken link with the accused but the sheer weight of such evidence given over days was sufficient to convince the jury. But your boss is going to want more than that. Where is he, anyway?'

'His snout wanted a meet. Said he had information to offer.'

Hennessey sighed as he looked around him. He didn't think he had seen such a collection of malcontents before in a single place at a single time. 'Shored-up?'

'Has to be here, Mr Hennessey.'

'It's been a pub in Doncaster . . . it's been the pathway outside Selby Abbey, and that was one of your more civilized rendezvous, I really quite enjoyed that . . .'

'And wasn't the information worth it?'

'Possibly . . . and then there was a crossroads in the middle of nowhere . . .'

'Again, for such gold dust, my esteemed Detective Chief Inspector.'

'But Rotherham!' Hennessey shook his head. 'Even for you, Shored-up, this is a new low.' He looked about him. The inevitable McDonald's even looked to him to be a struggling concern. The pedestrianized precinct, the toilets burrowed underneath the parish church . . . clever, sensitive town planning on someone's part, he pondered. 'In all the years of my life that I have spent in Yorkshire, I have heard of this . . . this . . . "place" and hoped against hope to avoid coming here . . . and what happens?'

'You have to stay up all night if you want to see the dawn, Mr Hennessey. I mean truly see it. Getting up an hour before dawn to see it, isn't quite the same somehow.'

'I never knew you were such a philosopher of the home-spun variety, Shored-up,' Hennessey replied sourly as he and his companion turned from the pedestrian precinct into the main street of the town. He didn't search for the name of the street on the wall on the building. He cared not to be in Rotherham at all. Ahead of him was the convex front of what appeared to be the offices of a newspaper. The Union flag hung limply from a flagpole on its roof and he noted, as often before, that people who have least often show the most loyalty to the Crown. The sky above was blue, cloudless; people about him dressed in lightweight summer clothing and all seemed to be putting such small-town mentality effort into being the same as each other. And this was high summer. Hennessey thought the town must be the end of the earth in winter.

'A man of many talents, Mr Hennessey. A man of many talents.'

'And guises,' Hennessey grumbled. 'What are you today, Household Cavalry, Major, retired?'

'Well, like I said, I am working on a new persona.'

'Oh yes, the Devonshire and Dorset Regiment, I forget . . .'

'Yes . . . the good old D & Ds, always there when needed – reading up on their exploits for the past twenty years. The inevitable tours of Northern Ireland, doing their bit to quell "the Troubles".'

'Well, all you need now is an emotionally needy but desperately wealthy spinster . . . but I warn you, all the good information you have supplied to the police in the last few years won't count for a thing if I should ever see you being at the wheel of a Rolls Royce . . . remember how the police work . . . if it doesn't look right, we pull it for examination and you driving anything but a supermarket trolley will look very suspicious.'

'You do me a great injustice, Chief Inspector.'

'You think so?'

'Oh yes . . . to think that if I were ever to pull off the big one, that I would be unwise enough to retain my current domicile in the "Famous and Faire" . . . not on your life, sunshine. I'd be off down Bournemouth way, where the pickings are rich, on a day-to-day basis, that is.'

'Why aren't you down there now?'

'Pull the big scam, then scarper, that's the plan. I don't really like the North of England, so I pull the big scam in the North and scarper to the South.'

Hennessey and Shored-up separated to allow a matted-haired, overweight woman who was ploughing a straight furrow through the pedestrians to continue on her deter-mined way.

'So,' Hennessey said, when he and Shored-up were once again walking shoulder to shoulder. 'Why have you insisted on this rendezvous? You could only have gold dust for me? To ask me to meet you here, it has to be gold dust.'

'Well . . .' Shored-up paused, 'I think we should go somewhere.'

'Oh, anywhere . . .'

The somewhere Shored-up proved to have in mind was a

car park on a slope at the edge of the centre of Rotherham, near the library.

'Just about as open as any open space can be,' Hennessey growled.

'Have met you in a pub once, in Doncaster, as you recalled, but I do like open spaces in which to meet. Nobody can eavesdrop. Long-range microphones exist but only work if they can be placed beforehand.'

'So I believe.'

'And even I didn't know where we were going to stand until I used the hour or so I had to fill before meeting you at the railway station. You never seem to use a car, Mr Hennessey. Why is that?'

'A very personal reason, Shored-up. A very personal reason indeed.'

'OK.'

'Now . . . information.'

'Well you asked me to inquire into the disappearance of the wife of Tommy "Blackhole" Ilford.'

'And?'

'Nothing. The consensus is that the lady disappeared.'

Hennessey checked his temper.

'Bottom of the Ouse, most like . . .'

'I am a busy man . . . I do not care for my time to be wasted, I do not care for my time to be wasted in a town such as this.'

'They're going to rob the Art Gallery.' Shored-up smiled. He enjoyed Hennessey's look of shock and then realization. 'Thought you'd appreciate that bit of information, Mr H.'

'Of course . . .' Hennessey gasped. Then mused: 'Digging for tin and striking gold.'

'So you thought there was something afoot?'

'Yes, a few roads seem to be converging, right enough.'

'Because the London criminal is in town?'

'You know about him?'

'Not much, but the feeling on the street is one of fear of

183

him; it would be an easier feeling if he and Blackhole Ilford were having a turf war . . . but they've teamed up . . . the little crims are quaking in their boots. And well they might . . . the London guy . . . . . . has a biblical name.'

'"Passover"?'

'That's it.'

'He cooled a guy on Sunday, yesterday . . . did it in front of Ilford's whole squad. It was a lesson in what happens if you cross the London guy, even Blackhole Ilford looked sick, so they say.'

'Who's they?' Hennessey no longer felt affronted by having to travel to Rotherham to indulge Shored-up in his games. This was indeed gold dust.

'Pretty well all of Ilford's crew, including Ilford's sons. What are their names? Leonard and Norman. Leonard didn't take it well . . .he's too soft so they say. Even Ilford's hard-nosed bit of stuff looked a little green about the gills.'

'This is firsthand?'

'Second, I am afraid, but people talk and the people they have talked to talk in turn. It's all a question of knowing where to place your ear upon the ground. I made a few new friends when I was in Full Sutton. Remember how I said I like to turn everything to my advantage if I can? It turned out by sheer coincidence that one other guest was . . . well, I won't tell you his name, but he was one of Ilford's boys . . . been done for stealing cars and selling the constituent parts to unscrupulous or unsuspecting customers . . . a replacement gearbox . . . good as new . . . a third of the normal second-hand price.'

'Ringing.'

'Is that the term used?'

'You know very well it is, you would have been carved if you put on your army officer airs in Full Sutton or any other nick, come to that.'

'Well, it does help to be a social chameleon at times and my native Yorkshire accent has saved me from a good kicking in the past, but you don't object if I use you to polish my act, I hope, Mr Hennessey?'

'I do mind frankly, though I doubt that will deter you.' Hennessey watched a cream-and-coffee-coloured bus drive slowly down the hill to his left and continued to watch as it stopped, gently, at the pelican crossing at the bottom. 'Well, said felon was quite relieved to be a guest because he felt Ilford wanted him to prove himself. He'd only got youth custody on his CV, so to speak. He told me you need to do time in the big boys' gaol if you are going anywhere . . . it's clearly a rite of passage, show that you can do time and not open your mouth . . . then you can move up. He actually implied that he allowed himself to be caught.'

'It's not unknown,' Hennessey growled, 'for reasons you've just put your finger on.'

'Well, we met, I knew where he drank and went there on the off-chance, dressed appropriately, and was obliged to drink pints of beer . . . ugh! He was there, he was shaky, he needed to talk . . . he'd seen a guy topped . . . bled to death, he said, slowly like they do to calves to produce veal.'

'You going to give me his name?'

'Oh, Mr Hennessey, really, I'd rather keep *my* blood within my body. The execution had a double purpose apparently, it was a revenge killing. Apparently a London gangster, Passover knew the guy from way back and the guy had given evidence against him. Must have thought he was safe in the North, then Passover walks into his boss's shop floor, they recognize each other and in an instant Passover felled this guy with a most mighty right hook. That was, I believe, on Friday last. Kept him alive for a day or so, then did the business on . . . well, yesterday morning. Waited until all Blackhole Ilford's crew could be assembled because, like I said, it was also to serve as an example of what ill could befall a gentleman should he betray Passover.'

'Sounds like Passover is taking over Blackhole Ilford's operation?'

'Well, this seems to be the thing, Mr Hennessey. It was, and I dare say still is, the opinion of my informant that Blackhole Ilford invited Passover up as a partner in a one-off operation, but rapidly found that he was expected to play lead support. I think the fate of your deceased was also intended for his eyes too. Worth a wedge, I think, Mr Hennessey?'

'Worth a bigger wedge if you can tell me when they are going to rob the Art Gallery.'

'Not known, but soon. The time is forced by the London man, Passover. Like most Londoners and those who live all points south, he is homesick when in the North, finds the accent incomprehensible, the air difficult to breath, the beer awful, and is anxious to go south of the divide before the first of the snow. So, soon.'

'Method?'

'Entering as tourists . . . finding a door which leads to the basement, waiting until it's locked up, emerging, over-powering the night staff and relieving the gallery of its art treasures. Odd crime . . . I mean where would you unload a well-known oil painting that the nation, the whole art world knows is stolen?'

'Two things you can do with a stolen Van Gogh or a Rembrandt, or any other famous painting,' Sherrie spoke in an authoritative tone. 'You can sell it for a substantial sum of money in the underworld to unscrupulous collectors who have their own private galleries and pass them on when they die, and so on. They then get handed down through the generations and anything up to two hundred years later they are allowed to surface as 'treasure-troves'. The person who "finds" it is compensated up to its true value and, once again, it is restored to public ownership. The other thing . . . and this is most likely, is that the paintings will be ransomed to the nation. A lot less risky than kidnapping a human being, just as lucrative and a lesser sentence if collared. Knowing Passover, he'll be planning a ransom.'

'Why the York Art Gallery?' Hennessey asked.

'Less security-conscious than the Tate, I would imagine, and not expecting anyone to knock over an exhibition of second-division landscape paintings, despite the fact that they could probably be ransomed for two or three million all told. Not a bad return for a few hours' work at zero risk. That's Passover's style.'

Hennessey tapped a pen on his desk as he thought. He glanced at his watch. Four thirty – getting to the end of the working day.

'What are you thinking, boss?' Yellich turned his gaze from the view through Hennessey's office window: the walls, the tourists, the pale-coloured battlements, the blue sky, the lengthening shadows.

'Whether to interview Ilford at his place of work or his home. As Mr Sherrie—'

'Philip, please.'

'As Philip says,' Hennessey smiled. 'As Philip says, he will be expecting us. It'll be odd if we don't call on him. He'll suspect something if we don't.'

'I'd better keep a low profile. If Passover sees me, he'll know the jig is up . . . and will abandon the art gallery job.'

'Yes . . .' Hennessey tapped his pen on the desktop again. 'We mustn't lose sight of that. We had better get a team of officers in plain clothes into the gallery . . . tonight and every night while Passover's in town.'

'I'd like to be part of that.' Sherrie raised his hand slightly. 'That'll be Passover's party. I'd like to be there to ruin it for him.'

'Be our guest . . . in fact if you could liaise with the Art Gallery . . . let them know what is happening.'

'Of course.' Sherrie turned to Yellich. 'Can I use the phone in your office?'

'Of course.'

*   *   *

Ilford's office was a cramped room above the shop floor of his garage. It was kept in a fastidiously clean and tidy manner with a window behind his desk which looked out on to the working area . . . fitters in overalls . . . cars on ramps . . . but didn't have a source of natural light.

'Know you.' Ilford leaned back in his hinged-back chair and beamed at Yellich. 'You did me once . . . funny name . . . Pellie . . . Wellie . . .'

'Yellich.' The reply was growled.

'Ah, yes . . . DS Yellich . . . you were in uniform then . . . come not a long way since then, I see.'

'As far as I want to go.'

'Not a man of ambition then.' Ilford was smartly dressed, not the normal dress of a garage proprietor in Hennessey's or Yellich's experience, not a man who likes a 'hands-on' approach to his work.

'Petty,' Hennessey said.

'Cash . . . officer . . . thief? Sorry . . . is this a word-association game? Sessions . . . Petty Sessions as was, at any rate.'

'Petty, Michael.'

'Ah, Michael . . .' But Ilford's warmth was false, the smile was forced.

'He works for you?'

'Does he?'

'So his wife says.'

'Well, he may do odd jobs but he's not on my staff. I only employ qualified mechanics. Mickey isn't qualified for anything except errand-running.'

'Know where he is now?'

'Nope . . . is he missing?'

'Not exactly.' Hennessey allowed menace to enter his tone. 'He's dead.'

'Oh, really?' Ilford didn't even feign surprise. 'How awful. An accident?'

'No . . . murder.'

'Ah . . . I see . . . and you think I had something to do with it?'

'We believe you may be able to provide information.' Hennessey stood beside Yellich, the two officers having declined the invitation to have a seat.

'Helping with enquiries? Love that phrase. Getting your head cracked open against a cell wall . . . that is what helping with enquiries means.'

'All right and proper these days, done according to P.A.C.E.'

'Pace? It has a speed?'

'The Police and Criminal Evidence Act. All interviews are tape-recorded, a lawyer is present at all times.'

'Oh . . . spoiled your fun, I bet.'

'Actually we prefer it like that.'

'Safe convictions come of it,' Yellich added. 'Very safe convictions.'

Ilford, small, stocky, looked stunned by the inference of Yellich's words.

'Very safe.' Hennessey noted Ilford's reaction and maximized the effect of Yellich's contribution.

'We are not talking about a few minor motoring offences here, Mr Ilford. This is big time . . . about as big as it gets.'

'Like porridge, do you?'

'Like lots and lots of alcohol-free sleep at the end of each day?' Yellich added.

'Where were you yesterday morning?'

'At home.'

'All morning?' Hennessey found it difficult to conceal his delight . . . an alibi, an alibi . . . a lovely, lovely alibi.

'Yes.'

'Anybody vouch for you?'

'My . . . lady.'

'Who is that?'

'A lady by the name of Sandra Picardie, if you must know.'

'Yes, we must. She will confirm that you were at home all morning yesterday . . . or were you at home for a longer period?'

'All day?'

'All day.' Ilford paused. 'Ate out at midday, though.'

'Oh?'

'Hare and Hounds . . . they do excellent Sunday lunches . . . roast beef, all the trimmings.'

'The Hare and Hounds? Which Hare and Hounds is that? It's not an uncommon name for a pub.'

'Sutton St Mary.'

'You live out there?' Yellich sounded surprised. 'You've come a long way since I last fondled your collar.'

'Further than you, Yessie.'

'Yellich. The name's Yellich.'

'Yellich,' Ilford parroted. 'I do apologize. But yes, I live out by Sutton St Mary.'

'Where is Miss Picardie now?'

'She'll be at home.'

'We'll have to call and see her. Just to confirm your alibi.'

'I am sure she will do that.'

'Well – ' Hennessey opened his briefcase and took out a writing pad – 'We'll just get this down in the form of a statement, ask you to sign it, then we'll be on our way.'

'Don't wish to detain you any longer than is necessary,' Yellich added, both sensing and sharing his senior officer's delight in being provided with an alibi by a man who obviously had much to hide.

'Frightened of Passover,' Hennessey said as Yellich drove the car away from Ilford's garage.

'You think so, skipper?'

'It's the only explanation . . . hasn't let the Law get near him for years, yet he gives and signs an alibi like a wet-behind-the-ears youth.' Hennessey patted the briefcase which he held on his lap. 'Did you think he looked frightened?'

'I did, in fact. Not the cool customer I have met in the past. So do we go straight to his house?'

'No . . .' Hennessey spoke slowly. 'Let's give him time to phone home, tell the good lady Sandra that we are about to arrive . . . let them get the script right and give them time to put Harry "Passover" Kennedy in the priest hole. Let's call in at the Hare and Hounds.'

'Bit early for a drink isn't it, skipper?'

Hennessey threw Yellich a pained and despairing glance.

The Hare and Hounds revealed itself to be a thatch-roofed building, which was unusual for the Vale of York, where slate roofs have long been preferred, but it was not at all unique. It was painted white, the timbers being picked out in black. The date above the door read 1710AD. Inside it was quiet – just one early evening drinker at the bar. The smell of wood polish was strong to the point of being overwhelming.

'Yes – ' the jovial nature of the white-shirted, bow-tied publican soured at the mention of Thomas Ilford – 'I know him. Comes in here sometimes. Can't stop him . . . never causes bother, but I still don't like him standing on my carpet.'

'Was he in yesterday?'

'When?'

'Lunchtime.'

'No.' The publican clearly searched his memory. 'Not yesterday lunchtime . . . I was here all lunchtime and like I said I know Ilford. If he was in the pub yesterday I would have noticed him . . . no . . . we were thankfully Ilford-free yesterday.'

'They didn't eat lunch?'

'Probably did, but not here. The dining area was closed yesterday.'

'No?'

'No. We had a bit of a disaster in the kitchen. Couldn't serve any meals at all yesterday.'

George Hennessey could not believe his good fortune, nor could he quite believe Thomas Ilford's folly. 'Would you mind giving a statement to that effect?'

The publican looked worried. He stroked his pencil-line moustache. 'Tommy Ilford has a reputation,' he breathed deeply. 'If I do stand up in court and give evidence against him . . . well, even if he goes down, his mates will see my pub torched . . . and it's my pub . . . I am the landlord. It's my home as well as my livelihood. I won't say I saw him, or I didn't see him. I won't mention him.'

'You don't need to.' Hennessey opened his briefcase and took out his notepad. 'Just a brief statement saying that this pub was unable to serve meals yesterday, the twenty-first of the month of this year.'

'That's all?'

'That's all.'

'Well . . . in that case . . . yes . . . yes, I will make and sign a statement to that effect. My pleasure.'

So this, thought Hennessey, so this is Sandra Picardie a.k.a. Tracy Morrison, one week ago unknown to the police in York, and now believed to be implicated in two murders, one disappearance, possibly an embezzlement, and witness to the murder of Michael Petty, bled to death 'like a calf for the production of veal'. Yellich, for his part, simply thought: It's been a long week . . . but here you are at last.

Sandra Picardie had hard eyes and a thin-lipped, cruel-looking mouth, so Hennessey judged. He also saw cold, piercing, suspicious eyes. She was dressed in a loud scarlet suit with pale-coloured nylons and red shoes to match the suit. A white blouse and a red scarf round her neck completed the visible clothing. Her fingers and neck were heavy with shiny metal, as were her earlobes. The living room of the house was lavishly furnished, in Hennessey's eyes; grey seemed to be the dominant colour – grey deep-pile carpet, grey sofas, two of them, huge matching grey armchairs . . . walls of a lighter grey paint on wallpaper. A cream-coloured vase, from which dry reeds projected, stood in the corner. A bookcase with a few book club editions behind the glass door, a television in the corner, one of the modern, wide-screen types. The lounge was a 'through lounge': the front window looked out on to the driveway and the greenery at the front of the house; the back window looked out on the meadow at the back of the house. 'Easy listening' music played softly.

'Can I ask what this is about?' Her voice was calm. 'My husband told me you were coming?'

'Your husband?'

'Mr Ilford. Well . . . we have a common-law relationship, we are not legally married.' She strove for 'received pronunciation', it seemed to Hennessey but the tendency to clip vowels spoke of Midlands working-class origins. She was Walsall more than Solihull.

'I see.' Hennessey paused. He allowed himself the luxury of enjoying the comfort of the sofa, facing Ms Picardie, who sat on the adjacent sofa. A glass-topped coffee table with stout wooden legs on which lay copies of *Country Life* and *Yorkshire Life*, separated Hennessey and Sandra Picardie. Yellich sat, as if consumed, in one of the armchairs. 'Now, the purpose of our visit—'

'Michael Petty. My husband told me you were investigating his death . . . how horrible.'

'You knew him?'

'Only by sight. He was employed at the garage.'

'As what?'

'As what? I don't know as what – whenever I went there he was sometimes there . . . gradually got to know his name.'

'I see. Can you tell me where you were yesterday?'

'Why? Am I under suspicion?' She laid her palm on her chest.

'Well, yes, you are, in the sense that at this stage everybody associated with Mr Petty is under suspicion, no matter how distant or fleeting is that association.'

'All right. I was here all day with my . . . well, with Mr Ilford.'

'Just the two of you?'

'Yes.'

'All day?'

'Apart from lunch. We went out to lunch.'

'Really?'

'Yes, the Hare and Hounds in the village.'

'All right.' Hennessey displayed no emotion but his heart leapt. Clearly, he thought, if you are adept at avoiding having suspicion fall on you and keep one step ahead of the police at every turn, the drawback is that you never develop any fencing skills necessary to survive being interviewed. Methinks, he further thought, methinks that madam is too used to getting away with it. 'So you and your husband spent the day together at home, apart from a pub lunch at the Hare and Hounds?'

'Yes. All day.'

'Well, we are really only interested in the forenoon of yesterday.'

'Long lie in . . . up at about nine thirty . . . pottered about, read the papers . . . out to the Hare and Hounds, back here by 2 p.m., in for the rest of the day and evening.'

'Well – ' Hennessey opened his briefcase – 'if I can just take a brief statement from you . . . get you to sign it . . . we'll be out of your house . . . in the kindest possible way, we don't want to be here any more than I am sure you want us to be here.'

'You're too kind,' said with a very insincere smile.

No, madam, thought Hennessey, as he began to write the statement, if you sign this, then it is you that is too kind. A few moments later, with pen held in long, slender fingers of painted nails, Sandra Picardie did indeed prove herself to be 'too kind'.

Driving away from the Ilford house, slowly, and so strongly transmitting the message that he was leaving on his terms, Yellich glanced to his side at Hennessey and thought his senior officer looked pleased with himself. He remarked on it.

'Well, I think I have reason to be. Two self-condemning alibis in the space of an hour . . . it's the crack in the wall of the dyke, Yellich . . . the net is closing in. There may be some much belated justice for Muriel Bradbury, skeleton in the rubble, after all.'

'And Janet Frost,' Yellich added.

'Yes . . . the snickelway victim. Would you mind working late?'

'Well . . .'

'Good chap . . . do you have your notebook with you?'

'Of course, sir . . . but it's gone six o'clock.'

'Good. I remember reading in your recording that Ilford has two sons.'

'Yes. What are their names . . . ? Leonard and Norman?'

'Yes . . . and you also recorded that of the two, one . . . Leonard, I think you said, was quite sensitive.'

'Aye . . . that's what Kate Ilford's sister said . . . his aunt.'

'Well, my snout . . . "Shored-up" . . . he said the same thing, said one . . . I think he said Leonard, looked very ill when witnessing the murder of Michael Petty.'

'As anyone would.'

'I think we ought to pay a call on Leonard Ilford, he might be shaken enough to cough. Have to catch him before he recovers his composure. You have his address in your notebook?'

'I think so, sir.'

'Well, pull over and look it up. We'll go there now. Tell me, have you ever been to Rotherham?'

'No, sir . . . I haven't.'

'Don't.'

*   *   *

Leonard Ilford was not, in Hennessey's opinion, a very criminal criminal, if he was even a criminal at all. It seemed to him that Ilford junior was suffered, tolerated, more than he was accepted. He was in the outfit because he was the boss's son. He had his father's stocky build but not his eyes . . . the eyes that Hennessey saw were frightened, childlike almost. He lived in a small terraced house within the walls, which in terms of its décor and furnishings was spartan. A bachelor's house. He sat in an armchair and seemed withdrawn into it, so Hennessey thought. Hennessey and Yellich also sat, as invited. Piles of newsprint that had lain too long in the sun made the rooms smell musty. A fly buzzed in angry frustration against the windowpane.

'I'm frightened of my father,' Ilford said. 'I'm frightened of the Law too. I suppose this is what is meant by a rock and a hard place.'

'I think it is, Leonard,' Hennessey spoke softly. 'Think that's exactly what it is.'

'What do I do?' The voice was plaintive, almost wailing. 'I'm not like my brother . . . he'd know what to do.'

'Well . . .' Hennessey adjusted his position in the chair. Unlike the chairs in Ms Picardie's home, the chairs in Leonard Ilford's house were aged and uncomfortable. 'If you are caught between a rock and a hard place you are going to be crushed.'

'Yes.'

'So, to avoid being crushed, you must clamber up one or the other while you can. You must chose the rock or the hard place.'

'Either you or my dad?'

'That's about the size of it.'

'I can't give evidence against my dad. Not my brother either. I won't.'

'You may not have to.'

Leonard Ilford looked eagerly at Hennessey. 'There's a way out of this without giving evidence against my family?'

'I think there may well be, Leonard.'

'How?'

'Well . . . tell us where Passover Kennedy hid the bits and bats he used to bleed Michael Petty to death in your father's garage yesterday morning.'

'You know about that?'

'Yes,' Hennessey said, although the reference to Leonard Ilford's father's garage was an assumption. Yellich, unseen by Ilford, smiled and winked at Hennessey. 'We know about that. He would have used a catheter to collect the blood from each ankle. Where are they?'

'Catheters . . . the tubes?'

'Yes, the tubes.'

'In my dad's garage.'

'Where? It's a big building.'

'In the rubbish. There's a stove made out of two oil drums, keeps the crew warm in the winter, anything that will burn goes in it . . . in summer it's not used, but stuff to burn once the cold weather comes is put in a box beside it. Passover chucked these tubes in amongst that lot.'

'He did?'

'Yes.'

'Was he wearing gloves?'

'No . . . don't think so. He was confident nobody would grass him up. We'd just seen what happens to anyone who does grass on him. And I am not grassing on Passover.'

Hennessey thought, You just have, but said, 'All right, we won't ask you to give evidence but you are clearly deciding which rock to climb up. Feel better about it?'

Leonard Ilford nodded. 'Yes, I do.'

'If necessary, we can offer witness protection.'

'It doesn't work . . . that guy that was bled to death was in witness protection, look what happened to him. He knew he was going to die . . . the fear . . . blood wasn't the only thing that came out of his body.'

'I can imagine.'

'He was alive, I mean conscious for nearly half an hour . . . but you can forget me giving evidence . . . like I said . . . witness protection doesn't work.'

'It does. Petty's problem was that he couldn't keep away from crime, he wandered back into the network and he bumped into Passover Kennedy. If he had kept his nose clean, he would still be alive.'

'Is that true?'

'Yes . . . that's how it happened. So it's a way out of the crime scene for you, if you want it. New name, new identity . . . you're a young man.'

'Twenty-eight. Not too young.'

'Time to do something with your life. You could study . . . you are not dim-witted.'

'Yes . . . I could . . . it's the way out that I want.'

'Help us, we'll help you.'

'I won't make a statement. If Passover can't get me, he'll nail my brother or my dad, or both. I'll give you information, but no statement . . . no evidence in court.'

'Probably no witness protection then. It's not called witness protection for nothing. It isn't "information provider protection" . . . it's *witness* protection. Something for you to think about. When is Passover going to do the Art Gallery?'

Leonard Ilford's jaw sagged. 'Is there anything that you don't know?'

'Not much . . . but as in all police work, there's a big gulf between what we know and what we can go to court with.'

'No statement . . . no evidence in court.'

'Just tell us what you know.'

'It's going to happen tonight.'

'Tonight!'

'Yes,' Leonard Ilford glanced at his watch. 'They'll be in there now if it's going to plan, but they won't start the robbery until after dark.'

Hennessey nodded to Yellich. Yellich fished his mobile from his pocket. He dialled Sherrie's number and after a pause was heard to say, 'It's tonight . . . OK . . . good luck.' Yellich looked at Hennessey. 'Sherrie's team is in the building, boss.'

Hennessey smiled his thanks. 'So it's all falling apart for Mr Kennedy.'

'And my dad, he's in the Art Gallery.'

'He's in there?'

'Where is Kennedy?'

'At home with Sandra.'

'Letting your dad take all the risks?'

'Yes . . . it's not like him, but Kennedy is . . . well, he's the boss.'

'How did they meet?'

'Unsure really . . . my dad told us that Kennedy was coming, didn't like the sound of the idea, said he wouldn't be staying long. It was as if Kennedy was inviting himself.'

'You think perhaps he had his eye on the touring art exhibition and decided to screw it in York . . . that he needed local assistance, press-ganged your father and his boys into providing the foot soldiers.'

'Could well be it. I've never seen my father pushed around before . . . this guy Kennedy, he's something else.'

'The Metropolitan Police have been after him for some time.'

'I can believe it.' Ilford was noticeably more relaxed.

'So . . . tell me about Sandra Picardie?'

'A cold, hard, calculating cow.'

'When did she take up with your father?'

'Shortly after my mum disappeared. Very shortly.'

'Were you close to your mother?'

'Yes,' Ilford nodded. He looked hurt.

'What do you know about your mother's disappearance?'

Ilford shrugged. 'What is there to know? She was there one day, gone the next . . . vanished . . . no trace . . . into thin air.'

'What was your parents' marriage like?'

'Strained. I think you could say it wasn't a marriage. My mum thought she was married to a garage proprietor who strayed a little. She couldn't even have suspected the extent of my dad's activities . . . unlike Sandra, who knows the full score. I think my dad is happier with Sandra.'

'Ever suspected what might have happened to your mother?'

'Suspect? Every day I wonder . . . but suspect . . . don't know what to suspect.'

'Or who?'

Ilford's eyes narrowed. 'What do you mean?'

'Were you close to your mother?'

'Yes . . .'

'Well, listen, Leonard . . . you have been of assistance to us, I will tell you something. Sandra Picardie is a woman with a history . . . she's been married twice.'

'She never told us that.'

'Well, take it from me. Both her previous husbands were wealthy widowers following upon the murder of their wives . . . both of them fell on hard times, upon which Sandra divorced them. She was known to both her husbands in an employment capacity before their wives were murdered.'

Leonard Ilford put his hand up to his mouth. 'But that's exactly what happened to my father. Sandra came to work for him as a sort of accountant, but she's not qualified as such.'

'We know.'

'Then mother disappeared . . . and she moved in with my dad.' Ilford paled as a realization was dawning.

'But your father is too cautious to marry . . . and so Sandra Picardie had to content herself with a common-law union. She still gets the good life but without the security. But to all intents and purposes, the pattern is the same.'

'She murdered my mum . . .' Ilford's voice faltered.

'It seems very likely, Leonard.'

Leonard Ilford glanced open-mouthed to one side but it did

not seem to either Hennessey or Yellich that he was seeing anything. The dreadful realization was continuing to dawn. The awfulness was being absorbed.

'So,' Hennessey said, 'I can understand your reluctance to give evidence about your father or Passover Kennedy, but can I assume that when it comes to Ms Picardie, you and I are on the same side?'

'Yes,' Ilford nodded. 'Yes, Mr Hennessey, you can that. What can I tell you? If she murdered my mother . . .'

'Well, did she have any friends outside your father and his gang . . . or his legitimate employees at the garage?'

'Only Monica . . . Monica Wickersley.'

Hennessey glanced at Yellich. 'That name has cropped up before in this inquiry, has it not?'

'Believe so, sir. I think both previous husbands have mentioned her.'

Leonard Ilford sighed. 'Both previous husbands . . . what did he bring into our family?'

'Well, let us both find out shall we, Leonard? Tell us what you know about Monica Wickersley.'

'Not much really . . . Sandra's age . . . she's married.'

'Do you know where she lives?'

'No, but Sandra's got a sieve-like memory, she has to write everything down . . . it'll be in her address book or her email if you can access it.'

'No other friends at all?'

'None . . . that I know of, anyway.' Leonard Ilford continued to stare into the middle distance, his voice was soft, faltering.

'Well, thanks anyway, Leonard,' Hennessey stood. 'You've been a great help. It may help us find out what happened to your mother.'

Leonard Ilford nodded. 'But I won't make a statement . . . not about Passover or my father.'

'Probably no need. If we can obtain the tubing from the garage and if it has Passover Kennedy's prints on it and the

DNA from the blood inside can be matched to Michael Petty, that in itself isn't proof but it gives Kennedy something to explain.'

A warrant obtained, the business premises belonging to Tommy 'Blackhole' Ilford was entered by the police and searched. Long opaque plastic tubing, two lengths of same, were recovered amidst a detritus of combustible material beside an 'intermediate technology' stove made from two oil drums, just as Leonard Ilford had described. Sandra Picardie and a surprised, indignant and 'full of his rights' Harold 'Passover' Kennedy were arrested, with warrants, at the home of Thomas Ilford. The house was also searched, with a warrant to search, and Sandra Picardie's address book was found in a drawer in her dressing table. Thomas 'Blackhole' Ilford, Norman Ilford and two other men were arrested within the premises of the York City Art Gallery in possession of equipment that could be used to steal oil paintings, to wit, very sharp knives and long sports bags. Upon the police leaving the building with four men clearly under arrest, a white van was observed to start up and drive away hurriedly. Neither it nor the driver was to be traced.

'It's late!'
   Hennessey didn't reply but knocked again on the door.
   'Who is it?'
   'Police,' he said. Then turned to Yellich and said, 'Late, 10 p.m. isn't late.'
   'Hardly late at all, boss. I've done this at 3 a.m.'
   'Haven't we all?'
   Then the door was flung open. A middle-aged woman stood on the doorstep. Her face was flushed with anger. 'Yes!'
   'Mrs Wickersley?'
   'Ms.'
   'Ms Wickersley . . . we'd like to ask you a few questions.'

'About?'

'Sandra Picardie.'

At the mention of the name, Monica Wickersley's face went white. 'I've got teenagers,' she said. 'Upstairs . . . playing on their computer.'

'How old is the oldest?'

'Seventeen.'

'Old enough to be left alone then, should we have to take you in for questioning.'

'Take me in?'

'It may not come to that, Ms Wickersley,' Hennessey said softly.

'Depends on how co-operative you are,' Yellich added.

Monica Wickersley's house was cramped and untidy in Hennessey's view, with the presence of teenage children in the household much in evidence, clothing abandoned here and there, school exercise books and textbooks lying on tables and chairs, the computer game being played upstairs clearly preferred. The officers were invited to sit and with some difficulty found a chair each.

'So . . .' Hennessey said. 'Sandra Picardie.'

'Yes?'

'How do you know her?'

'We used to work together at the building society.'

'The York, Harrogate and Ripon?'

'Yes.'

'You seem nervous, Ms Wickersley?'

Monica Wickersley shrugged.

'Ms Picardie's in custody,' Hennessey said quietly, but it caused Monica Wickersley to gasp.

'She is not a happy woman,' Yellich added. 'She's talking about plea-bargaining already . . . Likes the good life, doesn't she . . . the house she lives in, the car she drives?'

'She won't take well to a women's prison . . . especially for life.'

'Life!' Monica Wickersley gasped.

'She's been arrested in connection with a murder.' Hennessey held eye contact with Monica Wickersley.

'She's going to take anybody that she can down with her. She would do anything to win a reduction in her sentence.'

'It's a question of who speaks first,' Yellich added.

Monica Wickersley buried her head in her hands – eventually, sufficiently recovered she said, 'She was blackmailing me.'

'In respect of what?'

'I can't tell you . . .'

'Well, if you don't, she will. Anyway, what did she make you do?'

'Oh . . . she made me help her hide a body . . . it was . . . must be twenty years ago now. In a sense, I'm pleased you have come. It had to come out. I'm pleased my children are all but grown up . . . if I go to prison, they'll survive . . . they'll move in with their father.'

'So what happened?'

'Well, I stole some money from the building society.'

'It was you! The embezzlement . . . all those dormant accounts?'

'No . . . that was Picardie. But it was me who showed her how to do it . . . it was me that told her I'd done it.'

'But you did it as well?'

'I needed the money . . . really needed it. I found this account that had an enormous amount of cash in it which hadn't been touched for years. I was able to open an account with a fictitious name and address and transfer some of the money . . . just what I needed . . . but like an idiot I told Picardie what I'd done. She then used the same technique to milk every dormant account she could, then withdrew the money in cash . . . the address she had used was in student bedsit land . . . they couldn't find her . . . she kept the lot.'

'I see. You'll have to make a statement about this.'

'Yes.'

'So the body?'

'I was married . . . young, newly married . . . divorced now as you see, and went back to calling myself by my maiden name. My husband was a policeman.'

'A policeman!'

'Yes . . . he left the force to form a private detective agency . . . he's doing well . . . look at me . . . but if I was to be prosecuted, it would have destroyed him.'

'So what happened?'

'Well . . . the house we lived in had no garage but we rented a lock-up a few streets away and in the event only used it to store junk, we didn't go near it for days on end. Picardie said she wanted to store something there . . . just for a few days. Wouldn't tell me what. She said if I didn't, she'd confess to the embezzlement and take me down with her . . . it wasn't for me that I did it, it was for my husband.'

'Here I have to caution you, Ms Wickersley,' Hennessey held up a hand. 'You can have legal representation if you wish . . . if you want this to be done properly, you'll have to accompany us to the police station . . . so . . . . you do not have to say anything, but it may harm your defence if you do not mention, when questioned, something you later rely on in court. Anything you do say may be given in evidence.'

'It's all right . . . I want to tell you . . . I want it off my chest.'

'Very well . . . in your own words.'

'She had me wait for her at the lock-up . . . at night in the winter. She arrived in her car . . . made me unload something wrapped in a carpet.'

'A body?'

Monica Wickersley nodded. 'I didn't know it was until it was in the lock-up. Picardie said, "You're in it now . . . aiding and abetting." I said I didn't know it was going to be a dead body . . . and she snorted and said, "Course you did. I told you" . . . but she didn't. It would have been my word against hers. Then she said it would only be for a few days . . . once they've searched the garden.'

205

'She said that?'

'Yes . . . and she was as good as her word. She came to collect it a few days later but after that I was still in her pocket. Possibly even more so.'

'You helped her put it back in her car?'

Monica Wickersley nodded. 'Silly . . .'

'Downright stupid . . . up until you did that . . . well, your solicitor will be advising you, but I can tell you that you are helping yourself by giving this information.'

'Considerably so,' Yellich said with a smile.

'Well, she drove the body away, never knew what she did with it . . . by then the wife of one of our managers had been reported missing and a year or two later, Sandra Picardie became his young "trophy" wife.' She paused. 'Shall I get my coat?'

'Yes,' he nodded. 'And tell your children you will be late back.'

'You're not detaining me?'

'It's a risk, but no. We'll have to charge you with embezzlement and accessory to murder after the fact, but I don't think you'll flee the country or commit suicide.'

Monica Wickersley smiled and muttered, 'Thank you.'

The recording light glowed softly. The spools of the twin cassettes spun slowly. The silence in the room was oppressive. Sandra Picardie glared, glowered at Chief Inspector Hennessey. Yellich, sitting beside Hennessey, fixed his eyes intently on Sandra Picardie and sensed that she genuinely felt that she had been served an injustice. The fourth person in the room, a small, bespectacled man who had identified himself for the benefit of the tape as Roger Bowler of Bowler and Geeson, solicitors, shifted in his seat, nervously so, as if he felt uncomfortable with criminal law and was more at ease conveying houses.

'What's the best thing to do?' Picardie appealed to Bowler.

'Don't admit to anything, would be my advice.' Bowler

sounded to both Hennessey and Yellich as if he were irritated by the whole proceedings and seemed perfunctory in his manner. A man who clearly resented late working. 'But I would also advise you to play with a straight bat. The statement given by Ms Wickersley is sufficient to condemn you, and sufficient to earn her a reduced sentence, a considerably reduced sentence. You may care to take a leaf out of her book.'

'That's advice!' Picardie almost spat the words.

'Yes,' Bowler nodded. 'That's advice.'

'But I want advice that will get me out of here.'

Bowler snorted, 'You can forget that, Ms Picardie. You will not be walking the streets again as a free woman for a very long time. Not with this weight of evidence.'

'Can't we plea-bargain?'

'We don't plea-bargain,' Hennessey said. 'Our American cousins do that. We don't.'

'So why should I co-operate?'

'Because if you plead guilty, that will be reflected in your sentence and we will ensure that the parole board is fully acquainted with the extent of co-operation.'

'Or otherwise,' Yellich added.

'What can you prove?'

'The murder of Muriel Bradbury. Ms Wickersley's statement, plus the fact that you became the second Mrs Bradbury.'

'And added to the fact that you hid her jewels in the cellar, put them in a drawer in a desk, and hid them from view with a book about the Channel Islands. That book may have appeared old and useless to you but it was a treasured volume within the family.'

'No member of the family would have used that book to hide the jewels . . . had to have been used by an outsider.'

Sandra Picardie's head sank. 'I thought it was just an old book. I put it there to cover the jewels up . . . I intended to return and take them away to sell. Just never did though.'

'Be careful,' Bowler warned.

'Why?' Picardie forced a smile. 'They're right, all I can do is to co-operate.'

'So you did murder Muriel Bradbury?' Hennessey asked.

'Yes,' Picardie shrugged. 'Went to their home in Paxton on the Forest, banged her over the head. She was a bit groggy, pulled a plastic bag over her head to finish the job. Took her jewels while she was cooling, in case I needed to shift the blame.'

'To her husband?'

'Who else? It wasn't a happy marriage . . . but it never came to that. Knew the police would search the grounds as well as the house . . . . . . waited until they'd done that . . . went back and put her body in amongst a pile of rubble. And there it remained.'

'Until last Tuesday,' Yellich offered.

'And the embezzlement?'

'Guilty.'

'Thank you.'

'And the murder of Janet Frost, smashed over the head in a snickelway.'

'Not guilty.' She held Hennessey's stare.

'But you became the second Mrs Frost.'

'So?'

'You could serve two life sentences concurrently and not know the difference from serving one . . . but if we find proof about your involvement in Mrs Frost's death in subsequent years, you will be tried and convicted separately.'

'Never likely to get out.' Yellich raised his eyebrows.

'Please don't coerce my client, gentlemen.' Bowler allowed an edge to enter his voice. 'You've had my client's answer to the issue of that murder.'

'And the disappearance of Mrs Ilford, wife of your employer before you became his mistress?'

'Common-law wife,' she said indignantly. 'I am not a mistress! She disappeared. People do. It happens. Tommy thinks she committed suicide.'

'Really?'

'Really. Didn't like the way he lived his life . . . didn't like what he was doing to her boys. She got depressed, was on pills, so many pills it was a wonder she didn't rattle when she walked. Then one day she just wasn't there. Flung her silly self in the Ouse, I expect.'

'Her body would have been found.'

'Not if she tied something heavy round her neck, it wouldn't . . . tied it with a length of chain and a padlock, that would have kept her body down. Tommy says, anyway. Plenty of bits of metal in the garage . . . a cylinder head would have done it.'

'Is that what he used?'

Picardie glared at him. 'You'll have to ask him that.'

'Oh, we will. Will he tell us you were involved as well? You see, he's in the cells right now, we caught him bang to rights inside the Art Gallery . . . he'll be looking to help himself as much as possible . . . especially since he's being done for conspiracy to murder.'

'Conspiracy?'

'Michael Petty, bled to death by "Passover" Kennedy, inside your . . . your common-law husband's garage.'

'You know about that?'

'Practically got it on film,' Hennessey smiled. 'We've got the tubing and if Passover's prints are on it, he won't be going anywhere for a long time either.'

'It's falling apart,' Yellich said. 'You may as well salvage what you can.'

'I want to talk to my husband.'

'You can't. You can talk only to Mr Bowler.'

'If my client and I can have a few moments, please, gentlemen,' Bowler appealed to Hennessey.

'Certainly.' Hennessey reached for the on/off switch. 'The time is zero, zero thirty-two. Chief Inspector Hennessey and Sergeant Yellich are leaving the room to allow Ms Picardie to consult with her lawyer, Mr Bowler, in accordance with the

Police and Criminal Evidence Act.' He switched the machine off, and he and Yellich left the room.

Hennessey and Yellich put coins in the hot-drinks vending machine that stood in the corridor outside the interview room.

'You know – ' Hennessey looked at the machine as it whirred – 'this reminds me of that story . . . you remember, the one about the two leopards . . .'

'Oh . . . ?'

'Yes . . . grab the lot . . . you know, Yellich, sometimes, sometimes it just doesn't pay to do that . . . sometimes it pays to let one or two go . . . just to see where they run to . . . to see where they lead you . . .'

'Aye . . .' Yellich nodded. 'I see your point . . . She's crumbling, boss,' he added as he reached for his drink: tea, no sugar.

'As is the case in many instances, as is the mess that policing is.'

'Mess, boss?'

'Most people are victims of crime to a greater or lesser extent and most crimes are unsolved. If a criminal commits nine offences, he will get nailed for the tenth. It's going to be that way with milady in there. Guilty to murder, guilty to embezzlement, feeds us something about Passover Kennedy to help her negotiate an early parole. She won't admit to the Frost murder. That's a risk she'll take. But Kennedy's going to be difficult to crack. He's sitting there looking smug.'

'Really?'

'Phil Sherrie's doing handstands with delight. Passover's never been so long inside a police station in his adult life. Sherrie's still got an uphill battle though.'

'Aye . . . much helped if Picardie and Ilford will witness the murder of Michael Petty.' Yellich sipped his tea.

'They'll be scared of retribution?'

'Why? Passover's gang are like him . . . scared of the North of England, it could be a different planet for all they know or

All Roads Leadeth

care. Those London guys think you can see polar bears at Brookman's Park.'

Hennessey smiled at him. 'Remind Sherrie of that.'

'I will. Sherrie told me something. Do you know why photographers take "snaps"?'

Hennessey confessed that he didn't.

'Comes from the shooting brotherhood. Apparently guys in tweeds carrying their shotguns broken as they ought to . . . a feathered thing suddenly appears overhead, they snap the gun to and take a potshot . . . it's called a "snapshot". The term got hijacked by photographers to mean a quick shot . . . rather than a posed shot . . . so today holidaymakers show you their "snaps".'

'I am,' said Hennessey, 'enlightened, edified . . .' He sipped the remainder of his hot drink in silence and then said, 'Shall we see if she is finished consulting her brief?'

The interview having recommenced, the tape recorder again recording. Roger Bowler said, 'My client . . .'

'Name for the benefit of the tape, please,' Hennessey growled.

'Sandra Picardie,' Bowler said as if reluctant to co-operate, as if stung by Hennessey's reminder, 'wishes to make a statement. She will plead guilty to the murder of . . .' he consulted his notes, 'Mrs Muriel Bradbury; guilty to embezzlement and she will give evidence that she witnessed the murder of one Michael Petty by one Harold "Passover" Kennedy. My client, Ms Picardie, claims she is unconnected in any way with the murder of one Janet Frost, nor does she have any information concerning the disappearance of Mrs Katie Ilford. My client, Ms Picardie, also wishes it to be known that even though the murder of Michael Petty took place in the business premises of her paramour, Thomas Ilford, she will be making a statement to Mr Ilford's representative that it was her impression that Mr Ilford was coerced by Mr Kennedy into giving up his premises for the purpose of murder, and that it was not at all the case that he was a willing conspirator.'

'Thus making it difficult to prove conspiracy to murder.' Hennessey leaned back in his chair causing it to creak.

'Thus making it impossible, I would say,' Bowler said smugly. 'But you have your pound of flesh, Chief Inspector.'

'I'm going down for life,' Sandra Picardie spoke coldly, 'isn't that enough for you? How much blood do you want? How much do you need?'

'I'd like some justice for Mrs Frost,' Hennessey spoke equally as coldly, 'as I am sure her relatives would. And I am sure that Mrs Ilford's children would like to know what happened to their mother.'

'Well, I am very sorry, I can't help you there. What's the expression? Those cases will have to remain on file. Is that the expression?'

Hennessey pursed his lips. 'Well, that's your decision . . . but remember, if we can link you with either, then the charges start from that point, no matter how near your parole hearing . . . something for you to think about over the next few months in Foxton Hall.'

'Foxton Hall?' Sandra Picardie's eyes burned into Hennessey's face. 'What's that?'

'The women's prison for this area. There are worse places, or so they say.'

'Didn't think you'd come all the way to Yorkshire to chase me, Mr Sherrie.' Harry 'Passover' Kennedy smiled at Phil Sherrie.

'You know me, Harry, like a dog with a bone.'

Hennessey sat beside DS Sherrie and just as he thought when he first set eyes on Sandra Picardie, he thought again: So this is Harold 'Passover' Kennedy. He saw a smug-looking man in his middle years, well built, expensive clothing, who had a confident, you-won't-nail-me smile. By contrast to Roger Bowler, Passover Kennedy's lawyer was young, clean-cut, looked determined, hearing like a bat, eyes like a hawk. One hundred percent concentration.

'You've got a problem now, Harry,' Sherrie said.

'Oh?'

'Yes,' Sherrie smiled. Hennessey knew that Sherrie was enjoying himself . . . Heavens, he thought, he deserves it . . . He's been after this felon for long enough, but just like himself with Sandra Picardie, Sherrie would have to accept that many of the murders perpetrated by Kennedy would have to remain on file, but now at last . . . 'Yes, we are interested in your connection with the murder of Mike Petty.'

'Who?'

'Known to you as Michael Oates.'

Kennedy shrugged. Then he smiled. 'I'm still no wiser, Mr Sherrie.'

'Well, he's the guy who you strung up and bled to death in Thomas Ilford's garage, last Sunday morning.'

Kennedy became stone-faced but remained silent.

'We have a witness statement from Sandra Picardie,' Sherrie said quietly. 'You were seen where the body was dumped. And we have collected the plastic catheters you used to catch the blood . . . they're being tested for prints now. If your prints are on them, and we are advised that you didn't wear gloves, and the blood in the catheter matches up with Michael Petty's DNA, then you have some explaining to do. And the motive? Well, it's a matter of record that Oates a.k.a. Petty, gave evidence against you at the trial of which you were acquitted because key prosecution witnesses failed to appear and Oates subsequently went into the Witness Protection Programme. It's a watertight case.'

Kennedy paled, then flushed with anger and turned to his lawyer who said, 'Say nothing. Nothing at all.'

'It was a question of logic,' Hennessey said, 'before you turn your dogs on anyone. You've only one contact in these parts, that's Ilford. Pouring blood on Petty's doorstep is your hallmark. They don't call you "Passover" for nothing. You need premises to drain blood from someone like that . . . where else could there be but Ilford's garage? We got a warrant, found the bloodstained catheters in a pile of rubbish waiting to be burned.'

'You slipped up,' Sherrie said. 'You weren't grassed up, you slipped up. You had to, eventually. You're looking at life.'

'But Picardie . . .' Kennedy appealed, 'she grassed me up, you just said so.'

'Only after we told her we knew where you did the deed . . . only after that. She's already got her eyes on the parole board. If she keeps her nose clean inside, she'll be out in ten. And you can forget hunting her down, she doesn't need police protection to disappear. She's very good at it.'

'Don't,' said the youthful lawyer, 'say anything. Not a word.'

Harold 'Passover' Kennedy, having been charged with murder, Sandra Picardie also having been charged with murder and Thomas 'Blackhole' Ilford having been charged with unlawful entry with intent to steal, all three were escorted to the cells to await their appearance before York magistrates later that day, being the first step to their cases being heard at York Crown Court some months hence. A tearful Monica Wickersley was also charged with embezzlement and conspiracy to murder after the fact. She too was detained in the cells to await appearing before the York bench later that day, but in her case, and her case alone, Hennessey did not intend to request bail be denied.

'It's as I was saying to Yellich,' Hennessey said as he and Sherrie stood on the steps of Micklegate Bar Police Station enjoying the dawn rise over the still sleeping city. 'It's more of a mess than anything, but at least we'll get them for something.'

'Eventually,' Sherrie nodded. 'Eventually. It's been a long road. A hell of a long road.'

Later that day, after a nourishing sleep, Sergeant Somerled

Yellich drove out to the house at Paxton on the Forest, to where, just one week earlier, the case had been triggered by the discovery of a skeleton in a pile of rubble. He had to clarify some details for his report and needed to speak with the incoming owner of the property, the local lad who had made good in Canada. He parked his car at the kerb and walked down the drive, and as he walked past the house he saw a young woman stripping wallpaper. He'd seen her before, somewhere . . . she was dressed differently then, but it was the same woman . . . that tumbling head of golden hair . . . there was just no mistaking that head of hair.